TRICK ROLLER

SEVEN OF SPADES #2

CORDELIA
KINGSBRIDGE

RIPTIDE
PUBLISHING

Riptide Publishing
PO Box 1537
Burnsville, NC 28714
www.riptidepublishing.com

Cover art: Garrett Leigh, blackjazzdesign.com
Editor: Sarah Lyons
Layout: L.C. Chase, lcchase.com/design.htm

ISBN: 978-1-62649-636-1

First edition
January, 2018

Also available in ebook:
ISBN: 978-1-62649-635-4

TRICK ROLLER

SEVEN OF SPADES #2

CORDELIA
KINGSBRIDGE

RIPTIDE
PUBLISHING

For Samantha
Sister, best friend, inspiration

TABLE OF CONTENTS

CHAPTER 1

"**S**o it's late, the girls have been in bed for a while, and I'm nodding off myself." Dominic set his fork and knife on his empty plate and dropped his napkin on top. "I ended up falling asleep in front of the TV."

Across the small table, Levi was leaning back in his chair, as casual and relaxed as he ever got—which was to say not very. His keen gray eyes were intent on Dominic's face.

"I woke up with the sense that something wasn't right," Dominic said, continuing his story about babysitting his two young nieces. "Then I heard this kind of quiet, secretive giggling. And let me tell you, the last thing you want to hear when you wake up confused in the dark in a strange house is the sound of giggling children. Brings back the memory of every horror movie you've ever seen."

The corner of Levi's mouth tilted—a half smile that was for him what a broad grin would be for anyone else. Dominic took a moment to drink in the sight of it.

"But my mind cleared pretty quick, and I heard some sort of wet slapping noise on top of the giggling. I jumped up and ran to the girls' room. Vinnie and his wife shop at Costco, and for God knows what reason, they'd bought this five-gallon jug of olive oil—"

"Oh, no," Levi said, his eyes widening.

"Yeah. Those two little miscreants had snuck out of bed, dragged the jug from the pantry to their bedroom, and dumped the oil out all over the carpet. They'd created their own Slip 'N Slide."

Levi laughed quietly, and Dominic thrilled at the sound. Over the past few months, it had become his personal mission to make Levi laugh as often as possible. Levi was naturally solemn—not joyless, not by a long shot, but one of the most serious people Dominic had ever met. Bringing a smile to his face was a worthy feat in itself; getting him to laugh out loud was a deep source of pride.

"I almost didn't want to stop them, because they were having the time of their lives. But responsibility won out in the end. I managed to get them both cleaned up and most of the oil off the walls and the furniture. The carpet had to be ripped out and replaced, though." Dominic made a flourishing gesture with his hands. "And that's why I'm currently on babysitting probation."

His face still alight with amusement, Levi drank the last sip of his Boulevardier, the bourbon cocktail Dominic had introduced him to. He ordered one whenever he and Dominic went somewhere with a full bar, though half the time Dominic had to explain to the server or bartender in question how to make it.

"I don't know if I would have done any better," he said. "I'm terrible with children."

"You're great with Martine's kids," said Dominic, referring to Levi's fellow homicide detective and closest friend.

"They're teenagers. That's different. I have a young niece and nephew myself, and I don't know how to interact with them at all. Then again, I barely ever see them."

"Why not?"

Levi shrugged. "I don't like going back to New Jersey, and my sister doesn't want to bring them to Vegas."

They both fell silent as their server approached to clear their plates. "Any dessert tonight, gentlemen?" she asked.

Dominic hesitated and glanced at Levi.

"Get dessert," Levi said. "You know you want to. I'll have coffee."

After their server left, Dominic sat back in his chair with a warm sense of contentment. They were at Grape Street Café in downtown Summerlin, and on a Saturday night, there wasn't a single open table in the contemporary, brick-lined dining room. The food had been great, the company incomparable.

His eyes traveled over the man in front of him. Levi had a narrow, wiry build, his clothes concealing most of the incredible, lean musculature carved by over a decade of intense dedication to Krav Maga. He'd been growing out his curly black hair a bit, and his razor-sharp bone structure gave him a hollow-cheeked look that Dominic adored.

Levi lifted an eyebrow. "You're staring."

"You're gorgeous," said Dominic.

There it was—the slight blush spreading across Levi's cheeks as he turned his face aside with an eye roll and a tiny smile, embarrassed and pleased in equal measure. It was one of Dominic's favorite expressions on him.

They'd been dating for three months now, and the more time they spent together, the more fascinated Dominic became. He could admit that he was the type of person who relished a challenge, and Levi . . . Levi was a storm of intriguing contradictions, cool on the outside and boiling hot within, aggressive as fuck in certain situations and painfully shy in others. He was intelligent and driven and, every now and then, so unselfconsciously sweet that it made Dominic's chest hurt.

He'd never felt like this about anyone.

His dessert arrived along with Levi's double espresso. Dominic watched him drink it, knowing he would have ordered a triple if he'd thought the restaurant would serve it to him.

"Sure you don't want a bite?" Dominic asked, offering a forkful of profiteroles drowning in dark chocolate ganache and vanilla ice cream.

Levi eyed the fork askance. "I don't really have a sweet tooth."

"I know," Dominic said, and grinned. "I kind of hate that about you."

Levi gently kicked Dominic's shin under the table, then left his foot there, pressed up against Dominic's.

A short time later, they stood on the sidewalk in front of the restaurant, sweltering in the oppressive summer heat while they waited for the valet to bring Levi's car around. Side by side, their physical differences were more pronounced. Levi was a tall man, just an inch under six feet, but Dominic was still half a foot taller. He was more heavily built as well, his muscles thick and brawny whereas Levi's were lean and compact.

Dominic slid an arm around Levi's waist and bent to kiss him, not caring that they were in public. Most people—sober people, anyway—tended to avoid starting shit with a man his size no matter how homophobic they were, and anyone who thought Levi would make an easier target was in for a nasty surprise.

When he started to pull back, Levi surprised him by catching the lapel of his dinner jacket and keeping him close.

"It's been three months," Levi said, his voice pitched low. "Don't you think we've waited long enough?"

Dominic drew a deep breath. "You want to . . ."

"I want to spend the night with you."

Levi had left Stanton Barclay, his boyfriend of three years, only the day before he and Dominic had slept together for the first time. They'd agreed to take things slow from that point on, so that Levi would have time to grieve his lost relationship without the complication of jumping headlong into a new one right off the bat.

Despite their best intentions, they hadn't been able to *quite* keep their hands off each other in the weeks that followed. A few memories in particular stood out in Dominic's mind—dry humping like teenagers on the couch in Levi's new apartment, jerking each other off in Dominic's kitchen when they were supposed to be cooking dinner, Levi sucking his cock in the front seat of his pickup. That last had been made ten times more exciting by the fact that Levi was a cop.

There were two firm lines they hadn't crossed since April, however—no overnights and no penetrative sex.

Dominic had gone too long without responding. Levi let go and stepped away, a flicker of hurt and confusion crossing his face before it went blank. "You don't want to?"

"Oh, I want to," Dominic said honestly. *God*, did he want to. "That's not even in question. I just want to make sure you're ready for this." He had doubts that three months was long enough to move past a serious relationship—but then, he'd never been in one of those himself, so what the hell did he know?

"Dominic." Levi took his hand. "I want to be with you, move forward with you. I don't want there to be any barriers between us anymore. I'm ready for that if you are."

His expression was earnest, his voice sincere. After a moment's consideration, Dominic reeled him back in and kissed him again.

"All right," he said. "Let's go to my place."

Once the decision had been made, the half-hour drive across the city was pure torture. Dominic wrestled out of his jacket the moment they were inside the car. He hated wearing the thing even when it wasn't a billion goddamn degrees out, and the anticipation of fucking Levi again only had him running hotter.

Seeing Levi's self-control disintegrate, hearing his loud cries of pleasure, feeling that impossibly tight ass working his cock . . . Dominic was going to experience all that again, only this time with the advantage of knowing Levi so much better and caring about him so much more. His heart was already pounding.

Levi drove too fast and not a little recklessly. In record time, they arrived at Dominic's apartment building, a three-story concrete U shaped around a central courtyard with a community pool. Dominic let Levi precede him up the stairs and watched his round ass bouncing in his trousers all the way up to the second floor.

His dog Rebel, a German Shepherd–Rottweiler mix, awaited him just inside the door, sitting at attention with her ears pricked up. She stood and wagged her tail happily as Dominic crouched to greet her.

"I'm gonna take Rebel for a quick walk," he said to Levi. "Make yourself at home."

Levi nodded, stripping out of his own jacket as he headed for the living room.

Dominic and Rebel made a short circuit of the building's perimeter. Ordinarily, he enjoyed taking her on a long, leisurely stroll at night, using it as an opportunity to unwind from the stress of the day. Tonight, though, he hurried her along, anticipation building in his gut and itching beneath his skin.

The moment they reentered the apartment, he unclipped Rebel's leash and called out for Levi.

"In the bedroom!" Levi shouted back.

After stopping in the kitchen to grab a couple of bottles of water, Dominic backed into the bedroom, shooing Rebel away and apologizing to her even as he shut the door in her indignant face. Then he turned around and promptly fumbled one of the bottles, grabbing it with his free hand in a last-second save.

Levi had turned down the covers and was stretched out naked in Dominic's bed, jerking himself off.

"You said I should make myself at home," he said. His smirk was slightly undercut by the breathlessness of his voice.

Dominic moved to the side of the bed as if in a daze and set the water bottles on the nightstand without looking. He heard one of them roll off and thump onto the floor, but he couldn't have given less of a shit.

Levi's nude body always put him in mind of a jungle cat, lithe and graceful and undeniably powerful. Mesmerized, he reached out.

Levi pushed his hand away before he made contact. "No touching until you take your clothes off."

That got Dominic's ass in gear. He fished the lube out of the nightstand drawer and tossed it to Levi, then stripped as fast as he could. By the time he climbed onto the bed, Levi's cock and balls were slick with lube, and Levi was sliding a finger inside himself.

They rolled around in the sheets for a few minutes, kissing passionately and rutting against each other, all hands and mouths and rolling hips. That wasn't going to be enough for either of them tonight, though, and it wasn't long before Levi guided Dominic's hand where he wanted it.

Levi was even tighter than he remembered. He tried to take it slow, work Levi open gradually, but Levi was having none of it. Helpless against the combination of whispered demands and Levi's eager, arching body, Dominic found himself three fingers deep in Levi's ass within minutes, lavishing kisses against his sweat-damp throat.

The first and only time they'd done this, Dominic had taken Levi from behind; he wanted it face-to-face this time. Levi made no objections when Dominic spread him out on his back and knelt between his legs, lifting his hips to prop his ass on Dominic's own thighs. He just gazed up at Dominic with flushed cheeks and swollen lips, looking like sex incarnate.

Dominic rolled on a condom and draped Levi's legs over his arms, but he was distracted from his goal by the mouthwatering jut of Levi's prominent hip bones. He circled them with his thumbs, knowing how sensitive Levi was there.

Levi jerked against him and mewled like a kitten. Once he recovered, he thumped his heel against Dominic's shoulder and said, "What are you waiting for? Come on."

Smiling, Dominic lined himself up and pushed forward. Just like last time, Levi's tense body refused to take more than the first inch or so of his sizeable cock. He pulled out and pushed back in, managing to get a bit deeper on the second stroke.

He went on like that with slow, careful thrusts, easing his way inside. Beneath him, Levi was biting his lip, one hand on the headboard and the other squeezing his own cock as it dripped pre-come all over his stomach.

Levi might not like to admit this, but Dominic knew a size queen when he saw one, and he'd noticed how Levi's eyes glazed over and his mouth went slack every time he got a hand on Dominic's cock. Right now, Levi's trembling muscles and quiet moans made it clear how much he was struggling to convince his tightly wound body to accept what he so desperately needed.

"You gonna let me in?" Dominic asked. Then, remembering what had worked last time, he gentled his voice and said, "Gonna let me take care of you?"

Levi groaned, and his body relaxed a few degrees. Dominic alternated rocking and circling his hips, letting Levi get used to the thick girth of his shaft as he pressed gradually deeper. It felt fantastic, Levi snug and scorching hot around him.

"God," Levi said. He released his cock to grip at his hair instead. "Do you have any idea how much I need this? It's been three *months*. A dildo just isn't the same."

Dominic paused. "What?"

"I mean, it's better than nothing, but it can't compare to a real cock."

Dominic expelled a noisy breath. His brain was flooded with images of Levi sprawled out on his bed, pumping a dildo in and out of his needy ass, maybe thinking about Dominic while he did it—

"Are you trying to give me a stroke?" he said, his voice strangled.

Levi scowled at him like he didn't know *exactly* what he was doing, the teasing bastard. "I'm trying to get you to fuck me," he said haughtily. "But so far I'm not having much success. Maybe I should change tactics."

Dominic was still wondering what that meant when Levi braced both hands against the headboard, tightened his legs against

Dominic's arms, and lifted his back off the bed and his ass off Dominic's thighs. Using those two opposite points of tension for leverage, he maneuvered himself back and forth on Dominic's cock.

His mouth falling open, Dominic stared at the rippling muscles in Levi's abdomen. He automatically moved his hands to Levi's lower back, but Levi was supporting most of his own bodyweight, holding himself up with his shoulders just barely grazing the mattress like he was in the fucking Cirque du Soleil.

Levi was much less patient than Dominic. He drove himself onto Dominic's cock, forcing himself to take it, cursing and moaning the whole time.

"Shit," Dominic said. He started thrusting again, finally bottoming out. "Levi . . ."

"Give me more, come on—"

Dominic gave in and snapped his hips the way they both wanted him to.

"*Yes,*" Levi gasped. He released the pose he'd been holding, dropping back to the bed and Dominic's thighs. "Like that, Dominic, do it, do it—"

Dominic fucked him in a flurry of short, shallow thrusts, working his prostate over until Levi was crying out nonstop. Then he tossed Levi's legs over his shoulders, leaned forward on his hands, and screwed him deep and hard, surrendering to the urge to just fucking *ravage* the beautiful man writhing underneath him.

The headboard banged repeatedly against the wall—the wall he shared with Carlos and Jasmine, and there was no way they could miss the racket Levi was making. He'd buy them doughnuts or something tomorrow to make it up to them, because he wasn't stopping now.

He was gripped with the sudden need to kiss Levi, to have that second point of connection while inside him. Levi was flexible enough for them to kiss like this, but given their size difference, it still wouldn't be comfortable.

Instead, Dominic hauled Levi up onto his lap as he sat back on his heels. Levi yelped at the change in position.

"Ah, fuck, that's deep," he said, clinging to Dominic's shoulders. His fingernails dug in, sending a shiver of pleasure-pain down Dominic's spine.

Dominic shoved him against the headboard and fucked up into him, his pace every bit as relentless as before. "You like that, don't you, baby?" he growled, half out of his mind with the clutch of Levi's body around him. "Like taking my cock deep, getting fucked hard?"

Challenge sparked in Levi's eyes. He threaded his fingers through Dominic's thick hair and tugged with enough force to make Dominic moan. "Yeah, I like it," he said raggedly. "Love your big cock inside me, filling me up—"

Dominic seized his mouth in a savage kiss. Levi responded in kind, and it was vicious, as much teeth as lips and tongue. When he felt Levi tensing with approaching orgasm, he grabbed Levi's cock and pumped it in time with his aggressive thrusts.

Moments later, Levi screamed into Dominic's mouth as he came. His body shuddered, his phenomenally tight hole clenching and releasing around Dominic's cock in a breathtaking rhythm. Come splashed hot and messy over Dominic's fist and both their stomachs.

Levi slumped in his lap, his head dropping to Dominic's shoulder. Dominic didn't let up, straining toward his own climax, so close—

Levi's mouth roamed over his shoulder and the side of his neck, covering him with hot, open-mouthed kisses. Then Levi bit down on the juncture of his neck and shoulder and sucked hard.

Dominic shouted out loud, smacked his hand against the headboard, and rose up on his knees, burying his cock to the hilt in Levi's ass as orgasm swept through him. His hips hunched with every euphoric pulse until he was completely drained.

Dazed, he lowered himself back to his heels, Levi still straddling his lap and impaled on his cock. When Levi lifted his head, Dominic brushed a stray curl off his forehead and cupped his cheek, awash in tenderness.

Levi had a soft smile on his face; he was all but glowing. "That's gonna leave a mark," he said, grazing his fingers over Dominic's neck.

"Good," Dominic said, and kissed him again.

CHAPTER 2

Levi was a much earlier riser than Dominic, and he was just getting out of the shower when the summons to a new crime scene came in.

He sighed as he realized he'd have to swing by his apartment first for a change of clothes. If he'd been with Stanton, he could have just borrowed a clean shirt and called it a day, but borrowing a shirt from Dominic would leave him looking like a child playing dress-up.

He needed to shave and brush his teeth too. Maybe he should keep a few things here, just in case—

Whoa. He stopped that thought in its tracks. It was way too soon for a step like that.

When he returned to the bed, Rebel lifted her head off her paws and regarded him curiously. She'd slept with them last night, curled up between their feet, and he hadn't minded because she was so well-behaved.

Levi scratched her ears and looked at Dominic, sprawled on his back with the covers draped loosely over his waist. He took up a lot of room, his chest and shoulders impossibly broad and the bulk of his muscular thighs outlined by the sheet. A small circle of scar tissue just beneath his right shoulder marked the bullet wound he'd sustained in Afghanistan.

Propping one knee on the bed, he leaned over and ran his fingers along Dominic's strong, square jaw and the old break in his nose. "Dominic," he said.

Dominic's eyes fluttered open, and he gave Levi the wide smile that came so effortlessly to him. "Hey."

"I have to go. There was a suspicious death at the Mirage, and it's my turn in the rotation."

"Mmm, okay." Dominic turned his face so Levi's fingers fell over his mouth, then kissed his fingertips. Levi's breath caught. "Call me later?"

"Yeah."

Closing his eyes, Dominic rolled onto his side and pulled the sheet up to his shoulders, snuggling into his pillow. Levi watched him for a few more moments, wishing he could stay. Dominic's presence had a calming effect he was beginning to crave. He could relax and enjoy himself when they were together, with no need to keep his guard up because he knew nothing would hurt him. Even the recurring nightmares that had plagued him since childhood—dreams of being trapped and hunted by an unseen enemy—had ebbed over the past few months.

Levi kissed Dominic's cheek and headed out. He wasn't able to lock the door behind him, but he figured that anyone who broke into an apartment containing an ex-Army Ranger and a hundred-pound personal protection dog would regret that decision pretty quickly.

As he walked down the exterior hallway—Dominic's building was like a motel, all the apartments opening right into the outside— another door opened and shut behind him. He turned around to see Jasmine Anderson, who lived next door to Dominic with her boyfriend Carlos.

She was a total knockout, with light-brown skin covered in elaborate tattoos and long braids dyed a rainbow of colors. Her enormous eyes were emphasized with winged liner, and she'd changed out her lip piercing to a silver hoop in an intricately woven design. A hemp messenger bag was slung over one shoulder.

"Hey, Levi," she said, seeming unsurprised to see him. "You guys doing the sleepover thing now?"

"Looks like." He waited for her to catch up with him so they could walk to the stairs together. "Are you going to work?" Sunday morning might be odd hours for a tattoo artist to keep, but this *was* Las Vegas.

She shook her head. "Farmer's market. You gotta get in before all the good stuff's gone."

"Ah." Levi cast about for something to say while they went down the stairs. He liked Jasmine and Carlos, but he still felt uncomfortable around them—and not just because he was usually awkward around people he didn't know well. They were good friends with Dominic; no doubt they were judging him as an appropriate partner, and if they found him wanting, maybe Dominic would too. "Did you and Carlos have a good Saturday?" he asked, as they exited the fence around the property and entered the parking lot.

"Probably not as good as yours," she said, giving him a wink that made him immediately suspicious. "See you later!"

She trotted off merrily to her car. Levi narrowed his eyes, then shrugged and turned to his own.

Dominic's apartment near the University of Nevada, Las Vegas was much closer to the Mirage than Levi's new apartment in Rancho Oakey, so the detour put him well behind schedule. He hurried through the hotel's tropical rainforest-themed lobby, passing the enormous aquarium behind the reception desk, and drew up short in surprise when he saw Martine waiting for an elevator.

He and Martine were on the same six-detective squad in the Homicide Section; because they complemented each other's strengths and weaknesses well, they were often assigned to work the same cases. Martine lived out in Sunrise Manor, but she still should have made it here before Levi.

"I thought for sure I'd be the last one to show up," Levi said, joining her at the elevator bank. "What's going on?"

"My house is full of teenage angst, that's what's going on," Martine said in her strong Flatbush accent. Though she'd been born in Haiti, she'd grown up in Brooklyn. "Mikayla's been brooding and sulking all week, throwing epic tantrums I haven't seen since she was a toddler, and now it's spreading to Simone. The look on Antoine's face when I left this morning—it was like I was throwing him to a pack of wolves."

Levi winced in sympathy.

Martine had a petite, curvy build and rich dark-brown skin. Despite the frazzled air about her this morning, her short hair was done in perfect finger coils and she was as flawlessly put-together as always. There was also a too-perceptive light in her eyes that Levi didn't like as she scanned him from head to foot.

"So you and Dominic finally slid into home again?" she said.

One of the elevators arrived with a soft *ding*, expelling a chattering family of five. "How do you always *know*?" Levi hissed to Martine as they entered. They were the only ones who got on, but he still lowered his voice further as he added, "I'm not . . . am I *limping*?"

She pressed her lips together like she was trying not to laugh and hit the button for the twenty-second floor. "You're not, but thanks for that insight into your sex life. You just—you seem relaxed, you know? That's not something I'm used to seeing on you. Plus, you missed a spot shaving and your tie is crooked. Pretty much screams 'post-sex fog.'"

Cursing, he unknotted his tie so he could redo it.

A uniformed LVMPD officer stood guard outside the room where the body had been found. Levi and Martine signed the crime scene log, put on booties and gloves, and stepped inside.

The room wasn't large, but it was beautifully decorated, a vibrant color scheme of deep purples and reds contrasted against the snow-white sheets and curtains. Fresh flowers bloomed in a couple of crystal vases, and a flat-screen television was mounted on the wall opposite the king-sized bed.

Fred, the crime scene photographer, was already hard at work, along with a couple of CSIs and the coroner investigator. Standing out of the way in the corner was Jonah Gibbs, who could have been an excellent cop if not for his hot temper and absolute lack of anything resembling discretion or tact.

"What've we got?" Levi asked him.

Gibbs nodded to the deceased, who lay on the floor near the foot of the bed. "Dr. Stephen Hensley, fifty-three, hometown Baltimore. Here for some kind of palliative medicine conference that starts on Monday, but a bunch of them came in early to start things off with a bang—you know how it is."

"I will never understand what possesses people to host conferences in Las Vegas in July," Martine muttered.

"Heard that. Anyway, vic was found dead this morning by hotel security after one of his fellow docs told them he hadn't shown up for a scheduled breakfast and wasn't responding to phone calls or knocks on his door. She's on her way to the substation now. Pretty shaken up."

Levi nodded and moved toward the body. He kept his hands in his pockets to resist the unconscious impulse to touch—even wearing gloves, it was best to handle evidence as little as possible.

Hensley was a white man on the solid side, his dark-brown hair graying at the temples. He was wearing a hotel bathrobe, though Levi couldn't tell if he had anything on underneath it. No visible wounds, but there was a puddle of vomit near his head and more bile caked around his mouth and chin.

"Overdose?" Levi asked the coroner investigator, who was kneeling beside the body.

"Almost definitely," she said. "Early estimate for time of death is 1 to 3 a.m. That's pretty much all I can say until the autopsy."

Levi thanked her and continued on, surveying the room. There wasn't much space for seven people—eight if one counted Hensley—so he kept his movements as economical as possible.

The bed was rumpled, the pillows tossed every which way and the bedspread shoved haphazardly to one side. A nearby wastebasket held two used condoms. On the bureau beneath the television stood a couple of half-empty champagne flutes, one with a clear lipstick print, alongside a bottle in a silver ice bucket now full of water. Hensley was wearing a wedding ring, but if his colleague had been the one to raise the alarm, Levi was betting he hadn't brought his wife on this trip.

What was *missing* from the scene was just as important as what was present, and after a thorough search, Hensley's wallet and cell phone were nowhere to be found. There was also a tangle of chargers out on the desk but no electronics in sight.

"What do you think?" Martine said, as they met again by the door. "Trick roll gone wrong?"

That had been Levi's initial conclusion. A trick roller was a sex worker—or someone pretending to be a sex worker—who lured a john to a private location and then robbed them, often after knocking them out with drugs. It wasn't an uncommon occurrence in Las Vegas, though it wasn't usually fatal. If this was the work of a trick roller, the overdose had most likely been accidental.

However . . .

"If the sex worker was planning to roll Hensley, why bother having sex with him at all?" he said.

Always ready with a counterargument, Martine said, "Maybe she *wasn't* planning to roll him at first, but he said or did something to offend her, and she changed her mind."

"We don't know it was a her."

"Lipstick on the champagne glass," Gibbs cut in.

"That doesn't mean it was a woman," said Levi.

Gibbs blinked. "Yeah, okay, fair point. I think we can pretty safely play the odds here, though."

Levi shrugged; he was probably right.

Martine, meanwhile, was frowning across the room. "That's another thing—why leave such an obvious source of fingerprints and DNA behind after you've robbed someone, let alone accidentally murdered them?"

Now it was Levi's turn to play devil's advocate. "He could have still been alive when she left, and she may have been confident he wouldn't report the robbery given the circumstances. Or maybe she just panicked and ran."

"Not as exotic as a serial killer, huh?" Gibbs said with a smirk.

Levi glared at him. The Seven of Spades case had been closed despite his protests, the five murders attributed to the deceased Keith Chapman, even though Levi was sure he'd been framed. When he brought the final taunting message the killer had left in his hotel room to his sergeant, Wen had given him an odd look, said it was clearly a practical joke, and asked if he wanted to take some time off to "get his head on straight again."

Word had spread, and for weeks afterward, his coworkers had pranked him by leaving seven of spades cards with silly messages written on them all over the substation, on the windshield of his car, even in his jacket pockets when he left it unattended. Levi suspected that Gibbs had been behind at least half of them.

"Go start canvassing the rest of the floor," Martine said sharply to Gibbs. "Take note of anyone who's not in so we can get their information from the hotel."

Gibbs grumbled a bit under his breath, but he went out into the hall as instructed. Mouthing off to Martine was a good way to get a dressing-down that could blister the ears off a sailor.

The Seven of Spades was a sore spot between Levi and Martine, because she didn't believe the real killer was still at large either. So he just pretended the subject hadn't been raised at all. "You want to handle this like usual?" he asked, meaning that she would run the crime scene while he interviewed the first witnesses.

She agreed, and he was on his way a couple minutes later. He saw no immediate need to follow up on the statement Gibbs had taken from the hotel security guard, and Martine would ensure that all relevant staff from the night before were questioned. Instead, he drove further south along the Strip to the substation his squad operated out of to interview Hensley's colleague.

Dr. Anika Kapoor was awaiting him in the comfortably furnished room used to break bad news and question victims and witnesses of traumatic events. She was a plump woman who looked to be in her late forties, her face grooved with deep smile lines and her black hair cut in a short bob. Unexpectedly, she was accompanied by a tall, gangly white man much younger than herself.

Levi extended his hand to her first. "Dr. Kapoor, I'm Detective Levi Abrams. I'm so sorry for your loss."

"Thank you," she said, managing a weak smile through her tears. Gibbs had said she was shaken up; if anything, that was an understatement. Her eyes were bloodshot, and her nose swollen from hours of crying.

Though the man wasn't crying, he looked just as distraught, his face ghostly pale and his expression shell-shocked. Levi raised an inquiring eyebrow.

"Oh, this is Dr. Craig Warner," said Kapoor. "He's a research fellow under Stephen and myself at Johns Hopkins."

Her breath hitched when she said Hensley's name. Levi handed her a nearby box of tissues, then gestured for her and Warner to sit on the couch they'd risen from when he entered. He sat in the armchair across from them and pulled out a notepad.

"I know this is painful, but could you please tell me about the last time you saw Dr. Hensley alive?"

Kapoor swallowed hard and nodded. "The three of us had dinner last night with a few colleagues at Samba, right there in the hotel.

Stephen headed up to his room around ten, I think. Said he was going to call it an early night—jet lag."

"Did either of you communicate with him in any way after that point? Phone calls, texts?"

Both Kapoor and Warner shook their heads.

"Are you staying at the Mirage as well?" Levi asked.

"Yes, we're actually all on the same floor," said Kapoor. "They're part of the block of rooms reserved for the conference."

"Did you see or hear anything suspicious on the floor last night?" This time, Levi directed the question toward Warner, who had yet to speak.

"No," Warner said, in a voice that was surprisingly deep coming out of such a skinny frame. "I mean, there were people running up and down the hallway all night long, but ... it's Vegas, right?"

Kapoor agreed, and Levi spent a few minutes confirming the reason for their trip and their movements the night before. As Gibbs had said, they'd flown in early from Baltimore to do some partying before a national conference on hospice and palliative care that would officially begin on Monday. After dinner at Samba, their group had thrown back a few cocktails at one of the Mirage's many bars before scattering their separate ways.

Kapoor had hit the casino floor, not returning upstairs until almost 3 a.m. Warner, on the other hand, had gotten so wasted at the bar he needed two friends to help him back to his room, where he'd drunk-dialed his girlfriend in Baltimore despite the time difference and then passed out in front of a pay-per-view movie.

"I don't usually drink that much," he said, rubbing a hand over his face. "Now I have an angry girlfriend and the worst hangover of my life on top of everything else."

Welcome to Vegas, Levi thought, but he didn't say it out loud because it was insensitive even by his standards. "What raised your concerns about Dr. Hensley this morning?" he asked Kapoor.

"We had all planned to meet at Cravings this morning at nine for the breakfast buffet. Stephen is ... *was* ..." Kapoor closed her eyes briefly and then soldiered on. "Punctual to a fault. When he didn't show up, I texted him a couple of times, then called his cell. I even tried his room phone, but it just kept ringing and ringing. That's when

I knew something was wrong; I could *feel* it. I asked hotel security for help, and they let me into his room. He—he was—"

She started crying quietly again, pressing a tissue to her face. Warner put an arm around her shoulders.

Levi gave her some time before asking, "Was Dr. Hensley married?"

"Yes," Warner said. "His wife is back in Baltimore—shit, she doesn't know yet, does she?"

"Did Dr. Hensley have any other sexual partners either of you were aware of? A mistress, a girlfriend?"

Kapoor lowered the hand that had been covering her face and stared at him. "What?"

This was awkward, but it had to be discussed. "Dr. Hensley definitely engaged in sexual activity last night," Levi said. "Our top priority is finding out who was with him in his hotel room. Did he appear to be making romantic or sexual overtures to anyone at the restaurant before he left?"

"No," Kapoor said. "As far as I know, he went straight to his room."

"Is it possible he would have arranged a visit from an escort service?"

There was a short silence in which Kapoor and Warner exchanged uncomfortable sideways glances that told Levi everything he needed to know. "It wouldn't have been . . . out of character," she said delicately.

"Wait, hang on." Warner turned to her on the couch. "I thought Dr. Hensley died of some kind of overdose."

She took a shaky breath. "That's what it looked like from what I saw."

"But all these questions . . ." He frowned at Levi. "Do you think someone *else* overdosed him? Like he spent the night with a hooker and she killed him?"

Levi twitched in irritation at the term *hooker* and said, "We don't have an official cause of death yet. Until we do, I don't want to speculate. But regardless of the circumstances of Dr. Hensley's death, it's imperative that we find the person he was with last night."

"I'm sorry, I don't think we can help you with that," said Kapoor. "None of us have ever been to Vegas before. I don't know where Stephen would have turned for . . . for companionship."

Levi asked a few more follow-up questions but learned nothing else of relevance. "Are you still planning to attend the conference?" he asked, as they all stood. Tourist homicides could be a major headache when all the important suspects and witnesses flitted back to their hometowns, and there wasn't much, if anything, he could do to make them stay.

Kapoor nodded. "We're scheduled to present groundbreaking research later this week—research Stephen dedicated years of his life to. He'd want us to stay and go on with the presentation."

"Can I ask what topic your research is on?" Levi said, making a note for himself.

"The cellular mechanisms involved in pain signaling and perception," Warner said.

Levi gave both doctors his card with the usual instructions to call him if they remembered anything else that might help, then showed them out of the substation before heading for his desk. The first order of business was to call the Baltimore PD so they could send local officers out to notify Hensley's wife of his death in person. Then he'd need a slew of warrants—the hotel didn't have security cameras in the hallways, but they did in the elevators and lobby. He also needed access to the room's phone records and Hensley's cell phone records. If Hensley had booked an escort online, though, they were out of luck with his laptop missing.

After that, he'd vet Kapoor and Warner's alibis in the interest of thoroughness and maybe request some of the conference materials to get a handle on Hensley's background. He was definitely in store for a long day.

Mid-afternoon, he took a break to grab more coffee and a sandwich. Figuring Dominic would have left the weekly family lunch at his mother's house by now, he gave him a call while he ate.

"Hey," Dominic said, against background noise that suggested he had Levi on Bluetooth in his truck. "How's the case?"

"We're not a hundred percent sure there *is* a case yet." Levi scrubbed his napkin over his mouth. "Even if there is, it's looking like a possible manslaughter charge."

"Well, you'll crack it in no time."

Snorting, Levi said, "Thanks. How was lunch?"

"Pretty good. Gina's getting *huge*. She swears she's not carrying twins, but she's way bigger than any of the other women in our family were at six months."

"You didn't *say* that to her, did you?" Levi asked. Dominic was the third of five children, and Gina was his youngest sibling, currently pregnant with her first child.

"No way. I like my balls not smashed to a bloody pulp, thanks." Dominic paused. "My mom said it."

"Oh my God."

"Yeah, it ignited this huge debate about who had been how big at which point in their pregnancies—everyone with their cell phones out, digging back through their photos and shouting about it for over an hour." Despite this description of family drama, Dominic's voice was cheerful. "Anyway, I'm going to meet Carlos at the gym now, and then I'm interning at McBride tonight and tomorrow night. But I thought maybe we could meet up for lunch tomorrow afternoon?"

"Sounds good," said Levi. He was already looking forward to it.

"My schedule is more flexible than yours, so just give me a call and tell me when and where to meet you."

"All right. See you tomorrow."

As Levi hung up, he remembered a moment from the night before with crystal clarity—Dominic pressing him up against the headboard, surging inside him, calling him *baby*. It had been said in the heat of passion, and he didn't know if Dominic even realized he'd done it.

He'd always disliked pet names; he'd certainly never used them with Stanton. He thought about Dominic calling him *baby* again in that deep, rumbly voice. Though he should have hated it, all it did was make him shiver, because it was different this time.

Everything was different with Dominic.

CHAPTER 3

Dominic met Carlos at Rolando's, a casual, scruffy hole-in-the-wall gym not far from Downtown. The eponymous owner, an Afro-Caribbean man similar to Dominic in height and build, had been a champion heavyweight boxer a decade earlier, particularly beloved in Las Vegas. He'd opened the gym after he retired, resisting pressure to take it in a fancy boutique direction and keeping it stripped down to the bare essentials.

Carlos was waiting at the door, his lanky body clad in track pants and a zipped-up jacket despite the stifling heat. He was rocking the artful stubble look these days, and he'd recently cut his dark-brown hair into a shorter style.

Knowing that Carlos wouldn't want to use the locker rooms, Dominic had changed into his own workout gear before leaving his mother's house. He greeted Carlos with a fist bump, and they headed inside.

They passed a few cardio machines and the boxing area, where Rolando himself was patiently coaching a couple of young men. He gave Dominic a friendly nod, and Dominic returned the gesture. God, he'd had an insane crush on Rolando when he'd first started here. Too bad the guy was hopelessly straight.

He and Carlos stopped in the weight room. There were a few other people hard at work, grunting and sweating through heavy sets. This gym was popular with both veterans and bounty hunters—two communities that tended to have a lot of overlap—which was how Dominic had found it in the first place. People came here to push themselves.

"You gonna take your jacket off?" Dominic asked lightly, as he and Carlos set up by a couple of weight benches.

Carlos hesitated, glancing around the gym. Nobody was paying any attention to them.

A few months ago, Carlos had gotten top surgery to remove his breasts and reshape his chest. He'd been gradually resuming his previous exercise routine over the past six weeks, and now the surgeon had not only cleared him for heavy upper-body weightlifting, but had strongly recommended it.

"You're safe here," Dominic said. Even if any of the gym-goers pegged Carlos as trans, they'd know better than to shoot their mouths off unless they wanted Rolando to knock their teeth down their throats.

"I know. It's just . . ."

Carlos shook his head, unzipped his jacket, and peeled it off. After he set it aside, he went to cross his arms over his chest, then repressed the gesture with visible effort.

Looking down at the flat chest beneath his T-shirt, he said, "It still feels weird to be out like this without a binder on."

"It looks great," Dominic said honestly. The surgeon had done impressive work—as well he should have, considering how much Carlos and Jasmine had paid for the procedure. "Plus, remember what the doctor said: the more you build up your pecs, the more it'll improve the shape."

"Yeah. But I'm not looking for monsters like these, all right?" Carlos slapped his hand against Dominic's chest.

Dominic grinned. "Noted."

He guided Carlos through the upper-body superset circuit he'd designed himself, moving them along at the same pace so the only difference was the amount of weight they were lifting. They were about halfway through it, banging out a set of horizontal dumbbell rows, when Carlos said, "Jasmine told me she ran into Levi coming out of your apartment this morning."

"Yeah?" Bent forward with one foot propped on the bench, Dominic lifted his enormous dumbbell with a grunt until his arm was perpendicular to his shoulder. He inhaled slowly through his nose as he lowered the weight.

"It was a relief too, because after what we heard last night, we were afraid you might have murdered him."

Dominic gasped out a laugh. "Sorry about that. He can be pretty loud." The memory was distracting, and it wasn't until they'd switched arms and were rowing on the other side that it occurred to him to add, "Don't say anything to him about it, though. He'd be so embarrassed—dude, breathe *out* when you lift the weight."

Carlos, whose face was flushed and sweaty, took a short break to readjust his position and fix his breathing. "So you guys are doing good, then?"

"I think so," Dominic said with a smile.

The conversation ebbed for a while as they concentrated on the workout. Later, when they were doing side by side barbell curls in front of a mirror, Carlos said, "Do you want to bring him to the Andersons' party on Saturday?"

Dominic raised his eyebrows. Jasmine's parents were having a cookout on Saturday afternoon, a casual family reunion sort of thing, and they'd invited him weeks ago. "You sure? I didn't know if you'd want him there."

"Of course we do. He's your boyfriend, right?"

"We haven't talked about it yet."

Carlos rolled his eyes. "He's your boyfriend, trust me." His speech was ragged, the words punched out between heaving breaths. "I mean, Jasmine and I weren't sure about him at first, because he didn't seem like your type. He's a little . . ."

"Stiff?" Dominic suggested. He squeezed his biceps as he curled the weight toward his shoulders, relishing the burn in his muscles.

"Yeah. He loosens up when he's speaking to you or touching you, though. And the look on your face when you talk about him . . . anyone who can make you look like that is okay with us."

"Thanks." Dominic was touched. "I'll run it past him, see if he's free that day."

They finished out the superset and returned the weights. "I'm going to propose to Jasmine at the party," Carlos said, right as Dominic was gulping a mouthful of water.

Dominic coughed up his water and wiped the back of his hand over his mouth. "Seriously? How long have you been planning that?"

Wringing his towel between his hands, Carlos said, "I've wanted to do it for a while, but I couldn't afford a ring so soon after the surgery, so I thought it'd be a long time coming. Then I talked to her mom about it, and she gave me Jasmine's great-grandmother's ring."

"Holy shit." Dominic clapped his shoulder. "Congratulations, man."

"Thanks," said Carlos. "I'm freaking out about it."

"You know she'll say yes."

"And you'd think that would make it less nerve-wracking, but it really doesn't."

Spending the night with Levi, lunch with his family, now Carlos's happy news—this day kept getting better and better. Dominic was in high spirits when he returned to his apartment, and took Rebel for a walk before he showered and changed for his internship.

After the Seven of Spades case, Levi had suggested that he consider becoming a private investigator. Dominic, who had been coming to the realization that he didn't want to spend the rest of his life bounty hunting and bartending, no matter how much he enjoyed both professions, had jumped on the idea and ran with it. He was scheduled to take the licensing exam in a few months, and in the meantime, he'd been learning the ropes at McBride Investigations.

While not the largest agency of its kind in Las Vegas, McBride was by far the most prestigious, with a list of high-roller clients a mile long. Dominic's years as a bounty hunter had given him an edge; he spent a few weeks proving his worth by using the sly tricks and shortcuts he'd developed, as well as his extensive network of contacts across the Valley, to tie up asset investigations and other research-heavy cases in record time. Tonight, he was being sent into the field for the first time—supervised, of course.

The agency occupied the tenth and eleventh floors in a sleek high-rise right off the Strip. Dominic took the elevator and was shown into Kate McBride's office at once.

McBride had inherited the business from her father, who had taken it over from his father before him. She was a muscular, stocky woman with tanned skin and short hair. Her croaky voice was roughened from decades of heavy smoking, though she'd recently transitioned to vaping at the insistence of her wife—her much younger, drop-dead-gorgeous, showgirl wife. Dominic had never seen her without an e-cigarette in her hand.

She was holding one now as she waved Dominic into a chair in front of her massive desk. "We're gonna start you off nice and easy," she said, nudging a slim file in his direction. "Domestic case, cheating spouse—this shit is our bread and butter."

Dominic skimmed the file while he listened.

"Nervous housewife in Summerlin thinks her rich hubby is having an affair, and she's probably right. All the signs are there—staying late at the office, furtive telephone calls, lower sex drive, buying her flowers and jewelry for no reason. These cases confirm infidelity about ninety-five percent of the time."

He didn't need to be told that; he'd lost count of the number of married bounties he'd ended up tracking down at the home of a secret lover. "Basic surveillance job?" he asked.

"You got it. Cases like these, we keep the target under constant surveillance during the hours specified by the client, document all activities, and record video whenever legal." McBride took a drag off her cigarette and exhaled the vapor. "I want to stress *legal*. All of our evidence needs to be admissible in court if necessary. You're a bounty hunter, so I'm not too worried about it. You know the laws around trespassing and covert recordings."

That was true, though he'd also broken those laws when he'd known he could get away with it.

Pointing her cigarette at him, she said, "There is one challenge with you doing surveillance work. Seeing as you're roughly the size of an elephant, there aren't many environments where you could really blend in."

"Thanks," said Dominic, but he wasn't offended.

"How do you handle that when you're out hunting bail jumpers?"

"I usually try to stay out of sight as much as possible—tail them in a car if I can. Or I go the other way and make direct contact under some sort of pretext that lets me keep an eye on them without raising suspicions."

"Hmm." McBride tapped the fingers of her free hand against her desk, sizing him up. "Well, it shouldn't be a problem anyway. Justine Aubrey is the lead investigator, and she can follow the target anywhere you'd attract too much attention."

Aubrey was a surveillance specialist, as well as one of the most generic-looking human beings Dominic had ever met. He considered himself particularly observant, and even he would be hard-pressed to describe her in any meaningful way.

"She's downstairs with Isaiah getting her equipment. You'd better run down and meet her so she can explain the finer points."

"Thank you." Dominic put the file back on the desk and headed for the door.

"Russo," McBride said, when he had his hand on the knob. He turned back to see her unscrewing and refilling her vaporizer. "I've been impressed with what I've seen from you so far, and the bail agencies around here have nothing but good things to say about you. Keep on like this, and there'll be an investigator position waiting for you once you're licensed." She narrowed her eyes. "So don't fuck this up, you got me?"

"Yes, ma'am," Dominic said. As he left the office, he felt the strangest urge to salute, which was something he hadn't done in years.

CHAPTER 4

"That's definitely the same woman," Martine said.

Monday morning, she and Levi were standing behind Carmen Rivera's desk, comparing two pictures pulled up side by side on Carmen's computer. One was a driver's license photo from the DMV; the other was a still from the Mirage's elevator cameras, flagged by Levi as the most likely candidate for Hensley's nighttime companion. This woman had arrived on Hensley's floor around ten thirty and left shortly after 1 a.m., at the early edge of the established window for his time of death.

She was a statuesque beauty, all smooth olive skin and silky black hair, and her features had a distinct Mediterranean cast. In the camera footage, she was conservatively dressed in a plum sheath and low-heeled pumps, a duffel bag slung over one arm.

"No doubt," said Carmen, one of their young tech wizards. She had a habit of chewing on her lips when she concentrated, the end result being that they were permanently chapped. Her messy bun listed precariously to one side of her head. "Diana Kostas. No hits on the DNA, but the prints popped right up once the lab got around to them. She got fingerprinted here at the LVMPD for her work permit."

Levi frowned. The way escort agencies in Clark County were able to operate legally was to license themselves as "outcall promoters," referral services for entertainers sent to hotel or motel guest rooms. The outcall entertainers had to register themselves as such and obtain work permits. With careful semantics, all parties involved were able to avoid implicating themselves in actual prostitution.

Fingerprinting was a standard part of obtaining a permit, so Kostas would have *known* the LVMPD had easy access to her prints. Why leave them behind in such an obvious place?

"Any criminal history?" he asked.

"None."

"You have any idea which agencies she might work with?" Martine said to Levi.

"No, all the phone records were a bust. Hensley must have booked his appointment online." Turning back to Carmen, Levi said, "Did you find anything there?"

"Yep." She clicked her mouse, switching screens to a website with a sultry red-and-black color scheme and the words *Sinful Secrets* written in flowing script. "From what I could dig up, this is the only outcall promoter Diana Kostas works with."

Martine let out a low whistle, and Levi's frown deepened. Sinful Secrets was a top-tier agency, the kind that catered to celebrities and Fortune 500 executives. Their escorts' hourly fees were astronomical.

Carmen navigated through the website—which was actually quite tasteful—to one of the escorts' individual pages. "She goes by the name Pandora while she's working."

The woman in these pictures wasn't Kostas, but it wouldn't be; agencies like these used models on their websites to protect their escorts' identities. It was a close approximation, though.

"Why the hell would someone who's probably making thousands of dollars an appointment roll a john for a wallet and some electronics?" Levi said.

"We don't know that's what happened. There are other possibilities." Martine ticked them off on her fingers as she spoke. "Maybe they did the drugs together, and he had a bad reaction. Maybe she drugged him because he made her feel unsafe and she didn't think she could leave the room. Or maybe he took the drugs after she left."

"Then where's his stuff?"

She didn't have an answer for that.

"This doesn't feel right," he muttered.

"I know; I feel it too," said Martine. "But we won't know anything more until we question this woman. Carmen, you got an address?"

After Carmen provided them with Kostas's home address in Henderson, they stopped by their desks to grab their things. "Do you mind driving?" Levi asked. "I need to think."

"Sure."

Just as they were leaving, however, Levi's desk phone rang. Martine waved him toward it.

"You'd better get that. I'll start running the air-conditioning in the car. Maybe by the time you catch up, we'll be able to get in it without roasting alive."

As she continued on her way, Levi returned to his desk and picked up the receiver. "Detective Abrams."

"Hi, Detective. This is Dr. Maldonado from the coroner's office."

"Yes, Doctor, what can I do for you?"

"I'm calling in reference to the Hensley case." A clicking keyboard sounded in the background. "I'll be forwarding you the full report later, but I wanted to update you on the cause of death as quickly as possible. It was definitely an overdose—flunitrazepam, to be specific. Rohypnol. There's very little chance it was accidental."

His interest piqued, Levi asked, "Why do you say that?"

"Nobody could survive the massive amount of Rohypnol in his system. Whoever measured out the drugs either intended for him to die or had absolutely no idea what they were doing. I should also note that I can't rule out the possibility that the drugs were self-administered, though this isn't a common substance of choice for suicides."

Levi thanked her and hung up, even more dubious now that they were on the right track. He shared the news with Martine as they drove out to Henderson.

Kostas lived in a cute desert ranch on a quiet suburban block. Given the heat, very few people were out and about at this time of day. With Martine by his side, Levi walked up the flower-lined path and rapped on the front door.

Kostas answered a moment later; Levi was startled to realize she was barely an inch shorter than him, and she wasn't even wearing heels. "Can I help you?" she said.

"Diana Kostas?" he asked. When she nodded, he showed her his badge and said, "I'm Detective Abrams with the LVMPD, and this is

Detective Valcourt. We need you to come with us and answer some questions about Dr. Stephen Hensley."

Blanching, Kostas took a step backward. Before she could respond, there came the patter of small feet and a cry of "Mommy!" as a young boy of about four or five ran up behind her. He saw Levi and Martine and ducked behind his mother's leg, though Levi could still glimpse a head full of black curls and big, soulful eyes. He held a half-eaten cookie in one hand.

Another woman, this one pale and blonde, joined the growing group at the front door. "What's going on, Diana?" she said in a voice full of suspicion.

"Everything's fine. Can you take Mason back to the kitchen, please?"

Though the blonde woman cast Levi and Martine a narrow-eyed glare, she didn't argue, just took Mason by the hand and led him back into the house.

"Your roommate?" Martine asked.

Kostas shook her head. "Just my friend Julie. She helps keep an eye on Mason during the day so I can study."

"Would she be able to watch him while you come down to the substation?"

Folding her arms, Kostas said, "Am I under arrest?"

"Not yet," said Levi. "But Dr. Hensley is dead."

He watched the shock blossom across her face. She could just be a good actor, he reminded himself. A lot of sex workers were; it was part of the job.

"We have uniformed officers on their way with a search warrant for your house," he added. "So you might want to have Julie take Mason somewhere else for a few hours."

Kostas pressed her lips together and nodded shortly. "Give me a minute."

She walked away, leaving the front door wide open so Levi could see into the living room. It was a cozy space, with toys scattered across the floor and pictures of Mason all over the walls.

"Oh boy, this is gonna suck," Martine said.

On his way into the substation, Levi stopped outside the doors to give Dominic a call. "Hey," he said when Dominic answered. "I'm about to interrogate a suspect, but I should be able to take a break in about an hour and a half."

"Cool," said Dominic. "Where do you want to go?"

"Well . . . I was thinking maybe we could just eat at my place."

"Your place? Levi, I've seen your kitchen. You've got a couple cans of soup, a loaf of bread, and everything else is coffee."

Levi shifted from foot to foot, sweating through his suit jacket under the burning sun, and said nothing.

"Why, Detective," Dominic said, slow and delighted. "Are you trying to tell me you're in the mood for a nooner?"

"You're an asshole," Levi said, scowling even though Dominic couldn't see him.

Dominic laughed. "I'll tell you what—I'll pick up some takeout and meet you at your apartment, all right?"

"Fine." Levi didn't dare say more than that, not wanting to let on how aroused he was by the idea of using his lunch break to get fucked in the middle of the workday.

His voice sliding into a low, teasing register, Dominic said, "I'll get something that keeps well, so it can wait until afterward if you really need sex so—"

"Ugh," Levi said, and hung up on him. He felt both annoyed and amused, a common blend of emotions he experienced around Dominic, and he was looking forward to lunch so much he didn't know how he was going to make it through the interrogation.

Diana Kostas was sitting at the metal table in the interview room with her back straight and her hands clasped in her lap. She looked nervous, lips pinched and cheeks pale, but she was holding herself together well.

"Ms. Kostas," Levi said as he sat across from her, "can you please tell me where you were last Saturday night between 10 p.m. and 3 a.m.?"

She hesitated, her eyes flicking toward the camera in the corner of the room.

"I'm not interested in pursuing a solicitation charge," he said. "I wouldn't be able to prove it anyway. My only concern is with Dr. Hensley's death."

"All right." She took a deep breath. "I got the referral from Sinful Secrets early in the evening. The requested appointment time was ten thirty, so that's when I got to Dr. Hensley's room at the Mirage. I was there for . . . two hours, two and a half? I'm pretty sure I left around 1 a.m. Then I went straight home."

"Can anyone confirm that?"

"Yes, my babysitter."

So far, Kostas's statement synced up with the Mirage's security tapes. Levi made a note for himself to get the babysitter's contact information later.

"Did either you or Dr. Hensley take any mind-altering substances while you were in his room?"

"We drank some champagne, that's all." Her composure suddenly cracking a bit, Kostas leaned forward and put her hands on the table. "Look, he was *fine* when I left his room, I swear to God. In a great mood, even. I don't know how he died, but—"

"It was an overdose of Rohypnol. And several valuable items were missing from his room."

She blinked—and then, to Levi's surprise, fury twisted her features as she clenched her hands into fists. "Is that what this is about?" she spat. "You think I'm a fucking trick roller? Are you *kidding* me?"

"Ms. Kostas—" Levi started, but she barreled right over him.

"Do you have any idea how much money I make doing what I do? I don't need to rob *anyone*. And even if I did, I wouldn't be stupid enough to do it on a job I'd been sent to by people who know my real name!"

Her voice had risen to a shout by that point. He'd slid his chair back a few inches from the table, his hands half-raised, very aware that she wasn't cuffed to the table.

Abruptly, she closed her eyes and sat back in her chair. When she opened her eyes several seconds later, her voice was clipped but calmer. "I depend on referrals from Sinful Secrets for my livelihood. If I ever harmed a client and it got back to them, they'd never work with me again, and I'd be screwed. Whatever was taken from Hensley's room couldn't possibly have been worth that."

Levi was inclined to agree. He thought back to the video footage of Kostas leaving Hensley's room Saturday night. She'd appeared at ease, no signs of panic or distress. She certainly hadn't looked like someone fleeing the scene of a homicide, accidental or otherwise.

He spent another half an hour with her, going through her statement multiple times and following up on several questions, such as what she'd needed the duffel bag for (to carry the clothes she changed into once in the client's room) and whether she'd seen anyone else in the hallway when she left (just the usual drunken partiers coming and going). He was jotting down her babysitter's name and number for corroboration when there was a knock on the other side of the two-way mirror.

Levi excused himself and left Kostas alone while he went into the viewing room next door. In addition to Martine, he found a uniformed officer named Daley and an unfamiliar woman who immediately caught and held his attention.

He knew a trained fighter when he saw one. People who had dedicated serious time to the study of hand-to-hand combat tended to hold themselves with a loose, quiet readiness, their backs straight, weight evenly distributed, hands free in case they were needed for defense. This woman checked all those boxes and was in incredible shape besides, her lean, hard muscles obvious beneath her silk blouse and pencil skirt. She had golden-brown skin, a sharply defined nose, and black hair that was swept up in a simple ponytail.

"Levi, this is Deputy District Attorney Leila Rashid," Martine said. "Ms. Rashid, Detective Levi Abrams."

"Pleasure to meet you, Detective," said Rashid, coming forward to shake his hand. "I've heard a lot about you."

"I'm afraid I can't say the same."

"I'm relatively new to the DA's office—just started in March."

"Did you catch the Hensley case?" he asked. "I don't think we have anything solid for you yet."

"Are you sure about that?" She looked at Daley, who cleared his throat.

"The officers searching the Kostas home didn't find any of the stolen items," he said to Levi, "but they did find a shoebox stuffed in the back of the cabinet under the bathroom sink behind a bunch of other junk. There were a few unlabeled vials inside that field-tested positive for flunitrazepam. They're on the way to the lab for confirmatory testing, but it doesn't look good."

Astonished, Levi turned to the two-way mirror. On the other side of the glass, Kostas sat cradling her head in her hands.

"Are you going to arrest her now, or let her sweat it out for a bit?" Rashid asked.

"This doesn't make sense," Levi said, more to himself than to her.

She responded anyway. "Why not? I've reviewed the case so far. You've got her fingerprints and almost certainly her DNA at the scene, video evidence of her leaving within the window for time of death with a bag that could easily be carrying the stolen items, and now the possible murder weapon found in her home. What more do you want?"

"A motive would be nice," Levi snapped.

"Please," Rashid said, waving a dismissive hand. "I can think of half a dozen reasons for a sex worker to kill her client just off the top of my head without even bringing robbery into the equation. Have you considered the possibility that she took his stuff just to create the very doubts you're feeling now?"

Of course he'd considered it, but having Rashid throw it in his face only irritated him. He glared at her.

"Levi," Martine cut in, levelheaded as always. "Do you have another angle? Suicide, maybe?"

"In a guy who'd just had great sex, was about to present ostensibly ground-breaking research, didn't leave a note, and had been *robbed*? No." He shrugged. "But someone else could have killed Hensley and pinned it on her."

"Oh, floating the frame-job theory?" Rashid said pleasantly. "That's kind of a specialty of yours, isn't it?"

Levi went rigid. In his peripheral vision, he saw Martine wince, and Daley actually backed up a few steps.

"Okay," Martine said, after a loaded silence in which Rashid continued smiling at Levi like butter wouldn't melt in her mouth.

"We'll continue pursuing other avenues of investigation, but Levi, you know we have to charge Kostas based on what we have right now. I can do it if you'd rather not."

"I've got it," said Levi, his voice curt. He left the viewing room, restraining himself from slamming the door, and returned to the interview room.

Kostas lifted her head; when she saw Levi's face, she straightened up with an apprehensive expression. "What's wrong?"

"The officers searching your house found Rohypnol underneath your bathroom sink."

"*What?*" she said, her eyes going wide. "That's impossible. I'd never keep that shit in my house, and definitely not where Mason might get to it—"

"I'm sorry," Levi said. "Diana Kostas, you're under arrest for the murder of Stephen Hensley."

CHAPTER 5 ♠

"Oh my God," Dominic said, as Levi toppled off him and collapsed by his side. He stared at the ceiling for a few hazy moments before remembering he still had the condom on. Fumbling it off his softening cock, he tied it in a sloppy knot and tossed it at the wastebasket, making the shot more by virtue of luck than skill. Then he pushed his sweaty hair away from his forehead and looked at the panting man beside him.

When they'd met up at Levi's apartment twenty minutes earlier, Levi had torn into him, barely giving him a chance to drop the takeout on the kitchen counter before dragging him into the bedroom and shoving him onto the bed. Levi had been in a vicious mood, but since Dominic knew he wasn't the cause of it, he'd been happy to let Levi work out his frustrations by riding him like a champion jockey.

Now that Levi looked less like he was about to snap in half, Dominic rolled onto his side and skimmed a hand up Levi's thigh to squeeze his hip. "What happened at work to stress you out?"

"I don't want to talk about it," Levi said, though not rudely. He nestled against Dominic's chest, pressing a kiss to his collarbone. "I'd rather talk about *your* case. How was last night?"

"Pretty good. You know how boring surveillance can be." Dominic smoothed his hand up and down Levi's back as he spoke. "We're following this guy whose wife thinks he's having an affair. He's been telling her he has a standing Sunday night poker game at a buddy's house, and that checked out—he went to the right house, there were a bunch of other guys there, and he went straight home after a few hours. No detours."

Levi pulled back far enough to look him in the eye. "A poker game? Are you okay?"

"I'm fine," said Dominic. He couldn't resist kissing the tip of Levi's nose. "It's not like I saw them playing or anything; I was in the car the whole time."

Levi was always concerned about triggering Dominic's compulsive gambling. The truth was, if Dominic *had* been forced to watch the men playing poker, it would have been a big problem. At the very least, he would have needed to spend the rest of the night talking himself down. The urge to gamble was just as powerful now as when he'd gone into recovery over two years ago. But none of that had happened, so there was no point in thinking about it.

"Your guy will turn out to be a cheater, just wait," Levi said, his voice muffled as he buried his face back in Dominic's chest. "This is Vegas."

It occurred to Dominic that now might be a good time to raise the question of exclusivity between the two of them. The desire for serious commitment in a romantic relationship was totally foreign to him, but he couldn't deny it was what he wanted with Levi. In the end, however, he was too worried that Levi wasn't in the same place he was, so he kept his mouth shut and just held Levi in silence while they both wound down.

Last night really hadn't been as tedious as it could've been. Aubrey had led a crazy life, as exciting and remarkable as her looks were mundane, and her stories had kept them entertained for hours. Plus, though the case seemed frivolous, it was actually quite high stakes—there was a multi-million-dollar prenup hanging in the balance. Dominic would be assisting with surveillance of Geoffrey Rhodes for the rest of the week, or at least until they caught him with his hand in the cookie jar.

"I need to take a quick shower," Levi said a few minutes later. He began disentangling himself from Dominic. "I'd invite you to join me, but I don't think we'd both fit in there."

"No problem. I'll get the food set up."

Dominic was on the side of the bed closest to the bathroom, but instead of exiting on his own side and walking around, Levi just climbed over him. This seemed to involve a lot more sliding and rubbing than was strictly necessary, and as Levi got out of the bed, Dominic smacked his bare ass. Levi squawked in mock indignation and retaliated with a back kick, pulling it so his foot only gave Dominic's hip a hard nudge.

Chuckling, Dominic watched Levi disappear into the bathroom, then got up himself. He pulled on his boxers and pants but decided to forgo a shirt for now—the apartment was too warm even with the air-conditioning on full blast.

Levi's new place had hardwood floors and large windows that let in a lot of natural light, making it seem bigger than it was. The impression of space was emphasized by the fact that he didn't have much furniture. He'd donated most of his old stuff when he'd moved in with Barclay two years ago, and he'd only purchased the bare essentials for this apartment.

Dominic ambled into the kitchen to retrieve the sandwiches he'd brought over. He wouldn't have minded just eating his straight from the wrapper, but he knew Levi would want his on a plate, so he rummaged around in the cabinets for dishes and water glasses. Since he didn't come here very often—they usually went to his place instead—it took him a couple of minutes to remember where everything was.

Levi's taste in home décor ran to contemporary pieces with clean lines and an earthy, neutral color scheme. A sleek table and matching chairs stood in the small dining area off the kitchen, along with an incongruous armoire shoved against one wall—the tall kind with double doors that opened from the middle and two drawers beneath. Dominic had once asked Levi why he kept it out here, and Levi had shrugged and given him a vague answer about it being too big to fit in the tiny bedroom.

That was true, but the armoire didn't fit out *here* either, especially when someone Dominic's size was trying to maneuver around the table and chairs to clear Levi's work junk off to one side so they had enough room to eat.

It might not have been a problem if he hadn't still been sex-drunk and clumsy. As he was moving some of Levi's file folders, his elbow caught another pile and sent it teetering dangerously over the edge of the table. He lunged and grabbed them before they fell, but his stumbling momentum carried him sideways, and he banged hard into the armoire.

He winced at the thumping and rustling sounds of multiple stacks of paper falling over inside. One of the armoire's doors popped open, creaking under the weight of papers and folders slipping out further every second. He dropped his armful back on the table and hurried to rescue the armoire's contents before they could plummet onto the floor, shifting both doors wider so he could get a better grip. Of course Levi had to keep files in this thing instead of clothes like a normal person—

Dominic lifted his head, blinked twice in astonishment, and gaped.

The inner walls and doors of the armoire were plastered with graphic crime scene photographs, maps, and newspaper clippings, all focused on the Seven of Spades. There was the first-ever *Las Vegas Review-Journal* article on the subject, its headline blaring *SERIAL KILLER LOOSE IN LAS VEGAS*, and every related article since, including the one declaring Keith Chapman guilty of the murders. Colorful pushpins dotted maps of the Las Vegas Valley, tracking every known movement of the Seven of Spades—their five crime scenes, the hotel where they'd intervened to help Dominic protect Levi from Drew Barton's attack, the community baseball field in Boulder City where he and Levi had found Chapman having a meltdown. Everything in sight was marked up and underlined and scribbled over with Levi's spiky handwriting.

More papers were heaped on the bottom of the armoire, some stuffed inside folders and others left loose. It was no wonder they'd unbalanced when Dominic had bumped into the thing; the stacks were haphazard and crooked, a few far taller than the others for no reason he could discern. Levi's notes were even denser on these. He'd made himself goddamn spreadsheets and *charts*, for fuck's sake.

Dominic had known Levi planned to pursue this case on his own, even after his sergeant had ordered him not to, but this was no standard investigation. This was an obsessive shrine.

He felt Levi's presence behind him more than he heard him; Levi moved like a cat when he was barefoot. Slowly, Dominic turned around.

Levi stood a few feet away, dressed in trousers and a fresh shirt. His arms were crossed tightly over his chest, and a bead of water trickled down the side of his face from his wet hair. He glared at Dominic as if he were wishing he could burn a hole right through him by sheer force of willpower.

"I didn't mean to snoop," Dominic said. Privacy was important to Levi, and if he wasn't completely honest now, the results would be disastrous. "I accidentally knocked over the papers inside the armoire. I was just trying to keep them from falling out when I saw . . . this."

Levi's rigid posture didn't relax in the slightest. "I shouldn't keep it out here, but I didn't know where else to put it." It wasn't clear whether he meant the armoire itself or all the craziness inside. Probably both.

Dominic glanced over his shoulder and then back at Levi, at a loss for words.

"I thought you believed me that the Seven of Spades is still out there," Levi said. His voice was sharp and cold.

God, Dominic hated seeing him like this. He and Levi had known each other in a distant, professional sense for years before the Seven of Spades case had taught them that they didn't really know each other at all. It had been months since Levi had subjected him to this frosty-eyed, prickly façade he wore around everyone else—around people he didn't trust. Dominic couldn't bear it.

"I *do* believe you," he said. "I've always believed you. But Levi . . . part of you must know that this isn't healthy. How much time have you been spending on this?"

"All of it," said Levi, his gaze unflinching. "Whenever I'm not at work, or the gym, or with you, I'm here, working this case."

"Oh my God." Dominic scrubbed a hand down his face. When he looked up, he saw Levi retreating even further into himself, opening his mouth, no doubt about to kick Dominic out on his ass. "Wait. I'm not judging you, and I'm not trying to tell you how to do your job or control what you do with your time. I'm just worried. I want to understand—help me understand."

A muscle jumped in Levi's jaw. He glanced away, his aloof aura cracking a bit. "The day after Keith killed himself, Martine said I couldn't accept he was the killer because it meant I'd never have closure—he'd never be able to tell me why he specifically singled me out. She had a point. You and I agreed that the Seven of Spades is probably someone I know, or at least someone who knows me." He drew a shaky breath. "Every single day, I have to wonder if each person

I'm talking to and working beside is a serial killer. It drives me crazy that I could be looking right at them and not *know*. It gnaws at me all the time, and people make jokes but it's not *funny*—"

"I know," Dominic said, stepping forward to put his hands on Levi's shoulders. He wanted to hug him, but he didn't know if Levi would accept that in his current state. "It's awful. I'm sorry."

Levi stood still for a moment, vibrating with tension. Then he sighed and tipped forward against Dominic's chest, his arms falling to his sides as he rested his head on Dominic's shoulder. Dominic wrapped him up, gave him a squeeze, and kissed the top of his head.

"All right," he said. "Let's sit down and eat, and you can tell me what you've been working on."

While they settled at the table with their sandwiches, Dominic berated himself for being so oblivious. How could he not have realized how deeply this case was sucking Levi under? This obsession had been building for *months*, and he hadn't noticed. He'd known the Seven of Spades's clean getaway troubled Levi—hell, it troubled him too—but he'd had no idea Levi's anxieties had become so all-consuming.

In the course of his investigation, Levi had reinterviewed every witness even tangentially connected to the five murders, reanalyzed every piece of evidence, reevaluated every lead. One of the victims, Benjamin Roth, had been left in a car full of empty liquor bottles—the killer's pointed reference to his drunk driving—and Levi had contacted every liquor store in the area looking for anyone who'd purchased in bulk. He'd compared each name on the building security logs from one of the crime scenes to a list of people in the Las Vegas Valley who had a history of committing violence motivated by justice or self-righteousness. He'd personally run down every person who had known about the supposedly secret investigation into Phillip Dreyer's embezzlement and fraud, looking for a leak, only to discover the investigation hadn't been so secret after all.

Levi had even delved deeper into Los Avispones, the street gang the Seven of Spades had paid to knock over several veterinary clinics in the Valley for their ketamine. "I'm ninety-nine percent sure that's a dead end, though," he said, after swallowing a mouthful of roast beef. "That arrangement existed purely to frame Keith. I suspected from the beginning that the Seven of Spades might be obtaining their ketamine through legal channels, and I still believe that's the strongest possibility."

"How difficult would that be?" Dominic asked.

"For someone this intelligent?" Levi shrugged one shoulder. "Not very. Ketamine is a legal substance; it's just controlled. If you were able to forge the right paperwork, maybe have someone on the inside to grease the wheels . . . a clever person could pull it off. I've been looking into it, but it's the proverbial needle in the haystack. I can't even be sure they're getting the ketamine in Nevada instead of another state. Plus . . ."

"You don't know they're still getting it at all," Dominic finished for him. The Seven of Spades hadn't killed anyone since Keith Chapman's death—at least not with their old MO.

Levi glumly pushed his half-eaten sandwich away. Dominic almost protested, but thought better of it; Levi hated being pressured to eat.

"These are your suspects so far?" he said instead, picking up a thick sheaf of stapled papers. It was a printout of an Excel spreadsheet with each included person's connection to the case thoroughly documented. Still, he didn't know how helpful it would be, because it looked to contain half the LVMPD and a third of the DA's office.

"Yeah."

Dominic frowned as he flipped through the spreadsheet. "Hey, how come that loudmouth asshole you work with isn't on here? Gibbs?"

"Oh, come on," Levi said with a contemptuous snort. "He's an impulsive, tactless idiot. No self-control at all."

"That could be an act."

Levi rolled his eyes, but Dominic lifted a hand before he could respond.

"I know I said the same thing about Chapman, and I was wrong then. Nobody could fake being that ill for so long. A personality like Gibbs's, though? That could all be for show. It might even be fun for someone with a certain type of psychopathy."

Levi's brow creased as Dominic's words sank in. He chewed on his lower lip and stared into space, obviously deep in thought, while Dominic returned to the list.

"That rookie cop you liked isn't on here either," Dominic said a couple of minutes later. "The one who leaked the Seven of Spades story to the *Review-Journal*."

"Kelly Marin? Be serious, Dominic."

"I am." He dropped the spreadsheet and met Levi's eyes. "You can't rule people out based on your personal opinions of them. You have almost nothing to go on to begin with. The only people you can really exclude safely are—"

"The ones who were in the room when the Seven of Spades called me. Yes, I know that."

"Were either Gibbs or Marin there the first time?" Dominic knew they hadn't been there for the second call, because he'd been present for that one himself.

"No." Covering his face with both hands, Levi let out a low, frustrated groan.

Dominic reached out and tugged one of his hands away. "You're an amazing detective, Levi, but this case is too personal for you. Most of these suspects are people you work closely with every day. You're gonna miss things if you don't have someone helping you out."

"Sounds like you're volunteering," said Levi.

"Of course I am. I won't pretend to be impartial myself, not after everything that happened, but I'm not emotionally invested in these people the same way you are." Dominic hesitated, then asked, "Did you really think I wouldn't help you?"

"I . . ." Levi toyed with the crust of his abandoned sandwich. "No. I knew you'd help me if I asked, no matter what you thought of it. I kept this a secret because I was embarrassed. I can't control the way this whole Seven of Spades thing is affecting me, and I don't like that about myself."

Dominic understood. How much had he told Levi about his compulsive gambling, after all? Nothing more than the most basic details—not because he was worried Levi would reject him, but because he was so ashamed of his addiction and the things it had driven him to do that it was painful to talk about even with people he trusted.

"I get it," he said, and left it at that. "What's your next step?"

"Dr. Tran."

It took Dominic a second to place the name. "Chapman's psychiatrist?"

"Yes. I've always thought it was suspicious that she kept him on those antipsychotics even though he was so physically ill. We know now that he was being poisoned—she would have had plenty of opportunity to do that, and even if she didn't, why did she ignore his side effects? She brushed off all of Natasha's concerns every time Natasha reached out to her. Apparently that's not such an unusual dynamic between psychiatrists and social workers, but still."

Dominic nodded thoughtfully. "You have a plan?"

"Six weeks ago, I made an appointment with Dr. Tran for myself under a fake name."

"What?" Dominic said with a startled laugh. That sounded like something *he* would do. "Really?"

"I figured I could subtly feel her out, get a sense of who she is as a doctor and a person. See if there's anything there that merits further investigation."

Dominic imagined Levi sitting stiffly in a psychiatrist's office, pretending to be someone he wasn't, and cringed. No way that would end well. "Nobody there knows what you look like, right? Maybe I should do it instead."

Levi scowled. "No! Why?"

"I'm a better liar than you are."

"A better actor, maybe—"

"That's a nicer way of saying the same thing," said Dominic. "Look, this shrink treats a lot of cops, right? She's one of the LVMPD's go-tos. What if a coworker sees you there?"

Unmoved by this argument, Levi said, "What if they see *you* there? Half the cops in Las Vegas know who you are."

"That's true, but they'd never ask me why I was seeing a psychiatrist. You, on the other hand . . . Your sergeant specifically ordered you not to continue this investigation on your own. What do you think would happen if it got back to Wen that you were visiting Keith Chapman's doctor?"

"Ugh, fuck," Levi said a little sulkily, and it was ridiculous how adorable Dominic found that. "You have a point, I guess. You're sure you want to do this?"

"Absolutely."

"Fine. The appointment is Wednesday at 1 p.m."

"I'll be there." Dominic covered Levi's hand with his own and added, "I said I get it, and I do. I know what it's like not to be able to let something go. How many times did you tell me to do exactly that when the Seven of Spades was running around the city and I just flat-out ignored you?"

"Yeah, well, I know better than that now. You never do anything people tell you not to. You just smile and say something charming and do whatever the hell you were planning in the first place."

Levi said the words fondly, his eyes warm and his lips quirked. Momentarily flustered, Dominic dropped his eyes to his plate, so it caught him off guard when Levi leaned over the corner of the table and took hold of his chin.

They kissed softly, languidly, and Dominic couldn't help moaning into Levi's mouth. God, he was just about ready to go again. Levi worked him up like nobody else ever had.

They were interrupted by the ringing of Levi's cell phone across the room. Levi sighed, pressed one more kiss to Dominic's lips, and got up from the table. Dominic returned his attention to the remains of his lunch and willed away his burgeoning semi.

"Hi, Martine," Levi said, leaning against the counter that separated the kitchen from the living room. He was silent for a moment and then blushed a deep pink. "No, I'm not!"

Grinning, Dominic polished off the last of his sandwich.

Levi frowned as he listened to Martine, then said, "*What?*" in a tone that sounded shocked but not upset. "You're kidding me . . . Yeah. Yeah, of course. I'll meet you there. Bye."

"Everything okay?" Dominic asked when he hung up.

"It's the case Martine and I caught yesterday. It looked like a trick roll gone wrong—john dead of an overdose, valuables missing, the whole nine yards. We have the primary suspect in custody; she's on her way to the CCDC right now."

"And?"

"And someone just used the victim's credit card," Levi said.

CHAPTER 6

"**T**hese are weird charges for someone on a spending spree with a stolen credit card," Martine said.

She and Levi were sitting in her car in a parking garage Downtown, mapping the thief's movements on her tablet. In the time it had taken for the credit card company to notify Carmen Rivera of the activity and for Martine and Levi to coordinate their approach, the card had been used at a 7-11, an Economy Motel, a Laundromat, and a bakery. All the businesses were in the same general area, though there was no defined pattern. They'd sent uniformed officers out to start taking statements and checking for helpful security cameras while they waited for the next charge in hopes of catching the thief in the act.

Levi stretched out his legs and twisted from side to side to crack his back; he hated being cooped up in a car like this. "It's a good thing Hensley's wife agreed to leave his credit cards active so we could monitor them."

"Mmm-hmm. I talked to her a couple hours ago, by the way. She's flying into Vegas tomorrow morning."

"Nice of her to rush right out here."

Martine snorted. "Well, I did warn her that we wouldn't be able to release Hensley's body for at least a few more days. But yeah, I got the impression that she wasn't too broken up about his death. Are you really shocked?"

"Not much shocks me anymore," said Levi.

A message flashed on Martine's tablet. She swiped her finger across the screen and said, "It's from Carmen. Hensley's card was just used at the Market Street Café in the California Hotel and Casino."

"That's only a few blocks from here."

They drove to the hotel and left the car at the valet stand with apologies and a flash of their badges. Levi felt optimistic—the thief had probably left by now, but a restaurant meant a server who had personally interacted with them and would be able to describe them, maybe have an idea of where they were going next.

The Market Street Café was a casual 24-hour diner with a kitschy island theme. The hostess hurried them right to the back to speak to a manager, who called over one of the servers once they'd explained their purpose.

"Tanya, did you wait on a Stephen Hensley at Table 14 within the past hour?" he asked.

"His daughter," Tanya said. "She's still here, actually, just finishing up her dessert."

Tanya pointed across the restaurant to a corner table near the entrance—and God, it was just a kid, a skinny teenage girl with golden-brown skin and black hair in a messy ponytail. She was dressed in a baggy sweatshirt, hunched over her plate and shoveling pie into her mouth.

Martine reached out to lower Tanya's pointing finger, but it was too late. Across the restaurant, the girl's head jerked up like a deer scenting a hunter in the woods. She looked straight at them, and Levi saw her register them as enemies in the split second before she leapt from the table and bolted.

"*Shit*," he said, and ran after her.

"I'll call for backup!" Martine shouted.

The front of the restaurant had a few stanchion barriers set up to corral the long lines that formed at busier times of day. The girl slid right underneath them without missing a beat and took off across the casino floor. Too tall to do the same, Levi planted a hand on the bar and vaulted over instead.

Between the two of them, Levi was doubtlessly faster in terms of base speed—but he was wearing a suit and shoes not designed for running, and she had the adrenaline of fear on her side. He was just able to keep her in sight as he pursued her through the casino and into the lobby, where she nimbly darted around a heavily laden luggage cart a bellhop was pulling across the floor. With no time to change course, Levi hurdled the stacked suitcases to cries of shock and alarm.

The girl burst out the front doors and sprinted into the pedestrian crosswalk at the intersection of Ogden and Main despite the fact that the lights were decidedly *not* in her favor. Horns blared and tires squealed as cars swerved to avoid her. One car screeched to a halt right in Levi's path; he hopped up on the hood and slid sideways across it, ignoring the driver's cursing.

Somehow, they both made it to the other side of the street intact. The girl pelted down the sidewalk, but it was a straight shot with clear sightlines and little pedestrian traffic at the moment, so Levi started gaining ground.

That is, until she made a sharp left into the Freemont Street Experience.

"Oh, fuck me," Levi groaned.

The Freemont Street Experience was a pedestrian mall crowned by the world's largest video screen, a vaulted canopy suspended ninety feet overhead that extended the entire five blocks. It was too early for the light shows and live bands, but the place was *swarmed* with tourists drinking and shopping and people-watching—the perfect place to shake a pursuer.

Levi chased the girl through the thick crowd, dodging sightseers, break-dancers, street magicians, and even more exotic entertainers. There were distractions everywhere—music blasting from the speakers, excited whoops and hollers, screams from the people riding the zip lines that ran overhead. The girl knew what she was doing, too, creating a zigzagging path around souvenir kiosks and denser groups of tourists. It took all his concentration to keep her in his eyeline. His heart pounded in his chest, his lungs burning as he labored for breath.

Two blocks down, his cell phone rang.

"Now—is not—a good time," Levi gasped, not decreasing his speed at all.

"Just tell me where you are so I can get backup to your location," Martine said.

"FSE. Fourth Street side." He hung up without any pleasantries; she wouldn't care.

When they finally emerged on the far side of the Freemont Street Experience, Levi was flagging. He had great cardiovascular endurance, but running at top effort for over half a mile was ridiculous.

Fortunately, the girl wasn't immune to fatigue either. She slowed down as she ran past Crazy Ely's Western Village and then turned right down an alleyway. Levi put on a final burst of speed as he followed.

The alley was a dead end. Thank *God*.

He heard the girl's frustrated shout when she realized she was trapped. He stumbled to a halt about twenty feet away, panting, his hands on his hips. Sirens wailed in the distance.

The girl whirled around to face him in a fighting stance with her fists raised. Levi noted absently that her form wasn't bad.

Showing her his badge while spreading his own hands wide, he said, "I'm not going to hurt you. I'm a police officer."

Her expression only hardened. Obviously, cops weren't a source of reassurance for her.

Now that they were no longer running, Levi took a closer look. She was as young as he'd first assumed, fifteen or sixteen at the most, and she wasn't fast-metabolism skinny—she was not-getting-enough-to-eat skinny. Though her clothes were clean, they were worn-out and ill-fitting. Her battered sneakers were held together with duct tape, coming undone after the hard chase, and her fingernails were caked with dirt.

A black and white drove past the entrance to the alleyway, braked, and backed up. Two uniformed officers sprang out.

Levi came to a quick decision. He waved the officers off, instructing them to return to their car and kill the lights and siren. Then he turned back to the girl and said, "You're not in trouble. I just want to talk."

She didn't lower her fists. "About what?"

"I'm a homicide detective. The man whose credit card you've been using today—he was murdered on Saturday night."

The girl's eyes went round, and she dropped her arms to her sides. "I didn't kill him!" she said in a tone laced with panic.

"I know that. I'm not accusing you of anything, and you're not under arrest. I'd just like to talk to you for a few minutes. Maybe we could sit down?"

She hesitated, biting her lower lip, and then nodded.

They ended up crossing the street to sit at the bench in a bus shelter. Levi pulled off his jacket and loosened his tie; between the run and the terrible heat, he was soaked with sweat and a little dizzy. He'd kill for a bottle of water.

"What's your name?" he asked.

"Adriana. Adriana Velazquez."

"I'm Levi Abrams." He offered his hand, which she shook after a moment's pause. "You're not from Vegas, are you?"

She shook her head, clasping both hands in her lap and staring down at them. "Reno."

"How old are you?"

"Eighteen," she said, giving him a shifty sideways glance.

He raised an eyebrow.

"Sixteen," she muttered.

"Your parents know you're out here?" he asked, already anticipating her answer.

"No parents."

He considered her hunched, defensive posture, her swift flight from the restaurant, the hunted look in her dark eyes. "Foster family?"

She flinched and tried to cover it up with a nonchalant shrug. Levi sighed. He hated being right about things like this.

"The man the credit card belonged to—Stephen Hensley—he died Saturday night. His wallet, cell phone, and some other valuables were stolen. Can you tell me where you found them?"

"I didn't find all that! Just—just the card. It was laying out on the sidewalk."

"Where?"

She gave him a location Downtown, nowhere near the Mirage or anywhere Diana Kostas would have gone between there and home. Her feet shuffled as she spoke, her fingers twisting together, and she never looked him in the eye. It couldn't have been more obvious that she was lying.

She didn't trust him, and she didn't feel safe. What reason did she have to tell him the truth? There was no chance a homeless runaway with the history her body language suggested was going to confide in a strange male cop who'd just chased her through half the neighborhood.

"Adriana—"

"Am I gonna go to jail?" she interrupted. "I know I shouldn't have taken the card. I know it was wrong. I—I was just really hungry, and I wanted to take a real shower for once."

That explained the charge for the motel room. "You're not going to jail," said Levi. "I'll speak to his family and the DA's office and explain the circumstances. I'm sure we can work something out." Gently, he added, "But you know I can't let you run back out into the streets, right?"

She pressed her lips together, her gaze trained on her hands. Tears gathered in the corners of her eyes. "Please don't send me back there."

Levi looked up to where Martine was hovering half a block away, watching them closely. He nodded for her to join them and said, "Maybe you could come back to the substation with me and my partner. We know someone who might be able to help you."

An hour later, he had Adriana set up in a comfortable interview room with a soda and some snacks from the vending machine. Martine stayed with her while Levi waited in the bullpen for Natasha Stone.

A good friend of Levi's for several years, Natasha worked in the LVMPD's Police Employee Assistance Program. She'd counseled Levi himself after he'd shot and killed the perpetrator of a hostage crisis earlier that year. There was nobody he trusted more to handle a sticky case like Adriana's.

Natasha showed no irritation at being called back to work for something that wasn't even technically her job; she greeted Levi with the same calm, friendly energy that always surrounded her. Her very pale skin was dusted with freckles, and her rich auburn hair spilled loose over her shoulders.

"I'm sorry to call you in after-hours," Levi said. "I know you're not in victim advocacy anymore."

She smiled and squeezed his arm. "I'm a social worker, Levi. I'll always be in victim advocacy."

"I'm just not sure what to do here. I checked out her story, and she's in the foster system in Reno. Been missing three months. I didn't press her for details, but I suspect some form of abuse—physical, maybe sexual."

"Strictly speaking, we're supposed to send her back to Reno." Natasha lifted a hand before Levi could protest. "But obviously I'm not going to do that if there are abuse allegations. I have a few tricks up my sleeve, and I know how to game the system. I can work out a way to keep her in Vegas temporarily, buy us some time to find a more permanent solution that keeps her safe."

Levi let out a slow, relieved breath. "Thank you so much. I really appreciate it."

He brought her to the interview room, where Adriana and Martine were visible through the open blinds over the large window. Natasha slipped inside, exchanged a few words with Martine, and then sat in the chair across from Adriana while Martine left the room to stand beside Levi in the hall.

Within five minutes, Adriana was relaxed, smiling and chattering away like any normal teenager.

"How does Natasha do that?" Levi asked.

"She's a people person." Martine looked up at him. "Adriana lied to you, you know."

"Yeah. But if I'd pushed her any harder, we'd never get anything out of her. I thought maybe if we showed her we're on her side, helped her out with her situation and made sure there aren't any legal charges, she might be more forthcoming."

"No arguments here. That poor kid—she's jumpy as fuck. I don't know what happened to her, but it must have been some bad shit."

"There's one thing I *do* know for sure," he said.

"What's that?"

He turned away from the window and squared his shoulders. "Diana Kostas didn't kill Stephen Hensley."

CHAPTER 7

Geoffrey Rhodes had told his wife he'd be working late—and he did stay at the office a couple of hours past quitting time. When he left, however, he didn't head home. He went in the opposite direction, straight for the Las Vegas Strip.

"Think tonight's the night?" Dominic asked Justine Aubrey. They were following in her ubiquitous silver Honda Accord, a few comfortable car lengths behind.

"Could be," she said with a shrug. "Don't know why he'd go to the Strip to meet his mistress, though."

They trailed Rhodes to a parking garage. Rather than follow him inside, Aubrey stopped at the curb and said, "If he's going to be wandering around the Strip, we'll have to follow him on foot. I'll get out now and pick him up when he comes out. You park the car and hook up with me later—we'll leapfrog him so he's less likely to notice us."

"Sounds good."

Aubrey got out of the car and stood by the pedestrian exit, striking up a cigarette while she waited—though a close observer would have noticed that she barely inhaled when the cigarette touched her lips. Dominic came around to the driver's side, where he had to slide the seat all the way back to fit his legs in the footwell.

It took him a few minutes to find a spot. As he reemerged from the garage on foot, Aubrey texted him that she and Rhodes were in the Shops at Crystals.

Dominic walked with his hands shoved in his jacket pockets and his eyes focused straight ahead. Being on the Strip always made him tense. He'd rarely come here in the throes of his addiction, preferring the cheaper casinos Downtown and on the West Side that catered to locals, but there was no way to ignore the constant reminders of gambling on Las Vegas Boulevard. It was everywhere—the billboards, the ads, the fliers. Even the snatches of conversation he picked up from the tourists surrounding him were full of debates on gambling strategy and chatter about wins and losses.

He exhaled slowly and concentrated on the things he *did* love about the Strip: the diversity, the giddy high spirits, the pulsing, vibrating energy of thousands of people out having fun. These people in particular had braved the hellish heat of the Nevada desert at the height of summer for their vacations, and they weren't going to let anything stand in the way of their good time.

Following Aubrey's texts, Dominic resumed Rhodes's trail inside the blessedly air-conditioned upscale mall. He caught sight of her a hundred feet away; she gave him a barely perceptible nod and melted into the crowd.

Rhodes seemed more like he was killing time than doing purposeful shopping, just ambling around the mall and browsing the window displays of the various high-end stores. Dominic stayed well back, utilizing natural cover and reflective surfaces to his advantage whenever possible. Though he had a button camera on his jacket, it wouldn't be much use at this distance. He kept his cell phone in one hand; it was an easy way to look realistically occupied, and it also let him keep in constant contact with Aubrey.

When Rhodes stopped outside Bottega Veneta to fool around with his own phone, Dominic narrowed his eyes.

What kind of phone does Rhodes use? he texted to Aubrey.

iPhone 6. Why?

Because right now he's texting on a Samsung Galaxy.

Ooh, secret phone, she wrote back. *Nice catch. I'll see what I can dig up tomorrow.*

Rhodes wandered around the mall for forty minutes, checking his phone frequently. Dominic and Aubrey traded places multiple times. When it was his turn to tail Rhodes, Dominic had no trouble staying on task, but whenever he handed the guy off to Aubrey, he found himself more and more distracted. His thoughts kept straying to what lay just outside the mall's doors—this building was literally surrounded by casinos on all sides. At one point, he spent a good two minutes staring slack-jawed at an ad for the Bellagio, fantasizing about blackjack, before he was able to shake it off.

Dominic was the one on point when Rhodes finally made his way to the Todd English P.U.B., so he was the one who saw Rhodes remove his wedding ring and slip it into his pocket as he walked.

"Asshole," Dominic said under his breath.

He followed Rhodes into the restaurant, hanging back to watch him shake hands with a mixed group of men and women, all relatively young and attractive, before the hostess showed them to a table. After he updated Aubrey, the two of them ended up sitting together at the long bar in the middle of the restaurant with their backs to Rhodes's table. Aubrey had a hidden camera sewn into the lining of her purse, so when she set it on the bar at the right angle, they were able to monitor Rhodes's every movement via the feed on her cell phone without ever looking at him directly.

She was thrilled with this turn of events because they could expense their entire meal to the client, but Dominic couldn't muster up the same excitement. His stomach was too unsettled to do more than nurse a non-alcoholic beer and pick at the appetizers she'd ordered, trying to pay attention to the story she was telling instead of remembering the last poker game he'd played in vivid sensory detail. His foot tapped anxiously against his bar stool until the woman on his other side gave him the evil eye and he made himself stop.

"You okay?" Aubrey asked after a while, frowning at him. "You're sweating."

"It's hot in here," he said, which was true. He drained a long swallow of his beer and wished it were the real stuff.

She glanced down at her phone. "Rhodes isn't displaying any signs of intimacy with these women. I don't think any of them could be a girlfriend or mistress."

"Me neither." Dominic had been watching the feed too; Rhodes was flirting with all the women at the table, but only in a casual way, and with none more than any other. "I don't think any of them really know each other, actually. I saw them meet up—there was no sense of familiarity."

"Business dinner?" she said, though her tone was dubious.

"He wouldn't have taken his ring off for that." Dominic raked a hand through his hair. Why the *fuck* was everyone being so goddamn *loud*?

His mood steadily worsened through the rest of Rhodes's leisurely two-hour meal. When the group got up and left together in a happy, tipsy cluster, Dominic and Aubrey trailed along behind, arm-in-arm like a couple on a date.

It was clear that the night was far from over for Rhodes and his friends. *Go to a bar*, Dominic thought, glaring daggers at the back of Rhodes's head. *Go dancing, go to a strip club, go anywhere but—*

They walked out the back of the Shops at Crystal and right into the Aria Hotel and Casino.

Rhodes's group made a beeline for the casino floor, which was adjacent to the main lobby. The noises reverberated inside Dominic's skull, all of them deeply ingrained triggers—ringing bells, electronic beeps and whirrs from the slot machines, euphoric shouts around the craps tables. Bright lights were flashing everywhere and Dominic couldn't breathe.

He halted mid-stride just steps from the threshold. Aubrey, who was still holding his arm, stumbled against him with a startled yelp.

"I can't go in there," he whispered.

He wanted to, though. Right now, he wanted to go inside that casino more than he'd wanted anything else in his entire life.

"What are you talking about?" she said, disentangling her arm from his.

"I . . ." The word came out a dry croak. He swallowed and wet his lips. "I'm a compulsive gambler. I'm sorry, I can't go in there."

She stared at him. "You're addicted to gambling?" she said incredulously. She didn't have to say anything more; he could see the accusations in her eyes, because they were the same ones bouncing around in his own head. He should have anticipated that this might become a problem. He should have warned her.

"I'm in recovery, but I'm hanging by a thread. If I go inside . . ."

If he went inside, he'd feel *amazing*. That rush of adrenaline, the full-body thrill—gambling was better than alcohol, better than drugs, better than sex. Why was he trying so hard to resist it?

Dominic groaned in frustration and gave his head a sharp shake.

"Okay," Aubrey said. "I won't have any trouble keeping an eye on Rhodes in a casino. You go back to the car and wait for me. I'll keep in touch via text and let you know what's going on."

"All right." He realized his hands were shaking and hid them in his jacket pockets. "I'm really sorry."

She nodded, and he trudged away, feeling like utter shit.

He kept his head bowed the whole walk back to the parking garage, straining against the lure of the surrounding casinos as if they were emitting a tangible magnetic pull. Every step was like slogging through knee-high mud.

By the time he reached Aubrey's car, his breath was coming hard and fast. He got in the passenger's seat, threw his jacket in the back, and buried his face in both hands.

He could feel so *good*, if he just gave in. Poker, craps, even roulette—the game itself didn't matter, never had. It was the thrill that obsessed him, the euphoria of taking risks, laying everything on the line, chasing the big score and feeling brilliantly, powerfully *alive*.

Just one game . . .

Except it wouldn't be just one game. It never was for him. Most people could gamble with no problems, win or lose a little money and walk away whenever they wanted. For whatever reason, be it biological or psychological, Dominic couldn't do that. Once he started, he couldn't stop. And that was why he could never start again.

He slammed his fist against the dashboard so hard it rattled the car. That snapped him out of his fugue a bit. He went for his phone, then realized it was in his jacket pocket. Once he'd retrieved it from where it'd fallen out on the floor of the backseat, he called the first person who came to mind.

"Hello?" Levi said groggily after a few rings.

It was only a few minutes past midnight, but Levi had to get up early for work. Of course he'd been asleep. Dominic hadn't even considered it.

"I'm sorry," Dominic said, cursing himself for his thoughtlessness. "I shouldn't have called—"

"Dominic?" There suddenly wasn't a trace of sleepiness in Levi's voice. "What's wrong?"

"I . . ." Part of Dominic wanted to hang up and pretend this had never happened, but he knew he needed help more than he needed his pride. "Aubrey and I have been tailing Rhodes on the Strip. He—he went into a casino."

Blankets rustled and bedsprings creaked on the other end of the line. "Did you gamble?"

"No." Dominic closed his eyes, and the rest came out all in a rush. "But I want to, Levi. I was *right there*. It's pulling at me like it's hooked into my guts. I can't stop thinking about it, and I don't know how much longer I can control myself."

"Where are you right now?"

"Aubrey sent me back to the car to wait for her."

"I'm coming to get you," Levi said over the sound of drawers opening and closing.

"What? No!" Dominic was torn between tender warmth at Levi's reaction and horror at the idea of Aubrey thinking he needed his sort-of boyfriend to rescue him because he couldn't handle himself. "That's not necessary. I'm in an empty parking garage with nothing to trigger me. As long as I stay here, I should be okay."

"Did you and Aubrey drive there together?"

"Yeah. My truck is back at McBride."

"Uh-huh. And when Aubrey drops you off and you get behind the wheel all alone, are you going to drive home?"

Dominic clenched his jaw and banged his head against the headrest a couple of times. "I don't know," he said through gritted teeth, hating himself.

"Then I'll come pick you up at McBride whenever you're done."

"That could be hours from now—"

"I'll be there," Levi said, implacable.

Dominic's shoulders sagged, his anxiety subsiding somewhat. "Thank you," he said, though words were a weak way to express the depth of his gratitude.

"You're welcome." Levi was quiet for a moment. "We've never talked about this before, but . . . If you ever do try to gamble, would you want me to stop you? Physically?"

Dominic blinked. The possibility had never occurred to him—mostly because if the tables were turned, he wouldn't be able to make the same offer. He doubted there were any circumstances in which he'd be willing to use genuine force against Levi, even to prevent him doing something terrible.

Levi, on the other hand, had a streak of ruthlessness in him that Dominic didn't share. Dominic knew all the way down to his bones that if he gave his consent now, Levi wouldn't hesitate to do whatever was necessary to stop him from gambling. He wouldn't let Dominic ruin his life again, no matter what it took or what anyone else thought.

That was exactly what Dominic needed to hear.

"Yes," he said. The constriction in his chest eased, and he drew what felt like his first truly deep breath in hours. "Please."

"Okay. I'll stay on the phone with you until Aubrey comes back."

Dominic leaned back in his seat, trusting Levi unreservedly, believing now that he would be all right.

Levi was startled awake by the alarm clock on his phone. He slapped at it blindly until it shut up, then ground the heel of his hand against his dry eyes. Normally, he didn't mind getting up early, but he hadn't slept much last night.

He shifted onto his back underneath the covers. At the foot of the bed, Rebel lifted her head to look at him, then dropped back down with a tired doggy sigh.

Dominic was still asleep next to him, facing the opposite wall. The blankets had slipped down a bit, exposing the plane of his heavily muscled back and the tattoo of the Ranger crest that Jasmine had done for him.

Before Dominic, Levi had always preferred men with lean builds, and it wasn't *until* he'd slept with Dominic that he realized that wasn't a coincidence. Subconsciously, he'd always been disturbed by the idea of having sex with a man who could physically overpower him. But after everything they'd been through together and the multiple times Dominic had saved his life, Dominic's size and strength only engendered positive feelings in him—safety, comfort, and an aching lust he was still struggling to get a grip on.

Levi traced his fingertips over the colorful lines of the shield and the motto beneath. Dominic didn't react—he was a heavy sleeper, Levi was coming to learn—so Levi spooned up against his back, wrapping an arm around his chest and kissing the nape of his neck.

Dominic stirred and made a sleepy noise.

"Hey," Levi said, nuzzling his shoulder.

"Hey," Dominic mumbled. "What time is it?"

"Early. I need to start getting ready for work."

Dominic put his hand on top of Levi's. "I'm sorry you had to—"

"Shh. I didn't have to do anything. I chose to do this because I wanted to. We talked about this last night."

They'd talked about it far more than was necessary, in Levi's opinion. Dominic had been miserable when Levi picked him up at McBride Investigations; Levi hadn't seen him so on edge since the Seven of Spades had sent him that teasing gift basket back in April. He'd alternated between morose silence, snappish irritation, and self-flagellating apologies the entire drive to his apartment and even after they'd gotten in bed. Levi's repeated reassurances had gone in one ear and out the other.

Dominic was just as tense now, but he didn't say anything more. A few seconds later, he turned over in Levi's arms so they were face-to-face, hitched Levi's leg over his hip to pull him closer, and kissed him on the mouth.

"I forgot to ask you this yesterday," he said, "but you know the party I'm going to at Jasmine's parents' house on Saturday?"

"Yeah."

"Do you want to come with me?"

"Really?" Levi pulled back a little. "Am I invited?"

Dominic laughed, looking like his usual self for a few seconds. "Of course. Carlos and Jasmine want you there." He squeezed Levi and added, "So do I."

Levi was pretty sure Carlos and Jasmine didn't care about his presence so much as they did about making Dominic happy, but either way, he appreciated the gesture. "I'd love to," he said. "But you do know there's always a chance that something will come up at the last minute and I won't be able to make it, right?"

That had been a major sticking point in his relationship with Stanton, who had never been able to accept that his job entailed a 24/7 commitment. He wanted to be upfront about the possibility now, so it didn't become a problem down the line.

Dominic was giving him a strange look. "Well, sure. Obviously catching murderers takes priority. Chances are they won't bother you on your day off, though, and we can have a nice relaxing Saturday."

Levi brushed his hand over Dominic's jaw and then kissed him, uncomfortable with the swell of emotion in his chest. It *would* be nice to have something to look forward to this weekend. On Monday, he and Dominic were both testifying at the trial of Drew Barton, the man who'd tried to pin his wife's murder on the Seven of Spades and then assaulted Levi when he realized he wasn't going to get away with it. That was going to suck, so Levi would welcome the opportunity to decompress first.

He broke the kiss before things could go too far. Though his body yearned for more, he didn't have time, and he doubted Dominic was in the mood anyway.

His cell phone chirped, and he unwrapped himself from Dominic to roll over and grab it. Dominic sat up beside him.

"Who is it?" Dominic asked. He patted his thigh, and Rebel squirmed up the bed to put her head in his lap for an ear scratch.

"Natasha." Levi scrolled through the texts and sighed. "The girl I told you about last night—Adriana—she called Natasha this morning and said she needs to speak to me about the Hensley case. She won't talk to anyone else, and she has a meeting with Child and Family Services at nine thirty, so it has to be as soon as possible. I won't have time to drive you back to your car first."

"Don't worry about it. I'll ask Carlos to help me pick it up."

Dominic was an excellent liar, but Levi knew him well enough by now to be certain he would do no such thing. He would have hesitated to impose on Carlos under the best of circumstances; asking for help with this would mean explaining what happened, and he hated talking about his addiction even with his close friends. Either he'd pay for an Uber to take him to McBride or he'd just sit in the apartment all day, stewing in the same self-loathing Levi had seen last night.

Searching for a compromise that wouldn't hurt Dominic's pride, Levi said, "Why don't you just drive me to work and use my car this morning? We can do the swap on my lunch break. No need for Carlos to go out of his way."

"You sure?"

"Yeah. I don't actually need my car at work; Martine and I always take hers if we have to go somewhere."

"Okay." Dominic leaned over to kiss Levi's cheek. "I'm gonna take Rebel for a walk while you get ready."

At the word *walk*, Rebel perked up, leapt off the bed, and spun in excited circles before regarding Dominic with bright eyes and a wagging tail.

Chuckling, Dominic got out of bed as well. "All right, all right, let me get some pants on."

"You didn't have to walk me inside," Levi said as he and Dominic entered the substation.

"I want to say hello to Martine."

That might have been true, but Levi suspected that Dominic was delaying their separation because he still felt raw and didn't want to be alone. He'd been uncharacteristically clingy all morning.

They'd made a quick stop for coffee on the way—at least, Levi had. Dominic was drinking a syrup-laced, milk-loaded monstrosity that he insisted on calling coffee despite Levi's horrified protestations to the contrary.

Desperate for caffeine, Levi drank his in deep gulps that burned his tongue while they got Dominic a visitor's badge and proceeded to the bullpen. Dominic was a well-known bounty hunter throughout the Valley, and the people they passed greeted him with smiles and nods and a fist bump here and there. Most were far more pleased to see him than Levi, with whom they worked every day.

"How do you make friends everywhere you go?" Levi asked.

"I'm nice to people," Dominic said with a teasing note in his voice.

"I'm nice," said Levi, though he wasn't, not the way Dominic meant. Dominic was easygoing and gregarious and went out of his way to be friendly to everyone he met. Levi felt exhausted just *thinking* about how much energy that must take.

Shifting closer, Dominic murmured, "I think you're *very* nice."

Levi rolled his eyes, willing away his blush as they entered the bullpen. His and Martine's adjoining desks faced each other; she was already at hers, and Natasha was sitting at his, with Adriana in a chair that had been pulled up alongside.

"Morning," he said, setting his coffee down.

"Morning." Martine looked up—and then even further up. "Oh, hey, Dominic."

"Ladies," Dominic said. "Good to see you both again."

"Yeah, it's been a while," said Natasha, getting out of Levi's chair. "Are you still bounty hunting?"

Levi didn't listen to Dominic's response, because he was distracted by Adriana. She'd frozen in her seat, staring at Dominic in pure terror. Her face was drawn and gray, her breathing shallow, and her hands gripped the arms of her chair so hard they were shaking.

Dominic noticed right after Levi did. He took a few subtle steps backward, putting more space between him and Adriana, and his body language shifted in a clear attempt to make himself look less threatening. His arms hung relaxed by his sides, his empty hands wide open.

"Well, I should get going," he said, and even his voice was softer than it had been before. "I just wanted to stop in and see everyone, say hello."

"You and Levi should come to dinner at my place again sometime soon," Martine said. Her eyes glinted mischievously. "That is, if you're done hogging him all to yourself."

Dominic grinned. "I guess I can make an exception for one night. Just let me know when." He touched Levi's elbow and said, "Good luck with your case. See you later?"

Levi nodded. They'd never discussed acceptable PDA in the workplace—he wouldn't have minded a brief kiss on the lips, but Dominic didn't know that.

After a round of goodbyes, Dominic headed off. Levi, Martine, and Natasha exchanged silent glances, all of them aware of Adriana's anxiety but uncertain how best to address it.

"Adriana, do you want to go talk in the room we used yesterday?" Levi finally asked.

Startled out of her petrified state, Adriana mumbled agreement. He gestured for her to go first, then looked back over his shoulder as he followed. Natasha made a *call me* gesture, and he sent her a thumbs-up in response.

As soon as the door closed, Adriana said, "Who was that guy?"

"His name is Dominic Russo. Have you met him before?"

"No." She wrapped her arms around herself. "He just—he looks a lot like somebody I used to know. Is he a cop too?"

If she hadn't been in so much distress, Levi would have laughed. "Uh, no. Definitely not." He sat on the couch and observed the way she hovered at the edge of the room, hunched in on herself. "He's my . . . my boyfriend."

Okay, so maybe he and Dominic hadn't agreed on that particular label yet, but he needed to humanize Dominic for her, and he wasn't about to break down their entire romantic and sexual history to a teenager.

Adriana didn't look surprised—people usually assumed Levi was gay—but she did frown. "You're not afraid of him?"

"Why would I be afraid of him?"

She shrugged one shoulder, her arms tightening around her chest. "He's a lot bigger than you. It would be easy for him to hurt you." Averting her eyes, she said, "Make you do things you don't want."

Levi had to close his eyes to deal with the powerful surge of rage that tensed his muscles and turned his stomach. He took a moment to collect himself, not wanting Adriana to think his anger was directed at *her*. Only when he was sure he could control his voice did he say, "You're right. Dominic could probably hurt me a lot if he wanted to. But I trust that he won't. In fact, I feel safer with him than anyone else. You know, he once saved my life twice in one week."

"Really?"

"Yes. He got hurt himself both times, just because he was trying to protect me." Levi leaned forward, resting his elbows on his knees. "I understand if his size makes you uncomfortable, but I can promise you that he'd never harm either you or me for any reason."

"I . . ." Adriana exhaled heavily and dropped her arms. "I guess I didn't really think he would. It's just the way he looks—I wasn't ready for it. I didn't mean to offend him."

"You didn't," Levi said firmly. "I'm sure that's not the first time Dominic has gotten that reaction, and he'll know how to handle it. He'd be more worried about making sure you're okay."

She moved to the chair next to the couch, perching on the very edge of the seat. "I'm fine. Would you tell him I'm sorry?"

"Of course." He let the silence drag out a bit, but when she didn't volunteer anything more, he said, "Natasha told me you wanted to speak with me about my case?"

"Yeah." For the first time, Adriana looked him straight in the eye. "I lied to you yesterday."

"About what?"

Rather than answer his question, she said, "Natasha and I talked for a long time last night. She told me that you're a good man and a good cop. You guys are doing a lot to help me even though you don't have to, and I don't want to be the reason somebody gets away with murder."

She fell quiet then, and seemed to be working up the nerve to continue. Levi waited.

"I didn't find that credit card Downtown. I found it on the Strip." Tears welled in her eyes, and she bowed her head. "It—it was in a Dumpster where I was looking for food." Letting out a sob, she covered her eyes with one hand. "I didn't want to say anything because I was embarrassed."

"Hey." Levi put his hand on the arm of her chair, though he was careful not to touch her directly. "There's no shame in doing what's necessary to survive."

She shook her head, crying quietly, her hand still hiding her face. He handed her the tissues and then sat with her, not trying to rush or console her, just making himself available in case she wanted to tell him more.

After a few minutes, her tears slowed. She blew her nose and wiped her eyes before lifting her head with new resolve. "The card wasn't by itself, either—it was in a wallet, a nice one. I took that and one other card and all the cash and then left the wallet there."

"There was cash in the wallet?"

"Yeah, almost two hundred bucks. I already spent it all; I'm sorry."

"It's all right," said Levi. "I talked to Dr. Hensley's wife yesterday. There won't be any charges."

In fact, he'd been pleasantly surprised by how sympathetic Hensley's wife—Dr. Clarissa Northridge—had been once she learned of Adriana's situation. She'd volunteered to simply pay the credit card charges herself, so there would be no question of legal action.

"Oh," Adriana said, blinking. "That's good. Thank you." She scrubbed the back of her hand over her face. "Um . . . the wallet wasn't the only thing I found. It was in a big paper shopping bag from Macy's with a bunch of other stuff—a cell phone, a laptop, a tablet. It had all been smashed to pieces, so I just left everything there."

Levi sat back. As he'd anticipated, Adriana's statement blew any robbery motive out of the water. The murderer wouldn't have destroyed Hensley's valuable electronics and ditched cold hard cash if they'd been driven by monetary gain.

"Where was this Dumpster?" he asked.

The location she gave him was a short, easy walk from the Mirage. She had found the bag on Sunday, so the Dumpster had most likely been emptied by now, but they'd send an officer out to be sure.

"Thank you, Adriana," he said, after he'd jotted down all the details. "You've been very helpful."

"You're welcome." She'd stopped crying by now, though she still clutched a wad of tissues in one tight fist. "Will I have to testify in court or something?"

"I doubt it. Your official statement should be more than enough."

"Natasha said she would try to find a way for me to stay in Las Vegas." Adriana picked at the tissues she held, shredding them into bits. "I'm at a group home right now, but she's trying to get me transferred to the foster system here, so she can make sure everything's okay."

"If that's what she said, that's what she'll do. Natasha is an amazing social worker. She won't let you down." Levi stowed his pen and notepad in his jacket pocket and rose to his feet. "Are you ready for your meeting?"

"Yeah. I just need a minute."

Levi was halfway to the door when he hesitated, overcome by a sudden impulse. He turned back and sat on the couch again; Adriana gave him a puzzled look.

"When I was in college, a group of men hurt me very badly—so badly I almost didn't survive. I know what it's like to feel helpless and to be ashamed of that feeling. But whatever has happened to you isn't your fault."

She regarded him in wide-eyed silence before saying, "You don't seem helpless to me."

"Because I learned how to protect myself," he said. "How to fight back. I can help you do the same, if you want."

A ghost of a smile crossed her face, small but unmistakable. "Yeah. Okay."

What Levi didn't tell her was that the assault had left him with a deep well of inner rage that had only grown as the years passed. He knew how to protect himself now, true, and he'd learned how to control and channel that anger, but it was always burning inside him.

And he was afraid that one day it would rise up and swallow him whole.

CHAPTER 8

"**S**o," McBride said, studying Dominic from across her desk. "You're a gambling addict."

"Compulsive gambler," he said tightly.

"Right." She puffed on her e-cigarette. "And you didn't think this was important information to share?"

"I'm under no obligation to disclose my mental health history."

"True. But this is *Vegas*, Russo. It never occurred to you that this might become a problem? You can't tell me you never ran into this situation as a bounty hunter."

He shifted uncomfortably. Whenever his pursuit of a bounty seemed like it was veering into gambling territory, he just handed the assignment off to someone else. He should have known he wouldn't be able to do the same here without drawing comment. As a bounty hunter, he worked alone; this was a large firm with over a dozen investigators working in cooperation. McBride had no legal right to know this about him, but he wouldn't have been able to hide it for long regardless.

"If you're planning on firing me, please just tell me now," he said.

"Fire you?" she said with a snort that turned into a brief hacking cough. "For a mental health issue? No, thanks. I'd prefer not to invite a lawsuit, and besides, that seems like a shitty thing to do to someone." She tilted her head. "Aubrey said you're in recovery?"

"Yeah, two years now. I have it under control. I went to a meeting just this morning—"

McBride held up a hand. "You don't have to tell me the details. Just keep doing whatever you're doing, and make sure it doesn't interfere with your work here."

"It won't," said Dominic, dizzy with relief.

"That remains to be seen." She leaned back in her chair, inhaled deeply, and blew out a thin stream of bourbon-flavored vapor. "Now, as far as the Rhodes case is concerned—"

He cut in hastily before she could get any further. "I made some progress there on my own, actually." Knowing he'd have to prove his worth to get back in both McBride and Aubrey's good graces, he'd spent all morning—excluding the hour at Gamblers Anonymous—working a hunch. "Rhodes isn't having an affair."

Raising her eyebrows, McBride said, "Aubrey saw him leave the casino with one of the women he'd met for dinner and take an elevator upstairs in the hotel."

She hadn't been able to follow them without compromising her cover, and they hadn't engaged in any serious physical contact in sight of her camera, so while the situation was damning, it wasn't the definitive proof they'd been looking for.

"I didn't say he wasn't cheating. I said he's not having an affair." He got out his phone, fingers tapping across the screen as he spoke. "Mrs. Rhodes told us she suspected her husband had a long-term relationship, a mistress or girlfriend, whatever term you want to use. But his behavior last night—a second phone, non-stop texting, removing his wedding ring, meeting a group of strangers in public . . . It gave me an idea." He passed his phone to McBride. "These are Rhodes's profiles on Whim, Blendr, and Pure, all under false names."

"What am I looking at here?" she asked while she thumbed through the applications he'd pulled up.

"They're hookup apps for people looking for one-night stands. Really easy to use in Vegas, especially around the Strip, because of all the tourists flooding in and out."

Dominic spoke from experience. Before he started dating Levi, he'd used Grindr all the time.

"So instead of the affair his wife suspects, Rhodes has been fucking around with a bunch of different women he barely even knows?"

"Well, this isn't concrete proof—but yeah, basically. Sometimes people using these apps meet up in groups at first for safety."

McBride barked out a raspy laugh. "That crafty little bastard. No wonder his wife couldn't pin him down herself—she was coming at it from the wrong angle. So were we." She tossed Dominic his phone. "Nice work, Russo."

"Thanks. Think Aubrey will agree?"

"I'll leave that to her to decide, but I think you'll be fine."

Ten minutes later, Dominic sat behind the wheel of Levi's car, his internship safe but his mood no less grim. Though the urgent craving to gamble had receded, it had left potent shame and humiliation in its wake. He'd made an idiot of himself in front of a colleague, and then to make matters worse, Levi had seen him so pathetic and out of control. *Levi*, who was one of the strongest people he knew. How could Levi respect him now?

He rubbed a hand over his face. That was a ridiculous thought, but he couldn't shake it. This . . . this *failing* was his biggest weakness and his greatest source of shame. It was the ugliest thing about him. He hadn't wanted Levi to see it, but it was too late.

Right now, he was also facing one of the most threatening enemies of a compulsive gambler: free time. He wasn't expected anywhere for hours, not until his bartending shift at Stingray tonight. Most people he knew were working, and he didn't trust himself to pick up a bounty with his head all messed up. He could go to the gun range, but he'd never thought it was a good idea to fire a gun while upset.

There was only one surefire way to exorcise this stress. He started the car and headed for Rolando's.

"Are you serious?" Levi snapped into the phone. He'd called Leila Rashid about Adriana's statement, hoping she'd drop the charges against Diana Kostas. No such luck, as it turned out.

"Ruling out robbery as a motive doesn't mean she didn't kill him." Rashid sounded calm, even bored. "We discussed this earlier. She could have made it look like a robbery to throw suspicion off herself."

"You can't really believe Kostas is a murderer."

"It doesn't matter what I believe," she said, now with a bit of an edge. "What matters is what the *jury* believes. Look, Abrams, I understand that cops rely on hunches and instincts to do their work, but your gut feelings aren't admissible in court."

"I—"

"I cannot drop the charges against Kostas until you build a solid case against another suspect. You know why? Because the very first thing a defense attorney will do is hold her up as the murderer to introduce reasonable doubt. People love to demonize sex workers. What they don't love is to use their critical thinking and reasoning skills. So unless you give me hard evidence that exonerates Kostas and implicates someone else in a way so obvious a *kindergartner* could understand it, you're asking me to trust that the jury will be comprised of rational adults instead of twelve random mouth breathers. I'm not willing to take that chance."

By the end of her speech, Levi was sitting with his eyes wide and his mouth half open. Martine watched him curiously across their desks.

"All right," he said after a moment's delay. The truth was, he didn't disagree with her logic. "I'll bring you the evidence you need."

"Great." With that, she hung up on him.

He set his own phone in the receiver, stared at it, and then shook his head.

Martine laughed. "Yeah, she's about as good with people as you are."

Levi threw a pen at her; she caught it in midair. "There's one major question we have to answer before we can go any further," he said.

Nodding, she said, "Who was the primary target—Hensley or Kostas?"

"Exactly. Either Hensley's murder was the goal and Kostas made a convenient scapegoat, or someone's trying to frame Kostas for murder, and Hensley was just collateral damage."

"I'd say the first explanation was a lot more likely if it wasn't for the Rohypnol they found under her sink."

"Let's see what she has to say about it, then," Levi said.

Kostas had been released on bail; Martine called ahead to confirm that she was at home, and they drove over to Henderson. Once Martine had explained that they were trying to clear her name, Kostas was happy to see them. She invited them back to the kitchen and cleared a space at the table, which was littered with a laptop, textbooks, and reams of highlighted notes.

"Sorry about the mess," she said, as she shoved everything to one side. "I'm trying to finish my bachelor's."

She poured three coffees, and they settled at the table. Levi could hear Mason playing with her friend Julie in the living room.

"You really think I'm innocent?" she asked.

"We do," said Levi. "The DA's office isn't convinced, though. You were at the crime scene just before Hensley died, and the same drug that killed him was found hidden in your house."

"I had no idea that was there! I've never used Rohypnol, either on myself or someone else. Just thinking about how easily Mason could have gotten to it under the sink . . ." She shuddered.

"Do you have any thoughts about who the Rohypnol could have belonged to, then?" Martine said, notepad at the ready.

"I've been considering it." Kostas tapped her fingers against her mug. "Mason's father—Travis—we were on-again, off-again for years until a few months ago. He never officially lived with us, but he would crash here when he was in-between places."

"What's Travis's last name?"

"Merrow. He's the kind of guy who hides what a piece of shit he is behind good looks and charm. I fell for his act over and over again. Every time he promised it would be different, I believed him." She gazed into her coffee, self-disgust plain on her face. "I'm such an idiot."

Guiding her back on track, Levi said, "You said 'until a few months ago.' You ended things with him?"

She nodded. "He got angry with Mason and shook him. He'd never been violent before, not toward either of us, but once a guy crosses that line, he'll be willing to cross it again. I told him not to come around here anymore. He hasn't been back since—hasn't even tried to see his son." Glancing toward the living room, she muttered, "I guess he was never thrilled about being a father in the first place."

"Is there a specific reason you suspect him?"

Her eyes flicked once more toward the open doorway through which Mason's squeals of laughter could be heard. "He's a drug dealer," she said, lowering her voice. "Small-time, nothing major, but he'd have access to Rohypnol, and he's exactly the kind of asshole who'd hide it in his girlfriend's house. I don't know if he forgot it was there, or he just never had a chance to come back for it, but it has to be his."

"What about Julie?" Martine said. "She has complete access to your house, doesn't she?"

"*Julie*?" Kostas's eyebrows shot up. "No way. I mean, I get what you're saying, but there's no reason for her to have Rohypnol. She doesn't do drugs herself, and—well, she works for Sinful Secrets too. She'd have just as much to lose as me if she hurt a client. More, even, with her garbage boyfriend leeching off her all the time."

Martine's gaze sharpened. "Boyfriend?"

"Kyle Gilmore. He's the same breed as Travis—they're friends, actually. Not really dangerous, just . . . a user, you know? Shady and manipulative. I've tried convincing Julie to dump him a hundred times, but you can't make people see the truth until they're ready for it."

It was time to address the main purpose of their visit. "Ms. Kostas," Levi said, "is there anyone in your life who might actively wish you harm?"

"Wish me harm? I don't know what you . . ." She trailed off, looking back and forth between them, and comprehension dawned in her eyes as she connected the dots. "You think someone might have killed Dr. Hensley and hidden the Rohypnol here just to frame me for murder?"

"It's one of a number of possibilities we're considering." He knew it sounded far-fetched, but they had to at least rule out the possibility.

Waving a dismissive hand, Kostas said, "No. Definitely not. Travis is the only person I have any real problems with, and even he wouldn't go that far. Besides, to be frank, he's not smart enough to pull something like that off."

They continued that line of questioning for a few minutes; many people were quick to deny they had enemies, only to have second thoughts upon closer scrutiny. Kostas, however, remained adamant in her conviction that she didn't know anybody who both hated her enough to frame her for murder and was intelligent enough to do so.

After asking her to call if she remembered anything else that might be helpful, Levi and Martine headed back to the substation.

"I think she's right," Martine said, as she turned onto the Lake Mead Parkway. "Her shithead ex left that Rohypnol in her house, and she wins the Worst Timing Ever award."

Levi agreed. It had always been more likely that Hensley was the primary target, anyway. "We'll have to actually prove that to get Rashid off her back. Lawyers don't like coincidences."

"Neither do I. It's still suspicious as hell. But we'll get Merrow in for questioning and let him speak for himself."

When they arrived at the substation, they were greeted by a uniformed officer with the news that Dr. Clarissa Northridge was waiting to speak to one of them in Interview B. Levi thanked the officer and turned to Martine.

"You go ahead," she said. "I'm gonna do some background on Travis Merrow. Julie and her boyfriend too, just to be thorough."

With a nod, Levi broke off down a side hallway rather than continue with her to the bullpen. The woman waiting for him in the interview room looked a decade younger than he knew her to be, tanned, fit, and impeccably made-up. She stood at his entrance and gave him a polite smile.

Something about the way she moved struck Levi as so familiar that he paused on the threshold, taken aback. He was sure he'd never seen her before; he would remember a woman this attractive and self-assured.

"Dr. Northridge, a pleasure to meet you," he said, dismissing the odd feeling and shaking her hand. "I'm Detective Levi Abrams; we spoke on the phone yesterday."

"The pleasure's all mine, Detective. I'm sorry I couldn't come earlier. I had a surgery yesterday which couldn't be rescheduled."

He gestured for her to sit, and they passed several minutes with small talk while he expressed his condolences and explained the details of when and how the coroner's office would release her husband's body. He knew it wasn't fair for him to judge someone else's expression of grief; everyone mourned differently, and Northridge had already had a couple of days to process her husband's death. But he couldn't help comparing her demeanor to that of Drs. Kapoor and Warner, noting that both of Hensley's colleagues had been far more distraught than his wife seemed to be.

"I understand that you have a suspect in custody?" she said eventually.

"Well, she's been released on bail. The truth is, though, that we've been reconsidering our initial theory regarding the circumstances of your husband's death."

"Oh?"

Levi watched her closely. "Yes. The preliminary evaluation of the scene suggested an accidental overdose. But Dr. Hensley's test results indicate that the overdose was almost certainly intentional. He was murdered, deliberately."

Northridge sat back, her face paling and her mouth falling open. It was the most emotion he'd seen her display so far. "What?"

"The woman currently charged with his death—the woman he spent that night with—had no discernible motive to kill him on purpose, and in fact she had a lot to lose. Our working theory right now is that someone else killed him for their own personal reasons and set her up to take the fall."

"Christ," she muttered, pressing a shaking hand to her forehead. She took a deep, slow breath, then lowered her hand and said, "Who?"

"That's something I'd like to discuss with you. Is there anyone you can think of who would have wanted Dr. Hensley dead?"

Her throat bobbed harshly as she swallowed. She glanced away, wetting her lips, and was silent for a few long moments. "That's a difficult question to answer about your own husband."

"I understand," Levi said, "and I'm sorry to put you through this. But it does need to be asked."

She met his gaze straight on again. "Stephen was . . . an abrasive man. Impatient, demanding, occasionally cruel. Very challenging to live and work with. I don't know that anyone had a reason to *murder* him, but he was far from beloved."

Interesting. "We'd like to take a closer look at his life, see if we can work up a few suspects. I'll be getting a warrant for his text messages from his telecommunications provider, as well as for any email accounts he may have had."

"Oh, you don't need to do that. Or I suppose you might still need a warrant to read his emails, but you don't need to go through the providers—I know all of Stephen's usernames and passwords. I'll write them down for you."

"That would be very helpful. Thank you." Levi hesitated before asking the next question; it was even more awkward to broach this subject with Northridge than it had been with Kapoor and Warner. "It does seem that whoever killed Dr. Hensley knew him well enough to expect that he would have had an escort in his room that night. There's no other way they could have timed his death so well to coordinate with her visit."

With a bitter laugh, she said, "Anyone who'd even met him in passing could have known about that. Stephen never made much of a secret of his taste for prostitutes."

Levi wasn't sure how to respond to that, especially because his first thought was—

"I realize that sounds like motive for *me* to kill him," said Northridge.

"Being over two thousand miles away is a pretty solid alibi."

She smiled. "I'll do whatever I can to help you, Detective. I'm planning to attend the rest of the palliative care conference to support Anika. You may want to ask her if Stephen had any seriously bad blood with anyone in their field—research can be a petty, backbiting cesspool, and he didn't often discuss his work with me."

He thanked her for her time, got her contact information for where she was staying in the city, and showed her out of the substation. Then he returned to the bullpen and filled in Martine.

"We've got a real short window of time here," she said once he finished. "If Hensley's killer is attending the conference, they'll be gone in a few days. We need to get down there and re-interview everyone."

In the immediate aftermath of Hensley's death, they'd questioned the colleagues he'd spent time with the night before, but the red herring of Kostas's involvement meant they hadn't pursued that angle as aggressively as they would have otherwise. Now they'd need to do it all over again, pushing harder and broadening the suspect pool if necessary.

"What about Merrow and company?" Levi asked. "Anything interesting?"

"Merrow's got a hell of a rap sheet, but it's all petty crimes and drugs, nothing violent. Gilmore has a similar history. Julie is clean."

They decided to divide their efforts—Levi would get warrants for Hensley's communications and start putting together a list of people to interview while Martine stayed on the Kostas angle. In the early afternoon, Levi remembered that he still had to help Dominic pick up his truck. He dialed Dominic's cell phone without looking away from his computer screen.

The call went to voicemail. Had Dominic ignored it, or was he just busy? Only one way to find out.

Levi wrapped up what he was working on before tracking the GPS in his own car. The last address it had registered was a parking lot Downtown, near the gym Dominic belonged to. He was just working out, then, and had probably stashed his cell in a locker.

A small bit of tension Levi hadn't realized he was holding dissipated. The idea that Dominic might have purposely ignored his call had bothered him more than he cared to admit.

"I'm going out for lunch," he said to Martine.

"Yeah? You having Italian?"

"You're hilarious." He bumped his hip against her shoulder as he walked past, and she laughed.

He asked an officer heading Downtown to drop him off on the way. Twenty minutes later, he walked through the door of Rolando's, hoping Dominic hadn't already left.

He'd never been here before. It was shabby but clean, a functional, utilitarian space with no frills, quite unlike the fitness center he used in his apartment complex. Rock music pulsed through the speakers at a low volume, and even from the front door, he could hear the impact sounds of sparring.

A young woman was sitting at the reception desk, her tank top displaying an impressive set of shoulders and biceps. She barely glanced up from her magazine at his approach.

"I'm not a member," he said. "I'm just looking for someone."

"No problem." She looked him up and down, then dismissed him entirely. He guessed his business suit and lack of a gym bag made it clear he wasn't trying to score a free workout.

Levi wandered through the gym until he found Dominic in an area with mats on the floor and a few heavy bags against one wall. Dominic was wearing basketball shorts and a shirt with the sleeves ripped off, the latter of which was so drenched in sweat that it was plastered to his torso. He had on a pair of boxing gloves and was working one of the bags like it had insulted his mother.

Pausing by the far wall, Levi watched him for a couple of minutes. Dominic's stance, his footwork, his combinations—all of it screamed classically trained boxer. He never threw the same strike to the same area on the bag twice in a row, never wasted a punch, and stayed in constant motion, evading the counterattacks of an imaginary opponent. The heavy bag shuddered and bounced under the brutal assault; a person without similar training wouldn't last ten seconds against an onslaught like this.

Levi was no stranger to taking his stress out on the bag, and he could see from the tense lines of Dominic's body that he was still upset about last night. Yet his concern was quickly eclipsed by his admiration for Dominic's technique, for his remarkable speed and the insane raw power in every blow. Then *that* soon turned into appreciation for the way Dominic's gleaming muscles bunched and released, the shifting of his massive shoulders, the sight of his rock-hard ass in those clingy shorts—

Realizing that his trousers were becoming uncomfortably tight, Levi cleared his throat and started forward, crossing the mats so he came at Dominic from the side. The last thing he wanted was to catch Dominic by surprise in this kind of mood.

Dominic let up on the bag and turned around, his chest heaving with his heavy breaths. Surprise flitted across his face and was followed by an immediate smile. "Hey. How'd you find me?" Before Levi could respond, he said, "GPS in your car. Of course."

"I hope you don't mind," Levi said, only now aware of how creepy his actions might seem.

Dominic shrugged. "It's your car." He faced the bag again and loosed a jab-cross-lead hook combination so vigorous that Levi winced.

"How long have you been at this?"

"Half an hour, maybe?"

"Is it helping?" Levi asked quietly.

Dominic's response was a jab-cross-hook-cross, the last punch robust enough to send the bag swinging clear out of reach.

"I won't make you talk about this if you don't want to," Levi said, "but I don't know if it's the best idea for us to just forget what happened."

"Oh, there's no chance of that." Dominic's humorless laugh was quite unlike him. "There's no way for me to ever forget how fucking weak I am."

"It's not a weakness, Dominic, it's an illness—"

"That's not what it feels like sometimes."

He unleashed another flurry of jabs and crosses. Levi stood there in silence, at a loss for what he should do. When he and Dominic had started dating, he'd read every scholarly resource on compulsive gambling he could get his hands on. He knew it was similar in many ways to addictions to drugs and alcohol, and that recovery was far more complex than a simple question of inner strength or willpower. But while Levi could empathize with Dominic's distress, he'd never be in a position to truly understand what he was going through.

"You told me once that there's a part of you that's always angry, no matter how well things are going for you otherwise." Dominic swung at the bag again, halfheartedly this time. "That you carry that little kernel of rage inside you every second of every day."

Levi bowed his head. He'd only confessed that to Dominic because he'd been drunk at the time, though he hadn't regretted it afterward.

"For me, that constant nagging voice in the back of my head, that emotion that has its claws in me all the time—it's not anger. It's fear. There's a dangerous part of me I can't control. I wake up every morning afraid that this will be the day I slip up again and ruin my life. I live with my own worst enemy inside my head, and I'm *never* able to set that aside completely."

This was the most Levi had ever heard Dominic speak about his addiction. Moving closer, he said, "Last night, when I offered to physically stop you if you tried to gamble . . . Did you mean that, or were you just panicking?"

Dominic caught the heavy bag to halt its movement. "I meant it. Did you?"

"Yes. Though I'm not sure it's the healthiest coping mechanism we could come up with."

"That's up to us to decide. Nothing you could do to me would be worse than what I could do to myself. I trust you to stop me if I'm in trouble, and I'm giving you my consent to do exactly that. I don't care what anyone else thinks about it."

An idea for how to help Dominic purge some of these anxieties occurred to Levi then. "The thing is, we don't know for sure that I *could* stop you," he said, his voice slow and thoughtful.

Dominic frowned. "What do you mean?"

"I'm a well-trained fighter, maybe better than you, but our size difference isn't inconsequential. There's a possibility that I wouldn't be able to beat you even if I gave it my best effort." Levi moved into Dominic's personal space, crowding him. He had to tilt his head back to meet Dominic's eyes, but he wasn't intimidated. "So we should find out. Just to be safe."

"Levi," Dominic said, his face lighting up, "are you saying—"

"Fight me," said Levi.

CHAPTER 9 ♠

Dominic circled the mat, eyeing Levi over the few feet of space that separated them. As luck would have it, Levi kept a packed gym bag in the trunk of his car—in case he found time to squeeze in an extra session of Krav Maga training, he'd told Dominic. He'd paid the gym's guest fee and changed into loose sweatpants, a T-shirt bearing the logo of his Krav school, and a pair of MMA gloves. Now he stood across from Dominic in the same open-handed fighting stance Dominic had seen him use in a confrontation with three gangbangers in April.

Neither of them were wearing any protective gear besides their gloves, not even cups, so they wouldn't be able to go all out. Dominic was still on fire with anticipation, though. He'd been imagining this since he first learned what a skilled fighter Levi was.

"You sure you don't want to back out?" he taunted, bouncing on the balls of his feet, his own fists raised in front of his face. "I'd hate to put the LVMPD's best detective out of commission."

"Give it your best shot," Levi said.

Dominic started with a couple of feints, gauging Levi's reflexes, but Levi just kept his distance and gave him an unimpressed look. When Dominic threw a genuine left jab, Levi deflected it with his left forearm. In the split second it took Dominic to follow up with a right cross, Levi had already brought his elbow up to block it and was uncoiling with the force of his own momentum, bopping the side of his left fist against Dominic's cheek as he slid smoothly out of the line of direct attack. Dominic was able to block the couple of open-handed strikes that came next, though not the light, barefoot kick Levi landed on his stomach.

Levi disengaged, backing up a few feet. "If this were a real fight, I would've kicked you in the balls."

"If this were a real fight, I would've already knocked you on your ass," Dominic said. He waggled his eyebrows.

"That's big talk," said Levi, smiling.

Their next sally lasted longer. They traded blows back and forth, mostly able to block or evade each other, though they both managed to land a few glancing strikes that wouldn't have done much damage even at full force.

Then, as they got closer, Dominic went for a right hook. Levi threw his left arm up like a goalpost to block it and simultaneously counterattacked with an uppercut—but Dominic had anticipated that reaction, and he weaved out of the way as his fist connected solidly just under Levi's rib cage.

Levi gasped, barely redirected his next punch, and kicked him hard in the chest, sending him stumbling back several steps. They remained separated while they caught their breath, though they stayed in constant motion.

"You really like to kick," Dominic said.

"A person's legs are their strongest weapons." Levi raised a disdainful eyebrow. "That's one of the biggest problems with Western boxing—you ignore half your body."

They went again, and now Dominic was getting a better sense of how their fighting styles differed. It went deeper than form and function; there were psychological implications as well. For one thing, while Dominic had dabbled in various martial arts during his time with the Rangers, his training was solidly grounded in traditional boxing and wrestling. He *didn't* kick, partly because he hadn't been trained to.

But Dominic was also accustomed to being the biggest, strongest guy in any confrontation. He had the luxury of not using his legs to defend himself because he could rely on the power of his upper body alone. Levi, who didn't have the same advantage, frequently lashed out with kicks to keep him out of striking range, which helped level the playing field.

There were other dissimilarities. Levi tended to follow up defensive maneuvers with a series of ferocious, blindingly fast counterattacks before disengaging altogether, whereas Dominic preferred to stand his ground and go toe-to-toe. Dominic's blows had more force behind them when they made contact, but Levi threw strikes he wasn't used to—like elbows and open hands—that he found difficult to counter effectively.

On balance, they were evenly matched, at least in a training environment where a lot of things were off-limits. Ten minutes of energetic sparring later, they were flushed and panting, both having gotten in some good hits but neither having gained any real advantage.

Strength alone wasn't giving Dominic the edge he needed here. He'd have to use another strategy.

As a discipline, Krav Maga involved little grappling or ground work, and because Levi hadn't done much cross-training, he wasn't a strong ground fighter. Dominic, on the other hand, had been a state-ranked wrestler throughout high school and had continued training in the years afterward.

He waited until they were mid-exchange, feinted a jab, then ducked down and threw himself at Levi's midsection—keeping his head tucked against Levi's chest so Levi couldn't guillotine him. Levi yelped in shock and slammed both forearms against his shoulder. Dominic felt the catch, the point of leverage that would have stopped a smaller man in his tracks. He muscled through it, overcoming Levi's defense with sheer overpowering strength, and grabbed the backs of Levi's thighs to flip him on his back and follow him to the mat.

Levi made a valiant effort, writhing like an eel and working angles and pressure points while they tussled across the floor. In a real-life situation, he would have stood a better chance; he would have been able to go for Dominic's groin or eyes, improvise weapons from the environment, even bite. Dominic could actually *feel* him resisting the instinct to do exactly that.

In the end, the circumstances combined with Dominic's greater experience on the ground spelled Dominic's victory. He wound up clinching Levi from behind, one arm across his chest like a seatbelt and the other pressed against the hand Levi had brought up to protect his throat. His legs were wrapped around Levi's hips, though he knew better than to hook his feet together in this position. That was a good way to end up with broken ankles.

Levi went abruptly still.

If there was one thing Dominic knew about Levi, it was that he would *never* surrender a fight. He didn't ease up in the slightest, wary for whatever counterattack Levi was planning next.

Levi's body undulated within the confines of Dominic's grip, his ass starting up a slow grind against Dominic's cock. Dominic's breath caught and stuttered in his throat. At first, he thought Levi was just squirming to get away, but his movements were far too sinuous and rhythmic to be anything but deliberate.

"That's—that's cheating," Dominic said. His cock perked up at the slide of firm round muscles.

"There's no such thing as cheating in Krav Maga." Levi circled his hips lazily, giving Dominic a sort of sideways lap dance. "It's not a competitive sport; it's pure survival. I'll use every weapon at my disposal."

Dominic's eyes fluttered shut against his will. "That tight little ass of yours is a weapon, all right," he growled into Levi's ear.

Levi laughed, a soft, low-pitched sound, and that was it. The second Dominic let down his guard, Levi turned into a whirlwind of sharp elbows and knees. Before Dominic even processed what was happening, he found himself flat on his back with Levi astride his hips, both his hands trapped against his own chest. Levi's free hand flew toward his face, stopped at the last moment, and tapped him gently on the nose.

Dominic gazed up at him, captivated by his pink cheeks and bright eyes, and felt nothing but absurdly pleased. "You win."

"I fought dirty. Literally." Levi sat back, putting more weight on Dominic's stiffening cock.

"No such thing as fighting dirty in Krav Maga, right?" Dominic ripped off his boxing gloves, tossed them aside, and added, "Besides, I did the same thing. I know you're not as skilled on the ground and I took advantage of that."

"Mmm." Levi smoothed his gloved hands across Dominic's chest, biting his lower lip as he raked his eyes over Dominic's body. "I could be persuaded to a rematch. Under slightly different conditions."

"Like what?" Dominic ran his own hands up Levi's thighs.

Leaning down, Levi murmured, "Friday night. If you manage to pin me again, I won't try to escape."

Dominic groaned and yanked him into a kiss, threading his fingers through Levi's sweat-damp curls. Levi responded enthusiastically, wriggling against him, rubbing their bodies together—

A delicate cough sounded to their side. Levi jerked upright, and Dominic turned his head to see a small crowd had gathered at the edge of the mats, including Rolando himself. Their expressions ranged from wide-eyed astonishment to amused smirks.

Flushing a darker red, Levi leapt to his feet. Dominic stood more slowly, knowing his semi was obvious in his basketball shorts but not really giving a fuck.

"Sorry, man," he said to Rolando. "Got carried away."

"It's cool, guys." Rolando winked. "Just try to keep it PG out here from now on, huh?"

The gawkers dispersed, leaving Dominic and Levi in relative privacy. Dominic studied Levi, relieved that his embarrassment didn't seem to have ruined his mood.

"I can't believe that just happened." Levi ducked his head and looked up at Dominic through his eyelashes. On anyone else, the gesture would have been intentional flirtation; for Levi, it was completely unselfconscious. "You make me forget where I am sometimes."

Dominic grinned, light and happy, his earlier stressors fading away. He caught Levi's hand and reeled him in.

"Got time for a shower?" he asked.

Between the Hensley murder and the other homicides in their caseloads, Levi and Martine ended up working late. They shared dinner afterward at La Comida, a funky Mexican restaurant downtown with rustic décor and more tequilas behind the bar than there were seats out on the floor.

"I'll have all of Hensley's texts and emails ready to review tomorrow morning," Levi said, once they'd settled in with drinks. "And I made plans to speak with Dr. Kapoor in-between panels at the conference—"

"Please, no more work talk tonight," said Martine. She sipped her passionfruit margarita and let out a blissful sigh.

He eyed her warily. "All right . . ." Martine *loved* to talk about work—it was one of the many things they had in common. If she didn't want to discuss the case, that meant she had another topic in mind, one he probably wasn't going to like.

"You and Dominic seem to be getting pretty serious," she said.

Bingo.

Tequila didn't agree with Levi, so he'd opted for a glass of white wine. He picked it up now but didn't drink. "Come on. We've only been dating a few months. We're not even technically in a relationship, at least not an exclusive one."

"You slept at his place last night without having sex. That's a pretty big deal."

One of these days he was going to stop being surprised that she could read him so well. "That wasn't . . ." he said, and then paused. Martine didn't know Dominic was a compulsive gambler; he couldn't explain that last night had been a matter of necessity and not the cozy romantic cuddlefest she'd assumed. "It wasn't what you think."

"No?" She squeezed her lime wheel into her margarita, set it aside, and wiped her fingers on her napkin. "Out of curiosity, how long did it take for you and Stanton to get to the no-sex sleepover stage?"

He put down his wine without having taken a sip and reached for his water instead. "About six months, I guess."

The truth was that he didn't remember exactly, though it must have been at least that long. He had loved Stanton—*truly* loved him—but Stanton had needed to coax him along every step of the way. Their relationship had unfolded slowly as they'd learned to know and trust and love each other by degrees, and Levi had worked hard to bring his walls down enough to let Stanton inside.

Being with Dominic was nothing like that. It was more like jumping headlong off the top of a waterfall and enjoying every single moment of the freefall.

Across the table, Martine tilted her head. "You don't still feel guilty about the way things ended with Stanton, do you?"

"I . . . yeah, a little. I was falling out of love with Stanton long before this thing with Dominic started, and we would have broken up either way, but . . ." He trailed off as the server arrived with their food, thanked her, and waited until she left before he finished his thought. "I just wish there had been less overlap."

Martine hummed in understanding. She'd supported him throughout the breakup, which had been an absolute nightmare. After living together for two years, his and Stanton's lives had been enmeshed in ways that proved difficult to untangle, and Stanton had resisted the entire thing, pleading repeatedly for Levi to reconsider. Add in the fact that Stanton was a public figure—the Barclay family controlled a multi-billion-dollar hotel fortune—and the whole process had been agonizing from start to finish.

They fell quiet while they savored the first few bites of their food. Martine had gone for a smoked pork shoulder, while Levi had chosen sea bass *a la plancha*. It was delicious, as the food here always was.

"I get what you mean," Martine said, picking up where they'd left off, "but you can't plan for these things. Life happens. You didn't do anything wrong."

"I kissed Dominic before Stanton and I had broken up," he reminded her.

"Okay, so you could have handled that one better. But honestly, Levi, everything worked out for the best. You know I love Stanton, but you and Dominic just click. You have so much more in common."

"I agree. It still bothers me, though. *And*," he said as she opened her mouth, "you don't get to say anything about that, because you've never experienced a breakup in your entire life."

Martine's love story was the stuff of fairytales; she and her husband Antoine had been childhood sweethearts, growing up one block apart in Flatbush. They'd started dating in middle school and married while they were in college. Their relationship had its rocky moments, of course, but they'd never separated even temporarily.

"I know," she said, after she swallowed her mouthful. "We're #relationshipgoals."

Levi snorted into his glass so hard that some of the wine went up his nose. He coughed it out and grabbed his napkin to scrub his mouth. "Did you hear that from Mikayla?"

"Simone." Her smile dimmed. "Mikayla's not really speaking to me or her father at the moment."

"Things are still difficult?"

"They're . . ." Martine poked her food with her fork and said, "Shitty. No point in downplaying it. The thing is, I'm not even angry. I remember what it's like to be a teenager—your self-identity is constantly changing, your brain's going haywire, and everything feels like life or death. I just have to keep reminding myself that she'll come out on the other side a rational, empathetic human being again."

"You should let me take her and Simone to Krav," Levi said, an old point of contention between them. "There's nothing better for purging teenage angst than beating the hell out of a heavy bag. Plus, it would keep them safer."

Recalling the promise he'd made to Adriana, he made a mental note to check her status with Natasha the next day.

"I'd love that, but they just don't have time. They're overscheduled as it is, between all their homework and sports and clubs. It's insane what it takes for kids to get into a good college these days. When I was their age, you were set as long as you had decent grades, did well on the SATs, and had a couple of extracurriculars. Now they expect everyone to be a goddamn child prodigy . . ."

She went on in that vein, venting her frustrations, and Levi was happy to listen. He much preferred talking about Martine's life to talking about his own.

They went their separate ways after dinner, tired but sated. Levi was a couple of minutes into his short drive home when his cell rang. It paired automatically with his car's Bluetooth, so he just pressed a button on the dashboard and said, "Hi, Mom."

"Levi, it's your mother."

He rolled his eyes fondly. "What's up?"

"You're not still at work, are you?" Nancy asked.

"No. I just left dinner with Martine, and I'm on my way home."

"Oh, Martine is such a sweetheart. Remind me to email her this recipe for slow-cooker chicken chili I found online. But *you*." Nancy's voice, a usually gentle North Jersey twang, hardened in a way that made Levi cringe instinctively. "Explain to me why Lori Schneider says you haven't RSVPed for Matthew's bar mitzvah yet?"

Shit. "Um . . ." Levi cast about for an excuse, but he'd never been any good at lying to his mother. "I forgot?"

"You forgot," she said icily. "The due date was *three days* ago. Is this the way your father and I raised you?"

"I'm sorry. I'll call Mrs. Schneider first thing tomorrow morning. I can't go, anyway."

"Why not?"

"I have to work, Mom," he said. "I'm not taking time off and flying across the country to watch some kid I barely know flounder through his *haftarah* portion."

"You—"

There was a small scuffle, and then his father said, "Hi Levi, it's Dad."

"Hi—"

"I *told* your mother you wouldn't be able to come. You've got an important job to do; you can't just take off every time someone has a party."

"Lori Schneider is one of my closest friends!" Nancy said in outrage, her voice every bit as audible as if she'd been speaking into the phone herself.

"Since when?" said Saul. "Besides, that boy of hers is growing up into a snotty little prick."

"Oh, you—"

Levi drove into his building's parking garage to the background noise of their friendly bickering. It was comforting, in its own way—like a well-worn sweatshirt.

Once Nancy wrestled the phone back from Saul, she said, "I was thinking maybe you could make a vacation out of it, come see the family. It's been a long time since you were here last."

He parked in his assigned space and turned off the car, picking up his phone as the Bluetooth connection was severed. "I'd rather not."

She didn't respond right away, because she knew why Levi hated going back to New Jersey. It stirred up memories they all tried hard to forget. Plus, he didn't like being around his sister; Abby had never said outright to his face that he was to blame for the assault, but she'd heavily insinuated it in the months afterward. The damage that had done to their relationship was irreparable.

"You and Dad could come out here instead," he said, feeling guilty. He *did* miss them. "Once it cools off, I mean. Maybe after the High Holy Days?"

"That would be nice." Her voice perked up. "And it would give us a chance to meet that new young man of yours. I bet he's what's got you so distracted."

"Oh my God," said Levi, who hadn't thought through the implications of his invitation.

"Well, I'll let you go—I'm sure you're tired. We love you, *bubbeleh*. Stay safe."

"Love you too." Levi hung up, stowed his phone in his pocket, and grabbed his bag.

In his apartment, he showered off the stress of the day and changed into sweatpants and a T-shirt. He hadn't slept much the night before, he was exhausted, and he knew it would be another long day tomorrow. Still, instead of going to bed like he should, he found himself drawn to the dining area and the armoire that hid his work on the Seven of Spades.

He opened the double doors, recalling the gut-wrenching moment when he'd caught Dominic standing here with a look of utter horror on his face. Levi had seen himself through Dominic's eyes then—a morbid freak obsessed with a serial killer everyone believed to be dead—and he'd recoiled from that image of himself. He'd been so sure that Dominic would be disgusted; he'd frozen inside and out, prepared to reject Dominic first if necessary.

But Dominic had only given him empathy and support. He'd expressed concern, yes, but he'd also offered his help. Levi could spit on that kindness by wrecking himself staying up half the night indulging his obsession, or he could respect it by taking care of himself and getting a full night's sleep.

"Not tonight, Satan," Levi said to the armoire. He closed the doors, shutting away the blood-soaked images and frantically scribbled notes.

CHAPTER 10

"I t's no wonder Hensley was murdered," Martine said the next morning, looking up from her stack of papers. "I'd kind of like to go back in time and kill him myself."

"You're not kidding," Levi muttered. They'd spent the last two hours absorbed in printouts of every email and text message Hensley had sent and received over the past six months, and just reading this stuff made him feel the urgent need to shower.

Clarissa Northridge had undersold what a horrible man her husband had been. She'd used the words "abrasive" and "challenging"; Levi would have gone more with "vicious, hateful son of a bitch." His conversations with everyone he knew, from colleagues to students to family members, were bitter and rancorous, peppered with vile profanity and aggressive insults that crossed the line into straight-up verbal abuse. Though electronic communication with his wife was sparse, what little existed was so disrespectful Levi couldn't believe she'd never sought a divorce. And the guy's poor son was probably going to be in therapy for the rest of his life.

Sitting back in his chair, Levi said, "This isn't going to help us with motive. I wouldn't be surprised if a whole group of people got together to cook up a conspiracy to kill this guy."

"Hmm. Did you see this, though? Look at the way he communicates with Dr. Kapoor."

Martine pushed a pile of papers toward him. He flipped through them and then shook his head, giving her a questioning glance.

"He's way less gross with her than he is with everyone else." She tapped the top page. "He rarely curses, and he never insults her intelligence or competency, which is his go-to with all the other people in his life."

Levi took a second look at the printouts. Martine had a point—Hensley's texts and emails to Kapoor were still obnoxious, and nothing Levi would tolerate himself, but they were markedly different from his other conversations.

"They were research partners. Maybe it went against his best interests to be nasty to her." He caught the look on Martine's face and said, "You think they were sleeping together?"

"Why not?"

"Because . . ." Levi struggled to explain why the idea triggered such a deep aversion in him. "He may have been *less* terrible with her, but this is still not the way you treat another human being. I don't understand why anyone would sleep with a man like this unless they were being paid for it."

"There's no accounting for taste." Martine shrugged. "Is Dr. Kapoor married?"

Levi closed his eyes, thinking back to their brief meeting in the interview room. Kapoor had been wearing a wedding ring, a simple platinum band with no stones. "Yeah."

"So there's a number of possible motives. She got tired of him screwing around with call girls and decided to put a stop to it. Or she tried to end things, and he threatened to tell her husband. Or *he* tried to end it, and she wasn't having that."

"Normally, I'd be on board," Levi said, "but I don't think it was her. She's one of the few people who has a strong alibi—surveillance cameras have her well-documented all over the casino floor until almost three. Technically within the window for Hensley's time of death, but not smart if she was planning to frame a woman who left two hours earlier. And there's no way she could have slipped out of sight long enough before that to kill Hensley without it being noticeable in the security footage."

Martine pursed her lips. "That's probably true. Still, it won't hurt to ask her about it when you meet her later. It might rattle something else loose."

"Valcourt, Abrams!"

Levi and Martine looked up as their immediate superior, Sergeant James Wen, strode into the bullpen from his office. Wen had the military bearing of an ex-Marine, and he was always impeccably dressed and clean-shaven no matter the time of day or night.

"Got a new case for you," he said, stopping at their adjoining desks. "Homicide at a home in Copper Crest."

Levi exchanged a puzzled glance with Martine. They weren't next in the rotation, which meant—

"There's a possible connection to the Hensley murder."

"How so, sir?" Martine asked.

"The victim was working the front desk at the Mirage the night Hensley was killed," Wen said.

The crime scene was an attractive Southwestern ranch in a suburban housing tract northwest of the Strip. Levi made note of the Mercedes parked in the driveway as he and Martine walked up.

Hanna Ostrowski, the responding officer, met them at the front door. "Victim's name is Alan Walsh," she said while they put on their protective equipment. "Twenty-four. His girlfriend found him this morning—he hadn't been answering her texts all night, and she came over to confront him. Thought he might be cheating."

"Yeah, that's going around," Levi said under his breath.

Ostrowski blinked but didn't comment. Leading them deeper into the house, she said, "The coroner investigator isn't here yet, but the cause of death is pretty obvious."

Walsh lay awkwardly crumpled on his back near the desk in his living room, one arm flung out to the side. He was a short, chubby white man—*literally* white now, because he'd died of massive blood loss. No visible lividity at all.

"I know this guy," Martine said. "I talked to him on Sunday when I was questioning the hotel staff who'd worked the night of Hensley's death." She whistled as she circled around the body. "One direct stab to the carotid artery. From behind, judging by the blood spatter and the way the body fell. Either the killer got in a lucky hit or they knew exactly where to aim."

"Like a doctor would?" Levi said grimly.

No attempt had been made to conceal the murder weapon, a steak knife with a fancy engraved pewter handle. It had been left on the floor next to Walsh's body, still caked with blood. Walsh had a scratch across his forehead, though no bleeding or bruising—he must have sustained the injury after he'd been stabbed. Rigor mortis had fully set in, so he'd been dead for at least twelve hours unless there were complicating factors at work.

The Chopard watch on Walsh's wrist caught Levi's eye, and he frowned. "You're sure his girlfriend didn't live here with him?" he asked Ostrowski.

"Positive. He lived alone."

"This is a nice house." Levi gestured around the room. "Expensive furniture, top-of-the-line electronics, a Mercedes out front . . . how much do hotel desk clerks make?"

"Not enough to afford this lifestyle alone," said Martine. "Family money?"

"Detectives, I've got something here," one of the CSIs said. She was crouched a few feet away, passing a handheld forensic light source over the floor. When Levi and Martine joined her, she pointed to a fluorescing stain on the carpet. "Traces of recent vomit. Someone tried to clean it up, but they didn't do a thorough job. There may be enough for useable DNA."

Martine made a face and backed away. Levi had once seen her help a gunshot victim hold in his intestines with her bare hands, but she couldn't stand even the discussion of vomit.

"Has to be the killer's," Levi said. "That's the only explanation that makes sense."

"I don't disagree, but why would the killer throw up?"

Levi moved to the far side of the room and took in the scene as a whole, envisioning the sequence of events. Walsh had been standing right in front of the desk—looking at something on the surface, or maybe using the computer—and the killer had taken him by surprise from behind, jamming the knife into his carotid artery and quickly withdrawing it and stepping away.

Walsh would have instinctively grabbed for his throat, though it wouldn't have done any good. He may have managed to stay on his feet for a few seconds, but then he'd fallen to his knees, banging his forehead on the edge of the desk, and collapsed backward with his legs still tangled up underneath him. His death had been almost immediate.

Then . . . what? The killer had dropped the knife, stumbled away, and vomited.

"They weren't prepared for the way it felt," Levi said. "If this is the same person who killed Hensley . . . poisoning is totally different from stabbing. Using a knife is one of the most personal, visceral ways to murder a person. The killer was disgusted by it."

"This definitely wasn't your usual passionate stabbing, that's for sure," Martine said, examining the body more closely. "Just the singular wound, no other incisions or serious damage to the body. The murder weapon must have been a matter of necessity rather than personal preference. Why, though? There must be a stronger connection between Walsh and Hensley than just being at the Mirage on the same night, but what?"

Neither of them had an answer for that question, so they split up. Levi rifled through the desk while Martine went to search the bedroom—both good potential hiding spots for any secrets Walsh may have had. He inspected the papers littering the surface, careful not to disturb the body as he moved, but it was just bills and junk mail. His jaw dropped when he saw the charges on Walsh's MasterCard. Either Walsh had been living far beyond his means and was deeply in debt, or he had some other source of income.

The computer was silent, the monitor dark, so Levi had assumed it was turned off. When he crouched to search the desk's bottom drawers, however, he came face-to-face with the dim orange light on the computer tower. It was just in sleep mode.

Straightening up, he nudged the mouse with the tip of his gloved finger. As the computer stirred back to life, he sent up a short prayer that it wouldn't require a password.

For once, luck was on his side. The computer simply returned to the previous session in progress on the desktop. A folder had been left open, full of dozens of subfolders that were all named with strings of numbers in no obvious pattern.

He opened the first subfolder, trying to handle the mouse as little as possible. It contained a bunch of JPEG files with blank thumbnails, similarly titled with numbers. He clicked the slideshow button.

The first image popped up on the screen, and he sucked in a breath.

Though the lighting was dim, he recognized the interior design of the hallways at the Mirage. An older woman dressed to the nines and dripping in precious jewels was wrapped around a gorgeous man who couldn't have been older than twenty, kissing him fervidly. The slideshow continued, displaying a series of photographs documenting their groping, borderline obscene progress down the hallway until they disappeared into a room.

Levi navigated back to the original folder and repeated the process with the second subfolder. This time, the pictures had been taken in one of the Mirage's lounges. A man in a killer Balenciaga suit discreetly accepted a small baggie of pills from another man and passed him a wad of folded bills in return.

"Holy shit," Levi said, and then shouted, "Martine!"

She emerged from the bedroom with a small lockbox under one arm. "Look what I found under Walsh's bed—*whoa*. What's that?"

"Being a front desk clerk may not pay well, but blackmail sure as hell does." He showed her the first folder. "Walsh has been spying on the Mirage's wealthy guests and blackmailing them with their indiscretions; that's how he pays for all this. There are files here going back a couple of years. I bet when we run his financials we find a history of suspicious deposits for the same time period."

Her eyes wide, she said, "He knew who killed Hensley."

"And tried to leverage that information for a price. I'm thinking the same thing."

"What kind of idiot tries to blackmail someone who's already proven they're willing to commit murder? Dumbass." Martine looked at Walsh's body, winced, and crossed herself. "Ah, no disrespect."

"Walsh was standing at the desk with this folder open on the computer when he was killed. There's no signs of forced entry or struggle; he invited the killer inside."

"Yeah, to show them whatever evidence he had," she said. "I would have done the same thing—asked to see it in person so I would be able to get rid of it once Walsh was dead."

"Even if the files we want have been deleted, which seems likely, Carmen may be able to recover them." Levi pointed to the box Martine was carrying. "What've you got?"

"No idea. Let's find out."

One quick snip with a pair of bolt cutters, and they got the lockbox open. Its only contents were a portable hard drive.

Levi and Martine's eyes met as they let out simultaneous noises of triumph. "Let's hope Walsh had the sense to back up his files before letting a murderer into his house," he said.

Dominic's phone rang during the drive to Dr. Tran's office. He pressed the Answer button on his dashboard and said, "Hey, Jasmine."

"Hey, Dom. My dad just texted me about the cookout this weekend—he wants to know if Levi keeps kosher."

"Not completely. He doesn't eat pork or shellfish, but those are the only dietary rules he usually follows. He doesn't need separate cooking utensils or anything."

"It wouldn't be a problem if he did," said Jasmine. "You know how my family is. We're like the freaking United Nations."

Dominic chuckled. Jasmine was multiracial—her father was black and her mother half white, half Paiute Tribe—so her extended family was diverse in itself. But in addition to Jasmine and her two biological siblings, her parents had fostered more than twenty kids over the past two decades, all just as much a part of the family as those who had been born or married into it. As a whole, her family included more than a dozen ethnicities and national origins, five different major religions, and seven spoken languages.

"Anyway," she continued, "we're really glad Levi can come. My parents are looking forward to meeting him."

"It was nice of them to invite him."

Her smile was audible when she said, "I told them I've never seen you like this with any other guy."

"Levi's special," Dominic said absently, concentrating more on merging into the exit lane than the conversation.

Her soft laugh crackled over the speakers. "I know. Well, I've gotta run, but I'll talk to you later."

They said their goodbyes, and Dominic arrived at his destination a few minutes later.

Dr. Angela Tran's psychiatry practice was west of the city, on a street where various professionals' offices were clustered together in buildings that looked like attractive residential townhouses. Dominic had been here once before while searching for leads on the Seven of Spades; there was a private mailbox franchise less than a quarter mile away that the killer had used in their plot to frame Keith Chapman.

This time, he had left Rebel at home. He parallel parked his truck at the curb and mounted the steps to the front door, where he pressed a buzzer to be allowed inside.

The waiting room was what he'd expected—calm and quiet, furnished like a comfortable living room with the exception of the thick glass enclosing the receptionist's desk. Bland landscapes hung on the wall next to poster advertisements for various psychotropic drugs. *Seasonal Affective Disorder got you down?* read one with a picture of a beaming woman cuddling a dog in a meadow. *Ask your doctor about Hybitram today! A Solantia product.*

Nobody was waiting in the seating arrangement of a few plush loveseats clustered around a coffee table, which had been spruced up with some potted flowers and a little Zen garden. An end table held a pile of magazines along with a display of drug pamphlets. One quick scan proved they were all manufactured by Solantia Pharmaceuticals.

Dominic frowned, but he replaced the expression with a friendly smile as he approached the receptionist. She was already eyeing him with appreciation.

"Hi, I'm Adam Smith," he said, giving her the highly creative pseudonym Levi had booked the appointment under. "I have a one o'clock with Dr. Tran?"

"Welcome, Mr. Smith. Let me get your intake paperwork."

The false identity was possible because the appointment wasn't being paid for by insurance. Levi had handed him an actual envelope full of cash the other day, and his jaw had hit the floor when he'd seen the amount. He'd protested, thinking he should contribute part, even though he couldn't afford it, but Levi had waved him off. Only when Dominic pressed the issue had Levi admitted that because he'd paid for so few of his expenses during the time he'd lived with Stanton Barclay, he had almost two full years of his salary saved up.

He'd been so mortified that Dominic had changed the subject immediately—though not before experiencing a moment of self-doubt. What was it like for Levi to go from dating a powerful billionaire to a working-class guy with terrible credit and a mountain of gambling debts?

He shook off those stupid thoughts as the receptionist handed him a sheaf of papers through a window in the glass. Both the pen and the clipboard bore the Solantia logo.

"Thanks," he said, dialing up the brightness of his smile a bit. She giggled and tucked her hair behind her ear.

Settling on one of the loveseats, he reviewed his goals for this visit. Dr. Tran had continued prescribing Chapman antipsychotics despite what seemed to be severe side effects—though they'd discovered after his death that he'd been poisoned with a mix of contraindicated drugs—and had ignored Natasha Stone's repeated concerns about his physical and mental state. Dominic's purpose here was to assess Tran's personal qualities and clinical style to judge whether Levi needed to investigate her more closely.

As Chapman's psychiatrist, Tran would have known he'd make the perfect fall guy for the Seven of Spades. She would have had access to the drugs used to poison him, not to mention the ketamine used on the Seven of Spades's victims, and the mailbox used in the setup was a short walk from her office. One question needed to be answered: had her blasé attitude toward Chapman's difficulties been the result of clinical misjudgment or something more sinister?

Dominic filled out the paperwork with the cover story he'd devised, which was pretty much his own real story with just a few details changed. A lie was always most convincing when it resembled the truth as much as possible. He dreaded talking about his gambling for fifty minutes, but there was too great a chance Tran would call his bluff if he tried to fake something else. He could power through it.

After he returned the papers to the receptionist, he only had to wait five minutes before another man left the inner office, barely sparing Dominic a glance as he walked by. Tran herself emerged a short while later.

"Mr. Smith, I'm Dr. Tran," she said, extending her hand. "It's nice to meet you."

He tossed aside the magazine he'd been pretending to read and rose to shake her hand. "You too."

Tran was somewhere in her mid-forties, of average height, her black hair pulled up in a bun. She had a benevolent smile and gave off a composed, professional vibe as she showed Dominic into her office.

Unsurprisingly, there was no evidence just lying around that screamed *I'm a serial killer!* There were, however, a ton of drug posters on the wall, more even than in the waiting room. Dominic felt like he was at a Solantia convention as he took a seat in the cushy armchair Tran indicated.

She sat across from him with an open folio on her lap. "I've been reviewing your intake forms—I see you describe your condition as 'compulsive gambling'?"

He knew what she was getting at. "I've never been a fan of the term 'pathological gambling.'"

"Understandable. In fact, the new DSM doesn't use that term anymore either; the diagnosis is 'gambling disorder' now. But of course we'll use whatever language you're most comfortable with." Crossing her legs at the knee, she leaned back in her chair, pen at the ready. "Why don't we start with a brief history of the problem? Anything you think is important to my understanding."

Dominic gave her the bullet points—how he'd been fascinated by gambling throughout middle and high school, but it had only become an obsession after he graduated and was bored out of his mind at community college. Realizing he was on a dangerous path was one of the reasons he'd enlisted in the Army. Eight years of purpose and structure with the Rangers had kept him out of trouble; once he'd been discharged home, it had surged back with a vengeance. He'd spiraled out of control over the following two years, getting himself into some very deep shit, until a nasty shock with Rebel's health had driven him to commit to abstinence. He'd been in recovery ever since.

Tran gave him her full attention, listening without comment, jotting down the occasional note. So far, her behavior had been above reproach.

"Have you sought professional treatment for compulsive gambling in the past?" she asked when he was done, even though there was a section on the intake form where he'd put all that information.

"Yeah, I had a couple sessions of cognitive-behavioral therapy with a counselor when I first quit."

"Mmm. So—why now?"

"I'm sorry?" he said.

She smiled. "It's a question I ask all my new patients. What drove you to seek help now, as opposed to a week or a month or a year ago? Has something changed in your life? Some new source of stress, perhaps?"

My quasi-boyfriend thinks you may have killed five people and framed an innocent man. "Uh . . ." Dominic went with the first explanation that came to mind. "I started a new job recently, and I couldn't avoid being exposed to an environment I shouldn't have been in. It might happen again, so I thought it would be a good idea to get some help."

"I see. You're in . . ." She flipped back to his forms. "Personal security?"

"That's right."

"That must bring you into frequent contact with gambling triggers in a city like Las Vegas."

"They can be difficult to avoid, yeah."

Tran was quiet for a moment, tapping her pen against her pad. "Tell me, Mr. Smith, how do you feel when you gamble?"

He thought it was an odd question, but he didn't see the harm in an honest answer. He'd explored this topic ad nauseam in Gamblers Anonymous. "Excited, I guess. During the times I was gambling, it was my go-to whenever I was bored, which was a lot. I enjoy the social aspect, the skill involved—everything about it, really. I've always been kind of a thrill-seeker. I'm competitive, I like to take risks, and I like to win." Flashing a self-deprecating grin, he added, "But who doesn't, you know?"

"Sounds like it would be challenging to give up something you enjoyed so much."

"Well, I only enjoyed it while it was happening," he said. "Afterward I would feel sick and ashamed, especially if I'd lost a lot of money or if I'd had trouble stopping. And the things it did to the people I cared about—I know now that the consequences aren't worth the pleasure I might feel in the moment. For whatever reason, I can't gamble in a healthy way, so I shouldn't gamble at all."

She looked at him intently. "What do you think that reason is?"

Though he knew what she meant, he shrugged as if he didn't understand the question. Unease crawled across his skin.

"Why do you think gambling became a compulsive behavior for you, rather than remaining a relatively harmless leisure activity?" she said, undeterred by his evasion.

"Why does anyone get addicted to anything?" He forced a laugh. "We have no idea, right?"

"That's true. There's an enormous amount of controversy about the causes of addiction even after decades of research. But I'm not asking what you think about the field as a whole. I'm asking how you personally attribute the causes of your own addiction."

Dominic didn't answer; he couldn't. He swallowed hard and looked at the diploma hanging on the wall. There was a clock ticking somewhere in the room that was incredibly loud all of a sudden.

The silence dragged out for about a minute before Tran said, "You've been abstinent for two years. That's very impressive. But I have to wonder about your lack of support."

"I have support. My family, my friends, they've done everything they can to help me."

"That's excellent, and I'm happy to hear it. I actually meant *professional* support, though." She rifled through her papers. "In your own words, your attendance at Gamblers Anonymous is sporadic, and you don't have a sponsor. You haven't signed up for any of the voluntary self-exclusion bans offered by any of the casinos in the city. You ended your CBT counseling long before it could have had any measurable effect. You've created a debt repayment plan, which is commendable—but you haven't made any actual changes to the way you handle your finances, which is one of the first steps any clinician would advise to someone with a gambling disorder." Meeting his eyes, she said, "To me, this paints the picture of a man trying to white-knuckle his way through recovery."

He felt like she'd knocked the wind out of him, and he had to take a couple of shallow breaths before he could respond. "I'm here now, aren't I?" he said, more harshly than he'd intended.

She didn't even blink, just sat there with an expression of infinite patience.

Briefly closing his eyes, he got a grip on himself. He was letting her throw him off-balance, and that wasn't going to help Levi. "Look, I just—it's difficult for me to talk about this stuff. Nobody likes to think of themselves as a loser."

"A 'loser'?" she said slowly. "That's a particularly loaded term for a gambler, don't you think?"

Dominic rolled his shoulders uncomfortably. He didn't know why he'd said that at all.

"And I'd imagine a compulsive behavior that's difficult to control would be very threatening to someone whose self-identity is strongly rooted in their sense of competency and physical strength."

He stared at her, a faint ringing in his ears.

"You're obviously well-motivated to abstain from gambling, but at the same time, you've chosen not to pursue the many treatment options available to you," said Tran. "I have to wonder if maybe you view your compulsive gambling as an inherent weakness, a personality flaw that can be overcome with willpower, rather than an illness deserving of professional treatment and regular management."

"It is a weakness," Dominic whispered.

She nodded, though she seemed to be more acknowledging his opinion than agreeing with him. "Many people struggle to accept a medical model of addiction, especially with behavioral addictions as opposed to substance abuse. But the truth is that disordered gambling shares many features in common with addiction to drugs and alcohol—an inability to stop despite negative consequences, increasing tolerance, even withdrawal symptoms. You don't have to try to beat this on your own, and it's not a personal failing to admit that you need help. Coming here was a great first step."

He said nothing. He'd completely lost track of why he was here, and try as he might, he couldn't regain his equilibrium.

"I'm going to recommend a combination of CBT, psychodynamic therapy, and continued participation in GA." Tran glanced at the clock. "We're almost out of time, so we'll put together a treatment plan during our next session. In the meantime . . ."

She retrieved her prescription pad from the back of her folio, scribbled on the top page, and ripped it off. Dominic snapped out of his stupor as she handed it to him.

"This is an SSRI," he said. "I'm not depressed."

"I'm not prescribing it for depression. There's no FDA-approved pharmacotherapy for gambling disorder yet, but studies have shown promising results for off-label uses of SSRIs. The theory is that the brain activity involved in compulsive gambling has similarities to obsessive-compulsive disorders, so the dosage is similar to what I'd prescribe for that condition. It should help decrease cravings and mental preoccupation with gambling, though chances are it'll take about ten to twelve weeks to really start working."

"Trolexin—Solantia makes that, don't they?"

"Mm-hmm," Tran said, absorbed in her notes.

Dominic suppressed a snort as everything finally clicked into place.

She showed him to the door and shook his hand goodbye. In the waiting room, he politely declined to schedule another session with the receptionist and walked straight outside. Back in the bright sun and blazing heat, he caught himself on the bed of his truck and stood there for several minutes, breathing deeply.

Tran's words echoed through his head, bouncing around his skull like an out-of-control pinball. He had her number now, and he could tell Levi to scratch her off the list—but he wasn't sure it had been worth the cost.

CHAPTER 11

evi groaned in gratitude and relief as Dominic set a Boulevardier
on the bar. He took a sip, savoring the blend of bourbon, sweet
vermouth, and Campari. God bless Dominic for introducing him to
this drink.

"That rough, huh?" Dominic said, amusement dancing in his eyes.

"Long day," said Levi, though Dominic already knew that. They'd
been texting back and forth all afternoon, and it was Dominic who
had suggested Levi visit him at Stingray, the LGBT club where he
bartended part-time.

There was really no such thing as a slow night in Vegas, but it was
early enough that they could converse at a normal volume in-between
Dominic serving his other customers. He was working one of the
second-story bars tonight, overlooking the dance floor below. Blue
uplighting flickered off the glossy black and silver décor and gave the
entire place an underwater feel.

"I was so busy working the Walsh case that I had to postpone my
meeting with Dr. Kapoor until tomorrow." Levi rattled the ice in his
glass and drank another sip. "Martine and I are running out of time. In
a couple of days, the conference will be over, and if we haven't caught
Hensley's killer by then, we probably never will."

Dominic squeezed his free hand. "You'll get them."

Levi laced their fingers together, but Dominic was called away
moments later by patrons further down the bar. By the time he
returned, Levi had finished half his drink and was studiously ignoring
the leering man cruising him from a nearby table.

"You were going to tell me about Dr. Tran," Levi said.

"Oh, yeah. She's getting paid to prescribe Solantia products."

Levi almost dropped his glass. "What? That's illegal!"

"Sure, but you'd never be able to prove it," Dominic said with a shrug. "Pharmaceutical companies can pay doctors consulting fees. I'm guessing she gets a kickback for each prescription, disguised as something legitimate. That's why she never adjusted Chapman's meds."

"Shit. Are you sure?"

"I'm as positive as I can be without seeing her bank accounts." Dominic paused. "Which I would *never* do, because that would also be illegal."

"Yes," Levi said, holding his gaze. "You should definitely not do that."

Dominic winked, then moved away to greet some new customers. Levi only felt guilty for a second; he'd never be able to obtain Tran's financials through legal channels, but Dominic had plenty of ways around the system and no compunctions about using them. He could make his peace with the ethics violation in the interests of catching a serial killer.

Levi tossed back the last of his Boulevardier. Mere seconds later, his creepy admirer sidled up to him at the bar.

"Looks like you could use another drink," the man said.

"No, thank you," said Levi, his voice cool and prim. He didn't even look at the man.

"Come on. It'll loosen you up a little."

"I said no."

"Hey, I'm just trying to be friendly." The man put his hand on Levi's knee and slowly slid it up his thigh. "You could at least—"

Levi grabbed the man's hand with both of his and twisted his wrist around, bending the man's fingers toward his body while pressing his arm down and to the side. Yelping in pain, the man collapsed against the bar, half-hunched over Levi's lap.

"Don't fucking touch me," Levi said.

"Shit!" The man was already sweating, his body quivering like Jell-O. "Let go of me, you crazy asshole—"

Levi dug his thumbs harder into the back of the man's hand, drawing forth a sobbing moan. He knew how much it hurt to be on the receiving end of this kind of joint lock. A dark, secret part of him was viciously thrilled, pleased to see a man like this at his mercy—

"Problem?" Dominic said in a mild tone.

Levi and the man both looked up. With his build, Dominic could come off as intimidating even with the casual body language and amiable expression he was displaying now. His work uniform consisted of a black T-shirt so tight it could have been painted on; his biceps were all but busting out of the short sleeves, and the material clung to every thick muscle in his chest and abdomen.

The man shook his head somewhat frantically, and Levi released him. He yanked his arm against his chest as he backed away, hissing, "Fucking psycho," before he fled.

Dominic raised his eyebrows. Removed from the heat of the moment, Levi felt a little foolish.

"Sorry about that."

"Hey, he had no right to put his hands on you."

"And I could have communicated that without putting him in a cavalier," Levi said wryly.

Smiling, Dominic said, "Your words, not mine. *Do* you want another drink?"

"I'm good, thanks." Levi handed him his empty glass. "Is it terrible that I'm kind of disappointed Dr. Tran isn't the Seven of Spades?"

"Of course not. That would have meant this whole thing was over. Now you have to keep searching."

Levi watched him dump the ice and set the glass with the others to be washed. Dominic had been his usual cheerful self all evening, and his texts that afternoon had been as lighthearted and flirtatious as ever. Still, Levi knew what he must have spoken to Tran about; that couldn't have been easy, especially after his close call two days earlier.

"You haven't said anything about the session itself," Levi said, leaving Dominic the option to deliberately misinterpret the question.

He didn't take it. "It wasn't fun," he said, a hint of a shadow crossing his face. "But I'm fine."

"I'm sorry you had to do that."

"I didn't—I volunteered, remember? I know how important this is to you. I'd do anything to help."

Sighing, Levi folded his arms on the bar. "I wish you didn't have to work tonight." All he wanted to do was go to one of their apartments, have a satisfying orgasm or two, and fall asleep in Dominic's arms.

"Me too." Dominic mirrored Levi and bent down so their faces were only inches apart. "I need the money, though. My internship at McBride pays shit and cuts into the time I'd use to bring in bounties, so I have to pick up extra shifts whenever I can."

Levi swayed closer. "You know, I might actually miss telling people I'm dating a bounty hunter."

"Bail enforcement agent," said Dominic.

Levi laughed, his breath gusting over Dominic's lips. Dominic brushed his thumb along Levi's cheekbone with sudden tenderness.

"What?" Levi asked.

"I love it when you laugh," Dominic said, and kissed him.

Moaning, Levi leaned forward into what became a full-fledged make-out session over the width of the bar. A few wolf whistles sounded nearby, but Levi couldn't have cared less. Let them eat their jealous fucking hearts out.

"Levi?" a familiar voice said behind him.

Levi jerked away from Dominic so violently that his barstool pitched back on its rear legs; only Dominic lunging across the bar to grab his arm kept him from toppling to the floor. Once he'd steadied himself, he jumped off the stool and turned around.

"Stanton," he said.

Standing a few feet from the bar and gaping incredulously was his ex-boyfriend Stanton Barclay. He was a gorgeous man with a face that recalled the Golden Age of Hollywood, from his dimpled chin to his piercing blue eyes. His exquisitely tailored suit fit the long, lean lines of his body like a second skin.

The silence dragged out. Levi was just as shocked as Stanton seemed to be—in the three years they'd dated, he'd never seen Stanton in a place like this. Then again, Levi had never been one to frequent nightclubs himself.

"What are you doing here?" Levi finally asked.

"Some friends convinced me to come out tonight." Stanton half turned and gestured to a table near the dance floor. A group of familiar, judgmental faces looked back at them—the wealthiest and most socially prominent members of Las Vegas's LGBT community. They'd always been more Stanton's friends than his.

They'd all witnessed Levi's extreme PDA with Dominic. God, why didn't he just spit on the grave of his and Stanton's relationship while he was at it?

Behind him, Dominic cleared his throat.

"Oh," Levi said, startling. "Um, Stanton, this is Dominic Russo. Dominic, Stanton Barclay."

Dominic extended his hand across the bar. "Nice to meet you."

Ever the model of perfect courtesy, Stanton stepped forward and shook his hand. "Likewise." His eyes darted down to where Dominic's enormous hand engulfed his own, then traveled slowly back up Dominic's chest to his face before he let go.

The second silence was even more awkward than the first. "Well, I've got thirsty customers," Dominic said after a few seconds. "Excuse me."

He moved down the bar. Levi caught Stanton's elbow and led him further away, out of earshot. Stanton didn't resist.

"Wow," he said, his gaze still lingering on Dominic. "I guess there really were things I couldn't give you."

"Don't do that," Levi snapped. "You know I didn't leave you for Dominic, and even if I had, it wouldn't have been for some tawdry sexual reason. You're cheapening my relationships with him *and* you by suggesting otherwise."

Shoulders slumping, Stanton said, "I know. I'm sorry. It's just—it's not every day you see your ex hanging off the lips of a man who could body double for Dwayne Johnson."

Levi shoved his hands into his pockets and looked down at his feet.

"Don't you miss me at all?" Stanton said quietly.

Levi's head jerked up. "Of course I do."

"Really? Because I still wake up every morning feeling like my heart's been through a meat grinder. It's all I can do sometimes just to get through the day, and here you are having the time of your life with your hot new boyfriend. For God's sake, Levi, it's only been three months since you moved out." Stanton hesitated and then shook his head. "You never would have kissed me like that in public."

"I . . ." Levi's mouth worked open and shut. He couldn't defend his actions, because everything Stanton had said was true. "I know the timing is terrible. I do miss you, Stanton. I think about you a lot. But I didn't expect this thing with Dominic, and I can't just put it on hold while I wait for the rest of my life to catch up. I'm sorry. I'm not trying to hurt you—I would never want that."

They stood there without speaking for a moment. The volume in the club had picked up as it got busier, and there was a dissonance in having this heart-wrenching conversation against a raucous backdrop of laughter, tipsy cheering, and Lady Gaga.

"I suppose I shouldn't be surprised that you're handling the breakup better than I am," said Stanton. "After all, you're the one who left. I wanted you to stay."

"Our relationship wasn't working."

"We could have made it work."

"I disagree."

Stanton closed his eyes, exhaled, and opened them again. "I'm gonna go home."

"No." Levi reached out, but when Stanton shied away, he dropped his hand. "Stay. I was just about to leave anyway."

"I'm not really in a partying mood—"

"Stanton, please. Don't let me ruin your night. Stay and have fun with your friends."

Stanton wavered, looking torn. Then he nodded.

"Take care of yourself," Levi said, and returned to the bar. Dominic must have been watching from a distance, because he immediately waved Levi to the gap near the back where the bartenders entered and exited. Here, they could stand close enough to hear each other over the growing noise of the crowd without shouting.

"Everything okay?" Dominic asked.

"It's fine," Levi said automatically, and then sighed. "No, it's not. He still thinks I left him for you."

"I know that bothers you, but honestly, I'm not sure there's anything you could do or say that would convince him otherwise at this point. You may need to just let it go."

"Easier said than done." Levi squeezed Dominic's hand out of sight. "I'm going home. Call me tomorrow?"

"Yeah."

Levi went the long way around to avoid passing Stanton's table on his way to the exit. He'd had just about enough uncomfortable emotional conversations for one day.

Late Thursday morning, Levi was sitting at a corner table at The Roasted Bean, a vintage-chic bistro in the Mirage. He had his head propped dispiritedly on one hand and was sipping a cup of black coffee with two shots of espresso.

He looked up when Martine joined him, holding an iced coffee of her own and setting a plate of quiche in the middle of the table. "I've never heard so many people try to find a diplomatic way of saying, 'I didn't kill him but I'm glad he's dead,'" she said.

"At least yours softened it up. Most of mine came right out and said that verbatim."

They'd spent the morning interviewing Hensley's colleagues in-between panels at the hospice and palliative care conference. In Levi's experience, after a person was murdered, everyone who'd known them went out of their way to gloss over their negative traits and glorify their positive ones—the sanctification of the dead, Martine called it. The fact that nobody had reacted that way in the wake of Hensley's murder was a stronger testament to his character than simple words.

Martine pointedly pushed the quiche toward him.

"I don't want that," Levi said, annoyed.

"How about this? I won't badger you about eating it if you can tell me that you've ingested anything other than coffee today."

He scowled at her.

"You're so over-caffeinated you've got the shakes," she said, nodding to his hands. "Eat the goddamn quiche."

Heaving a groan, he dragged the plate closer and took a sarcastic, exaggerated bite. She just smiled sweetly.

The quiche *was* good—a fluffy concoction of broccoli and cheddar with a perfect flaky crust—so he stowed his attitude and tucked in. It wasn't like he deliberately avoided eating; it was just never his highest priority when he was distracted.

"So we have confirmation that Hensley was universally despised," Martine said while Levi ate. "But as far as serious motives for murder go, only one jumped out at me—Dr. Helen Dumont. I heard from a few independent sources that she and Hensley were bitter enemies even by his standards; he sabotaged her grant funding, and she was determined to pay him back. Yet the good doctor herself didn't mention anything about that to me when I spoke with her."

Levi swallowed his mouthful and said, "I heard about her too. And there was another name that kept popping up, a Dr. Arjun Bhatia. Apparently, Hensley ripped his research apart and dragged his professional reputation through the mud. His career still hasn't recovered."

"Is he attending the conference?"

"Supposedly. I haven't been able to track him down yet, though."

"Then we'll find him, grill them both a little harder, and check their alibis for Saturday night. Are you still meeting Dr. Kapoor during the lunch break?"

Levi nodded.

"This would be a lot simpler if Carmen could get the files we need from Walsh's hard drive," Martine said with a sigh.

The day before, Walsh's girlfriend had tearfully confessed her knowledge of his multiple ongoing blackmail schemes. He had never shared the details with her, and she'd never asked, content to enjoy the spoils of his dirty dealings without question. The only thing she'd known for sure was that he used burner phones to communicate with his targets. No such phones had been present at the crime scene, so it was a safe bet the killer had taken them if they existed.

Levi and Martine had ensured the delivery of Walsh's desktop computer and backup hard drive to the substation so Carmen Rivera could analyze them. That morning, she'd broken the bad news.

"The security on these is insane," she'd said. "Walsh must have hired someone to lock down his data, because this goes far beyond standard commercial protection. You got lucky that the system didn't require reauthentication when returning from sleep mode, though even that's probably just because Walsh turned that feature off. Most computer security problems stem from human laziness. But then the

CSIs had to turn the computer off to transport it, and the system reset."

"Are you saying you can't get in to either one?" Levi had asked.

"I *can*, it's just a matter of how and when. I'm worried that if I use a brute force approach, there may be a failsafe in place that corrupts the data. I'll have to finesse my way in, and that'll take longer."

So here they were, with the potential smoking gun that could solve their case locked up in a little black box they couldn't access. It was beyond frustrating.

"We know Walsh worked the front desk from midnight to 9 a.m. the night Hensley was murdered," Levi said now. "He saw something that was worth killing him for. We just have to figure out what."

He and Martine finished their coffees and then split up again, returning to the conference that took up the entire Mirage Event Center. A couple more hours of canvassing Hensley's erstwhile colleagues, and Levi was ready to pull his hair out. He'd never worked a case quite like this before, where the question wasn't who wanted the victim dead, so much as who of those many people wanted it *most*.

When the conference broke for lunch, Levi met up with Anika Kapoor on-site at Pantry, where they took a relatively quiet corner table.

"Thank you for being so accommodating," Kapoor said after they'd placed their order. "This schedule is running me off my feet."

"It's no problem," he said.

She folded her hands on the table. "Clarissa Northridge told me you no longer believe Stephen was killed by the escort he hired."

"That's correct. Our working theory is that someone attending the conference capitalized on the timing to murder him, knowing blame would fall in her direction first." Levi paused. "This is going to be painfully frank, but I'm sure you understand the difficulty we're facing in discerning motive. With your average murder victim, there's maybe a couple of people who genuinely wanted them dead. With Dr. Hensley, that list numbers over a dozen and is still growing."

She said nothing, running her fingers along the edge of her napkin over and over.

"The situation is complicated by the fact that because everyone's rooms are clustered so closely together, each possible suspect had plenty of opportunity to get into Hensley's room. And as for means—well, it can't be that difficult for a doctor to get their hands on Rohypnol."

"It's not," she said morosely. She lifted her eyes to meet his. "I'm well aware of how many people loathed Stephen with a passion. I can hear it in their voices when they express their so-called condolences—they're pleased he's dead. But there's an enormous difference between wanting someone to die and actually murdering them. I can't imagine anyone I know making that leap."

"Somebody did," said Levi.

Kapoor took an unhurried sip of water, her face clouded over. When she set down her glass, she said, "Do you think it was me?"

"I'm keeping an open mind."

"My relationship with Stephen was more amicable than perhaps any other in his life. I had less reason than anyone to kill him."

"That might be true, if you hadn't been sleeping with him."

That was a shot in the dark based on Martine's hunch, but it landed hard. Kapoor's eyes went wide, and she took a sharp breath. Then she swallowed and glanced furtively around the restaurant as if eavesdroppers might be lurking behind the nearby tables. "It's not what you think."

"But you don't deny it," he said, making a mental note to thank Martine for her insight.

"Stephen and I weren't having an affair," she said. "We slept together occasionally, but our relationship was never romantic. He respected me, as much as he could respect anyone, and that meant more to him than any kind of love."

"What about you?"

"I . . ." Her expression turned wistful. "Stephen was a brilliant physician-scientist, a true genius. I *know* that doesn't excuse his many flaws, or the way he treated people. I know that. I could never have loved him the way I love my husband. But there was always a spark of attraction there—a meeting of the minds as important as that of the flesh."

Her eyes were misting over, so Levi gave her a moment to pull herself together. Then he asked, "Does your husband know?"

She shook her head.

"Dr. Northridge?"

"Yes," Kapoor said, surprising him. "She's always known. She and Stephen have lived apart for years; their marriage was just a formality."

Levi frowned. "Then why not get a divorce?"

Shrugging, she said, "I don't know all the details, but the Northridges are old money. Clarissa and Stephen didn't have a prenup, so in a divorce, he might have been able to lay claim to some of her family's assets. It was easier all around for them to stay married."

Well, that was one of the more depressing things he'd ever heard. He filed that away and continued his questioning. "When we spoke on Sunday, you said you were aware of Dr. Hensley's habit of hiring escorts while on business trips. That didn't make you jealous?"

"Of course not. I told you, my relationship with Stephen wasn't romantic. There was nothing to be jealous of."

He had no grounds to challenge that statement, so instead he pulled a photograph of Walsh from his jacket pocket and slid it across the table. "Do you recognize this man?"

"No," she said, after giving it a cursory glance. "Should I?"

Before he could respond, a server approached with their food in hand—a chicken Caesar salad and a plate of steak and fries. It wasn't the same server who'd taken their order, and without asking, he began to set the salad in front of Kapoor.

"It's the other way around," Levi said. The reprimand came out more rudely than he'd intended, but he hated when people made gendered assumptions.

Mumbling an apology, the server switched the plates and scurried away. Levi poked the salad with his fork; he was still full from the quiche, but he'd felt like he had to order something.

"I understand your suspicions, Detective," Kapoor said. She picked up her own fork along with the steak knife that had been brought out on her plate. "But I also know that casinos are some of the most heavily surveilled places in the world, and I was at the Mirage's when Stephen died. There must be plenty of—"

She kept talking, but Levi was no longer listening. He stared at her hands as she cut into her steak, then reached across the table and snatched the knife away from her.

Though she yelped in shock, he was too preoccupied to apologize. The steak knife had an intricately engraved pewter handle, an abstract pattern like vines twining up its length.

This was exactly the same type of knife that had been used to kill Alan Walsh.

"Obviously there's no way for them to tell if a single knife is missing," Martine said over the phone. "But the Food and Beverage Manager confirmed that the steak knife found at the Walsh scene is one of a design manufactured exclusively for the Mirage's use in several of their restaurants as well as room service."

Levi paced back and forth outside of Pantry. "Room service, of course. It would have been easy for the killer to stash a knife in their room and then slip it up their sleeve when they went to visit Walsh."

"If we had any doubts that Walsh and Hensley's murders are connected, they're gone now."

"Why leave the knife behind, though? They were so careful with the first scene."

"I think you were right about why the killer threw up after they murdered Walsh," she said. "They must have gotten flustered and either forgot the knife or didn't consider that we'd link it to the Mirage. They also didn't think to shut down his computer. We got lucky that the experience of stabbing someone unnerved them so much."

"Well, I just finished up with Dr. Kapoor." He glanced at his watch. "I'm going to head back to the substation, triple-check alibis and follow up with forensics on the Walsh scene. There must be something we're missing."

"All right. I'll see you there."

Levi hung up and started for the lobby. He and Martine had driven here together in her car, but it would be no problem to catch a quick taxi back. The Mirage was only four miles away from the substation, a straight shot down the Strip—or the parallel Las Vegas Freeway, which would probably be faster.

As he walked through the casino floor and passed the aptly named Center Bar in the middle, one of the patrons caught his eye. Pale, gangly Craig Warner was slumped on a stool, both elbows on the bar while he nursed an enormous drink. Levi hadn't been able to find him all morning; this explained why. By the looks of things, the cocktail in his hand wasn't his first of the day.

Joining him at the bar, Levi said, "Little early for a Mai Tai, isn't it?"

Warner blinked at him blearily, seeming not to recognize him right away. "Not in Las Vegas."

Good point. Levi sat on the stool next to him and waved off the approaching bartender.

"You know, I'm supposed to be in a lecture on managing geriatric delirium right now," Warner said. He guzzled his drink noisily through his straw.

"Mind if I ask what you're doing here instead?"

Warner didn't answer immediately. He was gripping his glass with both hands like somebody might take it away if he let go for even a moment.

"I'm glad Hensley's dead," he said.

He was clearly gearing up to say more, so Levi waited without comment.

"When Dr. Kapoor told me the news on Sunday, the first thing I felt—the very first thing—was relief." Warner closed his eyes. "I guess I'm having trouble dealing with that."

"I understand Dr. Hensley was difficult to work with," Levi said carefully.

Warner let out a bitter, snorting laugh. "Difficult? It wouldn't be an exaggeration to say he made my life a living hell. But still—to be happy that another human being was *murdered*? That's sick." He gave Levi a beseeching look. "How am I supposed to reconcile that part of myself?"

Unbidden, Levi's mind flashed back to the hostage situation at the Tropicana months earlier—the panicked robber police had cornered in the lobby, the little boy he'd been using as a human shield. The *crack* of Levi's own bullet as it hit him dead center in the forehead.

When Dale Slater collapsed, with the boy still alive and well, Levi had felt a moment of the purest, most intense satisfaction he'd ever known. The nauseating shame that swamped him seconds later still persisted today, though Natasha had helped him process the worst of it.

"You're asking the wrong person, trust me," he said.

Fidgeting with the pineapple garnish on the rim of his glass, Warner said, "I've thought about going home to Baltimore, and just screw our presentation tomorrow. But Dr. Northridge talked me out of it."

"Yeah, she mentioned that she was going to come support you and Dr. Kapoor."

"She's a great doctor—a great woman. Much better than Hensley deserved. I'm surprised she flew out here so soon after he died. In her place, I don't know that I would have bothered to come at all."

"You call a full forty-eight hours later 'soon'?" said Levi.

Warner's brow furrowed. "Well, we didn't find out until Sunday morning. Monday afternoon isn't that much later."

"Dr. Northridge flew into Vegas on Tuesday," Levi said, puzzled. "Did you see her on Monday?"

"Um . . ." Clearing his throat, Warner straightened up. "No, you know, I must be confused. I've been so stressed out all week, the days are all blurring together." He gestured to the bartender and added, "Hey, can I buy you a drink?"

"No, thanks. I'm on duty." Levi took in Warner's twitchy body language, then hopped off his stool. "And I've got to get back to work. You might think about doing the same. I don't want to minimize what you're going through, but it's probably not worth ruining your career over."

"Thanks, Detective," Warner said, toasting him with his glass.

Levi pulled out his phone while he strode through the Mirage's rainforest-themed atrium. Clarissa Northridge had been in Baltimore when Hensley had died, which was as ironclad as an alibi could get. There was no real reason to doubt that.

Still, it wouldn't hurt to confirm a few things.

CHAPTER 12

ominic threw the tennis ball in a neat arc that sailed down the length of the dog run. Rebel took off after it, kicking up grass in her enthusiasm. She snatched the ball up seconds after it landed and bounded back to him. Rather than drop the ball at his feet, she sat and waited for him to extend his hand for it.

"Good girl," he said. He tilted the ball back and forth. "You want this?"

Her ears pricked up, her eyes trained as intensely as a laser beam on each miniscule movement. She stood in a tense half crouch, every muscle primed to spring into action.

He faked her out a couple of times, but she was too smart to fall for that. When he finally let the ball fly, she bolted away at top speed.

He smiled as he watched her go. In the cooler months, he took her with him on his long runs, but that was out of the question in the middle of summer. Even when he ran outside himself, early in the morning or late at night, he was too concerned about her overheating to bring her along. Playing at the park near his apartment provided a safe alternative.

Dusk was falling when he called a halt—he had plans to meet Aubrey in an hour to continue their Rhodes surveillance. He clipped Rebel's leash to her collar, and they ambled back to his truck, where he poured a small amount of water into a collapsible dog dish.

Mid-slurp, Rebel's body stiffened. She lifted her head, water dripping from her muzzle, and stared across the parking lot with her ears pushed all the way forward.

Her body language wasn't aggressive, just curious, so Dominic wasn't alarmed. He looked in the same direction and tried to figure out what had caught her attention. There were people out playing with their kids and dogs, a few intrepid joggers, a group of teenagers on skateboards—nothing out of the ordinary for a neighborhood park on a Thursday evening.

Rebel didn't relax, though; she stood like a statue, only her eyes moving. Dominic had never seen her act like this. She was a trained personal protection dog, and if he were in danger, she'd warn him in no uncertain terms. Right now, she wasn't displaying any of those signals. So what was going on?

He trusted his own instincts too, and he didn't sense any danger. But he was starting to get a little creeped out.

Suddenly, Rebel huffed and returned to her water as if nothing had happened. Dominic scanned the environment one last time and then bent to pick up the bowl. "Come on, let's go home," he said.

When he pulled into the lot outside his apartment complex, he saw his neighbor Mrs. Muñoz struggling to corral her three rambunctious young children while also retrieving several large grocery bags from the trunk of her car. Looping Rebel's leash around his wrist, he jumped out of his truck and hurried over. She stayed close at his heels and happily accepted the children's lavish attentions as they flocked around her.

"Let me help you with those," he said.

"Oh, *mijo*, thank you." Mrs. Muñoz handed him the bags with a sigh of relief. "Such a sweet boy."

She clapped her hands sharply, shooing her kids toward the gate in the complex's chain-link fence. Dominic followed, only to be brought up short when Rebel whirled around and stared across the street with the same stiff posture and focused concentration she'd shown in the park.

Once again, Dominic couldn't identify the source of her fixation, and this time it made him even more apprehensive.

"What is it, Rebel?" he asked.

Whining low in her throat, she backed up a few steps and paced forward again. She looked up at Dominic, wagged her tail hesitantly, and then looked back across the street. She seemed more confused than anything else.

"Is everything okay?" Mrs. Muñoz called from the gate.

"It's fine," said Dominic. "Must be a new dog in the neighborhood or something."

He clicked his tongue and tugged lightly on Rebel's leash. If she sensed a genuine threat, she would ignore him until he acknowledged it. Instead, she turned around and trotted at his side into the complex, glancing over her shoulder just once on the way.

His unease persisted as he brought Mrs. Muñoz's groceries up to her apartment and then returned to his own, where he fed Rebel her dinner and ate a quick meal himself. He wished he could take her along tonight; he was used to having her at his side when he pursued bounties, and he was loath to leave her alone after her unusual behavior. But he couldn't explain that to Aubrey, who would probably find Rebel's presence an unwelcome distraction.

Aubrey had continued keeping tabs on Rhodes the past two nights while Dominic was bartending at Stingray, but Rhodes had just gone straight home from work both nights. Tonight, however, he'd told his wife he'd be working late again. Dominic hooked up with Aubrey in the parking lot outside Rhodes's office just in time to see the man get into his own car.

"Looks like he saves his bad behavior for you," Aubrey joked as she turned the key in the ignition.

"Lucky me," Dominic said.

They followed Rhodes to a rowdy dive bar Downtown. It was crowded enough inside for them to risk close personal observation, so they took a table in the corner and ordered a couple of drinks for appearance's sake. Rhodes hung out by the bar for a few minutes, texting intermittently, before greeting a pretty brunette and settling down at a table of his own.

"Sometimes I wonder if Rhodes suspects his wife is having him followed," Aubrey said, after they'd watched him and the woman flirting tamely for a while. "I mean, I don't think he's ever made us, but he's oddly careful about not crossing the line with these women in public."

Dominic shrugged. "Could be. Or maybe he's concerned about the possibility of running into someone he and his wife know. You don't have to be a PI to snap an incriminating picture on your phone."

For the umpteenth time that evening, he swiveled around in his chair, surveying the bar. It was second nature for him to pay close attention to his surroundings, marking exits and escape routes, staying alert to any activity or movement or other visual cues that were out of place. But tonight the nape of his neck was prickling in a way that prompted more deliberate scrutiny. The worst part was that he couldn't be sure if that was because he was picking up on something subconsciously, or if he was just being unnecessarily paranoid due to Rebel's earlier behavior.

"You're on edge." Aubrey narrowed her eyes. "Are you, um . . . having problems again?"

"What?" he said, his attention snapping back to her. "No, it's nothing like that. I'm just keeping an eye out."

A stunning young woman walked into the bar then, a quintessential blonde bombshell in an eye-popping dress who turned heads all over the room. She didn't return any of the admiring glances, though, scanning the crowd as if she were searching for someone in particular. When she saw Rhodes, she locked on and headed straight for his table. He seemed surprised but not at all displeased by her approach.

"Think he accidentally double-booked himself?" Dominic asked.

"That, or he's trying for a threesome," Aubrey said with a smirk. "In which case I doubt he'll succeed."

Indeed, the introduction of a rival had the brunette spitting fire. Dominic and Aubrey watched with fascination as a war was waged for Rhodes's attention in venomous glances, tossed hair, and painfully fake laughter. Rhodes was the only one enjoying himself, apparently oblivious to the fact that the women were one snapped thread away from leaping across the table and clawing each other to shreds.

"This is better than Animal Planet," said Aubrey.

The brunette put up a good fight, but in the end, the blonde's more aggressive affections won out. As the brunette slunk away in defeat, the blonde curtailed Rhodes's protests by curling up in his lap, playing with his tie while she whispered in his ear.

Frowning, Dominic said, "I'm getting a weird vibe off this woman. Rhodes is a good-looking guy, but is he really worth this level of dedicated effort?"

"Yeah, I know what you mean. There are plenty of hot guys in here, but when she came in, it was like she was looking for Rhodes specifically."

"And it didn't seem like he was expecting her."

Less than five minutes later, the blonde hopped off Rhodes's lap, coaxed him to his feet, and led him to the door. He stumbled along behind her, a glazed, lust-drunk expression on his face that Dominic could empathize with. He was sure he looked the same way half the time he was in Levi's presence.

He and Aubrey turned aside as the couple passed them, but they needn't have bothered—Rhodes only had eyes for the woman. They trailed them outside, remaining at a discreet distance while Rhodes and the woman called for an Uber, then tracked them to a motel a few miles away.

"Classy place," Aubrey said, parking at an angle that gave them a good view of the front of the building. "You ready?"

Dominic nodded, hefting the camera and lowering the passenger-side window. He snapped a continuous series of shots as Rhodes and the woman left the Uber hand in hand, laughing and canoodling on their way to one of the first-floor rooms.

"They didn't check in," Aubrey said. "Does one of them already have a key?"

That question was answered when the blonde withdrew a keycard from her purse and waved it playfully at Rhodes, who said something they were too far away to hear. She smiled in response, backed him up against the wall outside the room, and kissed him hard.

Dominic continued photographing them while Aubrey made a quiet, triumphant noise beside him. Rhodes and the woman separated just long enough for her to unlock the door and were already kissing again by the time it closed behind them.

Dominic lowered the camera and leaned over so he and Aubrey could both review the photos as he cycled through them. The clear, crisp images caught Rhodes with his unfaithful hands all over a woman who was decidedly not his wife, and the setting left no doubt as to his intentions. Combined with the photos Aubrey had taken in the bar with her hidden purse camera, this spelled doom for the cheating bastard.

"Got the money shot." Aubrey leaned back in her seat with a contented air. "Now we just wait, get a few more shots of him coming out with a post-sex glow, and our client's got her profitable divorce in the bag."

Expecting to hang around for an hour or two, they made themselves comfortable, and Aubrey started telling a story about the time she'd gotten lost in Marrakesh while stoned out of her mind. They both startled when the door to Rhodes's room flew open not ten minutes later.

The blonde darted out, stuffing something into her tiny purse and struggling to close the clasp. Dominic and Aubrey instinctively flattened themselves against their seats as she looked back and forth across the parking lot and then took off running, leaving the door to the motel room half-ajar.

"Holy shit, she just rolled him!" Dominic said. He grabbed the camera and took a few more quick shots.

"We don't know that."

He pointed to the far corner of the lot, where a dark sedan's lights flashed as the blonde unlocked it remotely. "You think she's going out to get condoms?"

Maneuvering with impressive agility on her stiletto heels, the blonde dove into the car, started up the engine, and peeled out of the lot to the sound of screeching tires. Dominic reached for his door handle, but Aubrey caught his arm.

"What are you doing?" she asked. "You'll blow our cover."

"Seriously? She could have drugged him, stabbed him—he could be dying right now."

"Our first responsibility is to our client."

He shook his head in disbelief. "I'm sorry, but my first responsibility is to my fellow human beings."

Ignoring her protests, he got out of the car and hurried toward the room. The heavy door had begun to creep shut, but he caught it at the last second before it hit the jamb. He nudged it back open, crouched low, and peered inside.

Rhodes was sprawled unconscious on the bed, his shoes off and his shirt half-unbuttoned. Though the room looked otherwise empty, Dominic drew his gun and cleared it anyway, in case the blonde had an accomplice who'd been lying in wait. Once he was sure nobody was hiding in the bathroom, the closet, or under the bed, he moved to Rhodes's side.

Rhodes was breathing fine and his pulse was steady, but he didn't respond at all to Dominic's vigorous attempts to wake him. A couple of red Solo cups were set out next to the TV alongside bottles of vodka and orange juice. No points for deducing what had happened here.

"Christ," Dominic muttered. He rolled Rhodes into the recovery position on his left side before pulling out his phone.

Someone knocked on the door. He checked through the peephole, then let Aubrey inside.

"I thought you weren't interested in helping," he said.

"I wanted to make sure you weren't going to do something stupid." She nodded to the phone in his hand. "Like call 911."

"He's been drugged—"

"Russo, for God's sake, would you think this through for a minute? McBride promises its clients absolute discretion. If we're here when the cops show up, our names will be in the paperwork. We'll have to give statements. Rhodes will find out who we are, and it might even get out to the press. This could destroy the firm's professional reputation."

Torn, Dominic glanced back at Rhodes. Not calling for help wasn't an option. They could call 911 anonymously and get lost before the cops showed up—but the idea of leaving a drugged person alone and unprotected disgusted Dominic to his core, and that would also mean the blonde probably getting away with her crime. There had to be an alternative.

"How about a compromise?" he said. "My boyfriend is a detective with the LVMPD. I'll call him, and he'll handle this in a way that keeps our names and the firm out of it."

"You think he'll be willing to do that?" Aubrey said skeptically.

"He will for me," said Dominic.

Dominic watched Levi speaking quietly to the paramedics wheeling Rhodes's stretcher out of the room. There were no sirens, no flashing lights; Levi had called the ambulance himself and arrived on the scene without any uniformed officers. Most of the motel's residents would never know anything remarkable had happened here tonight.

Levi could almost always be found in a well-tailored suit, but it was late enough that he was dressed more casually—in *jeans*, which Dominic had only seen him wear once or twice before. His gun rested in a hip holster rather than his usual shoulder rig.

Dominic's contemplation of the denim hugging Levi's round ass and strong thighs was cut short when the ambulance drove off, and Levi rejoined him and Aubrey.

"Rhodes will probably be fine," Levi said. "I'll call the uniforms in once you guys are gone. The official story will be that I received an anonymous tip, thought it was bogus, and checked out the scene myself before calling for backup. I found the memory stick from a camera laying next to the body, but there was no way for me to know who left it."

"Thank you," Dominic said, squeezing his shoulder. Aubrey echoed the sentiment.

"Of course. Can I see the pictures of the woman who did this?"

Dominic handed the camera over. Seconds later, Levi's jaw dropped.

"You've got to be kidding me," he said in a voice faint with shock.

"What is it?" Dominic asked.

Levi looked up, a dumbfounded expression on his face. "I know her."

CHAPTER 13

"Police, open up!" Levi shouted, banging on the door to Apartment 3B.

Martine stood next to him, sleepy after being roused from bed but still ready for action. He heard rustling and thumping inside the apartment, then silence.

Slamming his fist against the door again, he said, "Open this door right now or I'll break it down."

Across the hall, the door to 3C creaked open, and an elderly man's face peeked out to glare at them. Martine shooed him back inside.

Footsteps sounded inside 3B, but nothing else happened. Then, just as Levi was about to step back and kick, the door opened the tiniest sliver.

"Julie Emerson," he said, "We have a warrant for your arrest as well as one to search your apartment."

"What for?" she asked, though her face was ghostly pale and her lower lip was trembling.

"I have evidence that you drugged and robbed a man named Geoffrey Rhodes earlier this evening. And I'm guessing that the Rohypnol in Diana Kostas's house belonged to you as well."

She glanced over her shoulder, muscles tensing as if preparing to take flight.

Levi placed his hand on the butt of his gun. "Please don't."

A few fraught seconds ticked by while he wondered if she was really going to make him force his way into the apartment at gunpoint. Before the situation reached critical mass, however, she let out a sob and opened the door the rest of the way.

Martine entered first, gesturing for Julie to turn around and put her hands behind her back. "I'll bring her down to the car while you start the search," she said to Levi.

He nodded. Martine handcuffed Julie and read her rights while she escorted her out of the apartment, leaving the door open.

His nose wrinkled as he looked around the small, messy space. He couldn't help contrasting it to Kostas's cute house in Henderson. The two women worked for the same elite escort agency, and Julie had to be pulling a similar income. What was she doing living in a shithole like this, or rolling random johns in fleabag motels?

He checked the handful of rooms to ensure Julie had been home alone, then returned to the main living/dining area. Clothes were tossed haphazardly over the mismatched furniture; empty beer cans and used paper plates littered the coffee table and even the floor. He had to navigate around actual piles of trash as he started his search.

A dozen baggies of pot, coke, and Ecstasy tablets were sitting in plain view on the dining room table, which saved him a lot of time and energy. Rolling his eyes, Levi tagged them and moved on, running through a mental checklist of criminals' most favored hiding spots.

His search brought him to the small galley style kitchen, which was tucked in a corner off the dining area with a wall separating it from the living room. He rummaged through the cabinets and drawers, but it wasn't until he opened the freezer that he hit the jackpot. Buried underneath packages of pizza rolls and fish sticks was an enormous freezer bag full of wallets.

He unzipped the bag and flipped through a few of them. They'd been emptied of cash, but the driver's licenses, cards, and even photographs were all still intact.

A simple thief would have taken the cash, maybe a few credit cards, and dumped everything else far from their home. If Julie had risked keeping this stuff, she was probably dabbling in identity theft as well.

Levi went rigid at a creaking noise from the room beyond. He looked up just in time to see a big, burly man rounding the corner into the kitchen.

"Mother*fucker*," the man spat, lunging toward him.

Levi dropped the freezer bag and wrenched the refrigerator door open as a shield. When the man ran headlong into it and bounced off, Levi slammed the door shut and threw a defensive front kick with all the power in his hips, driving his foot into the man's chest. Though it didn't knock the man down, he did reel backward out of the kitchen, coughing.

Levi had to get clear of this literal dead end he was trapped in. He darted out at an angle, grabbing the nearest dining chair and tossing it in the man's path before drawing his gun.

"Police," he said. "I have a warrant to be here. If you don't stop, I will shoot you."

"Is that right, pig?" The man kicked the chair out of his way, though he didn't come any closer.

Levi stood his ground in a two-handed stance, his gun aimed at center mass. Then he blinked, and he was no longer in that dingy apartment. He was in the lobby of the Tropicana, at the center of a storm of chaos, boiling over with fury and horror as he prepared to kill Dale Slater.

Another blink, and he was in a crowded alcove in the ER, watching history repeat itself as a desperately ill and terrified Keith Chapman took a rookie cop hostage in the moments before he turned his gun on himself.

Levi shook his head, trying to dispel the images. If this man charged him with clear intent to continue his attack, Levi was supposed to shoot him.

But if he did that, the man could die, and what then? Another life on Levi's conscience? More endless weeks of nightmares and flashbacks and suffocating remorse?

Or worse—what if none of that happened? What if killing someone was easier the second time around?

Perhaps sensing Levi's paralyzed indecision, the man snatched several baggies off the dining table and whipped them at his face. Levi flinched under the rain of pills and pot, and had a moment to be grateful none of them contained coke before the man came barreling toward him at full speed.

In the split second Levi had to react, muscle memory took over. He threw a high front kick, the heel of his foot smashing into the underside of the man's chin and decisively halting his momentum. The man bellowed in pain and collapsed to the floor.

Shifting his gun to his right hand, Levi went for his cuffs—but the man wasn't as incapacitated as he'd assumed, and he didn't see the metallic glint of the blade until it was too late.

The knife shot out, scoring a deep cut into the back of Levi's hand. He yelped, reflexively dropping his gun, but he had no time to recover it. Even as the man rose to his feet, the knife came swooping toward Levi's guts in a low underhand stab.

Levi hollowed his body out and slammed his left forearm down to block the strike; the blade halted mere inches from his shirt. Before the man could draw back for another try, Levi slipped his arm around the man's, wrapping it up and trapping it against his own chest. With the man's stabbing arm locked out, Levi grabbed him at the shoulder and kneed him in the groin.

The man grunted, hunching forward. Levi peeled off to the side, twisting the knife out of his hand and kicking him in the face for good measure as he disengaged.

Straightening up, the man grinned at him through bloodied teeth, unfazed. Levi noticed how blown his pupils were and groaned—this guy was high as a kite.

He *hated* fighting intoxicated people. Their judgment, their sense of self-preservation, their capacity to feel pain, all of it was compromised. A couple of solid punches wouldn't do the trick here.

The man came at him swinging, not in the style of a trained fighter but more like a schoolyard bully who'd never developed beyond the playground. Still, he was a big guy, and there was considerable power behind his wild blows. Levi dodged and blocked and counterattacked with the knife, raising thin red lines all over the man's arms and hands, but he was relentless.

Nothing was worse than fighting with knives; they turned every situation into a total clusterfuck. Every second this blade was in play, there was a chance it could be taken away or turned against him. He couldn't even fully commit to using it, because he just wasn't willing to stab an intoxicated man.

If he could get to his gun, he could shoot the man in the knee or the foot and end this without a fatality. He had to do it soon, because he was going to burn out before the man lost his drug-fueled steam.

The man stood in-between him and the place the gun had fallen. Levi chambered his right leg, intending to unleash a flurry of swift kicks to create space.

Unfortunately, the man was wise to him by now. When Levi kicked, the man absorbed it with a grunt and hooked his arm around Levi's leg. Grabbing Levi's waist with his other hand, he lifted Levi in the air and hurtled forward, throwing him onto his back on the dining table with a bone-rattling crash.

Levi coughed, the wind knocked out of him, and lost the knife in his shock. He still had enough presence of mind to draw his knees up to his chest, keeping his legs between himself and the man so the man couldn't bear down on him with all his weight.

As they struggled, the man threw a punch too fast for Levi to avoid; it connected solidly with his mouth, splitting his lower lip against his teeth. Then both of the man's hands closed around his neck.

Not hesitating for a second, Levi jabbed his fingers hard into the notch at the base of the man's throat. The flinch from that form of contact was reflexive, not tied to a pain response, and the man's hold loosened enough for Levi to release the choke with an explosive plucking motion. Because he already had his legs coiled up, he was able to smash his feet into the man's chest forcefully enough to send him staggering away.

He couldn't give the man any quarter; nothing short of a knockout was going to take him down. Levi leapt off the table, picked up one of the rickety wooden chairs, and hit the man with it, battering him over and over again until the thing fell to pieces.

Still the guy managed to stay on his feet.

"Oh, come *on*," Levi groaned. He could see his gun; it wasn't far. He circled around, edging into the living room—

And lost his footing in the trash strewn across the floor, falling hard against the arm of the couch.

The man pounced. Levi barely managed to block an incoming punch, then lashed out with a desperate kick to the groin. The man grimaced but didn't so much as buckle.

Fuck—

Martine ran in through the door, absorbed the situation in a split second, and kicked the man in the back of the knee. Crying out more in surprise than pain, he collapsed to the other knee, his hands touching down for balance.

Levi didn't waste any time. He blasted the man with the most vicious hook punch he could muster and followed it with an uppercut.

The man was *still* upright, though he was dazed and swaying, his eyelids fluttering. Martine planted her foot in his back and pushed him forward onto his face, then followed him down and knelt between his shoulder blades while she handcuffed him.

Wiping the back of his uninjured hand over the blood streaming from his mouth, Levi heaved himself off the couch.

"Two for the price of one," Martine said happily.

"He made me do it," Julie said, giving Levi a pleading look across the metal table. "You don't understand."

"Then explain it to me," he said.

She raked her fingers through her disheveled blonde hair. He'd had her uncuffed for the time being, hoping it would make her more comfortable and loosen her lips.

Unsurprisingly, the man who'd attacked him in Julie's apartment had turned out to be her notorious boyfriend Kyle Gilmore. He and Martine had let them both cool their heels—and in Gilmore's case, sober up—at the Clark County Detention Center overnight, then transported them to the substation the next morning for interrogation.

"Kyle's never been able to hold a job for very long," she said. "It's not his fault. He just—he's a passionate man. He feels things very deeply. People don't get that about him."

Controlling his expression, Levi nodded for her to continue.

"But we tend to go through money really quickly. It was Kyle's idea to start rolling tourists; he would get me the drugs and find the guys. I didn't want to do it."

"Did he threaten you?"

"Uh . . ." She hesitated, chewing on her lower lip. "No."

A toddler would have been able to tell she was lying. Confronting her about it would be pointless, though, so Levi didn't bother. "Then why go along with it?"

Julie looked down at her hands, where she was worrying one of her cuticles into a bloody mess. "We needed the money. I know it was wrong, but those men were rich assholes who were usually cheating on their wives or girlfriends. It's not like they were innocent victims."

"Did the Rohypnol we found in Diana's house belong to you?"

"Yes," she whispered. "It was in my purse that first day you and your partner came to her house. I thought you might search me, and I panicked. I didn't know what to do, so I hid it under the bathroom sink. She had no idea it was there."

Well, at least that should get Kostas off the hook for Hensley's murder, but it would come at the cost of discovering what a shitty friend she had in Julie. This was just not her week.

"What made you go after Geoffrey Rhodes?" Levi asked.

Julie frowned. "I told you, Kyle always picked the guys. He was out last night, but he texted me Geoffrey's photo and where to find him. Said he was a prick with a lot of money who'd make an easy mark—and he was right."

Sitting back abruptly in his chair, he stared at her while he processed what she'd said. He had a hard enough time accepting the coincidence that the break in his case had come from Dominic's own investigation. To learn that Julie had been deliberately aimed in Rhodes's direction—what were the chances?

Perhaps sensing his disbelief, she leaned forward on the table and said, "The texts are still on my phone. You have it, right? You can see for yourself."

"I'll check it out."

As he gathered his notes, preparing to leave, she said, "Did Kyle do that to your face?"

He lifted a self-conscious hand to his mouth. An angry purple bruise had bloomed in the lower left corner since last night, and the cut on his lip was still raw and red.

"I've had worse," he said.

After a brief check-in with Martine, who hadn't been able to get anything out of Gilmore, and a quick examination of Julie's cell phone, Levi headed into the adjacent interrogation room to take a crack at Gilmore himself. According to Martine, he was claiming to have no memory of the night before—which wasn't outside the realm of possibility, between the drugs and multiple blows to the head.

Gilmore sat slumped in his chair, handcuffs threaded through the loop at the edge of the table. He looked like he'd had a rough comedown, his eyes bloodshot and his face mottled with the bruises Levi had given him in return. A bandage was taped over the bridge of his broken nose; more bandages swathed his arms and hands, covering the lacerations from the knife.

His amnesia story couldn't be totally true, because recognition crossed his face when he saw Levi. Smirking, he said, "Nice fat lip you've got there."

"Have you looked in a mirror today?" Levi asked, gesturing to the two-way glass.

Gilmore rolled his eyes. "You know, whatever that little bitch told you—"

"Shut your mouth," Levi said coldly. He approached the table but didn't sit, just set down Julie's cell. "You think I haven't seen a hundred assholes just like you sitting in that chair? You're bitter and resentful; you think the world owes you something, so you feel free to take whatever you want. You binge drink, you get high, you steal and gamble away your girlfriend's money, and then exploit her to get your hands on more. You're a toxic, manipulative leech."

Gilmore's nostrils flared as he glowered at Levi. "I wasn't anywhere near her when she rolled that guy."

"But you told her to do it. Went as far as to pick out the specific man and tell her where to find him."

"What? No I fucking didn't!"

Levi called up the texts on Julie's phone and pushed it across the table. Gilmore peered down at it, and his face twisted.

"I didn't send these," he said.

"You really expect me to believe that?"

"I don't remember anything that happened last night!"

Levi crossed his arms. "I know you remember me."

"I . . ." Clenching his jaw, Gilmore exhaled harshly through his nose. "Look, most of last night is a blur. I was hanging at a bar with my buddies, I felt weird, and next thing I know I'm waking up in jail. I only remember bits and pieces in-between, crazy flashes of stuff."

"You said you felt weird—weird how?"

"Weird like fucked up, man, and not in a way the shit I'd taken would make me feel. I swear to God someone slipped me something."

"Why would anyone want to drug you?" Levi said with a snort.

"Fuck if I know. Maybe they got the wrong drink by accident. Felt like Special K with a goddamn angel dust chaser."

A chill ran down Levi's spine. "You think somebody slipped you ketamine?"

"Not just that, but yeah, I was definitely lost in the K-hole for a while there."

Levi stood motionless while the floor seemed to fall away beneath him. An abusive douchebag drugged with ketamine, fake texts that had driven the exact person Levi needed right into Dominic's path . . . this was no coincidence.

The Seven of Spades had set this up.

When Levi returned to the bullpen, Dominic was sitting at his desk, deep in conversation with Martine.

"Whoa," Dominic said, springing out of the chair as he saw Levi coming. He caught Levi's chin and turned his face into the light, then glanced down at his torn knuckles and bandaged hand. "What happened to you?"

"Ran into a door?" Levi said.

Dominic arched an eyebrow.

"Got into a knife fight," Levi admitted. He braced himself for the reprimands that were sure to start flying. Every time he'd been injured in the line of duty, Stanton had nagged and guilted him about it for days afterward. *You need to be more careful, don't you know how much I worry about you, how do you expect me to sleep at night—*

Dominic laughed, released his chin, and slapped his shoulder. "I'd hate to see the other guy," he said, before turning back to Martine.

Levi blinked, his mouth half-open. It took him a few seconds to realize Martine was addressing him.

"Sorry, what?" he said.

"I said, did you have better luck with Gilmore than I did?"

"Yes." It was impossible to soften what he had to say, so he just laid it out. "The Seven of Spades is responsible for this."

"*What?*" Martine and Dominic said at the same time but in very different tones—Dominic concerned, Martine incredulous.

Levi relayed Gilmore's story and his own conclusions. "There is no way this situation wasn't deliberately engineered," he said when he'd finished. "And there's only one person who would do that."

Dominic was quiet, a line etched between his brows and his eyes unfocused. Martine, on the other hand, regarded Levi with clear irritation.

"Levi, come on," she said. "Do you hear yourself? You're saying that a serial killer—who almost everyone believes is dead, by the way—helped you catch a criminal related to an ongoing investigation."

"It's not unprecedented. The Seven of Spades exposed Loretta Kane's history of taking bribes for generous plea deals."

"Yeah, after he slit her throat in her living room!"

"Why is it so important for you not to believe me about this?" His tone came out embarrassingly plaintive. But it *hurt* that Martine, who had always been on his side, stood with everyone else when it came to the Seven of Spades.

She dropped her gaze to her desk and took a deep breath. Then she looked back up and said, "Because I'm terrified of what it would mean."

"You think I'm not?"

"I know you are. But you're also intrigued by the challenge. An elusive, seemingly omniscient killer who helps the police catch criminals while getting away with their own vigilante-style murders? That speaks to something in you."

Levi had no response for that. As always, Martine's assessment was painfully accurate.

"It doesn't speak to anything in me except horror," she said. "Thinking there might be someone this intelligent and ruthless out there watching us and pulling our strings like puppets—just the idea of it makes me want to move my family out of this city and never look back."

An uncomfortable silence fell and stretched out. Levi had never been able to navigate emotional confrontations well, and even though he knew Martine wasn't angry with him, his first instinct was still to escape this conversation in any way possible.

"Is there anything I can do to help?" Dominic asked, breaking the tension. He still had a distracted air about him.

"I don't think so, but thanks," said Levi. "Just be on your guard."

"Okay." Dominic inclined his head in a wordless request for Levi to move with him to the side of the room. Once they had a relative degree of privacy, he said, "Are we still on for tonight, or would you rather reschedule?"

"There's nowhere I'd rather be tonight than with you," Levi said honestly.

Dominic's warm brown eyes crinkled at the corners. "I was thinking a quiet night in, since you're probably looking at a long day. Maybe I could cook you dinner at your place?"

"That sounds amazing." Levi pulled his key ring out of his pocket. "Here, you should take the key in case I end up running late."

He worked his apartment key off the ring and handed it over. When Dominic started to move away, Levi put a hand on his arm.

"You can kiss me," he said.

There was always the chance that Dominic's discretion stemmed less from respect for Levi's boundaries and more from his own reservations about kissing a cop in the middle of a crowded police station. Knowing Dominic, however, Levi seriously doubted that was the case.

Sure enough, Dominic smiled and leaned down, pressing a gentle kiss to the uninjured side of Levi's mouth. A wolf whistle sounded from the bullpen, which Levi knew without looking came from Jonah Gibbs. He gave the man the finger and received scattered laughter in response.

"See you tonight," Dominic said as he pulled back. "Text me if you need me."

Levi watched him walk away before returning to his desk. Martine was intent on her computer, and he was happy to avoid another argument, so he said nothing as he settled in to work.

Julie and Gilmore were both waiting for their public defenders; it was a coin flip as to whether the lawyers would show up before they were transported back to the CCDC. The deciding factor would be who was busier today. In the meantime, he could call Leila Rashid about dropping the charges against Diana Kostas.

His desk phone rang as he reached for it. He picked it up and said, "Detective Abrams."

"Hi, Detective. This is Officer Jason Tanaka from the Baltimore PD. Sorry I wasn't able to return your call last night."

"It's no problem. Thanks for getting back to me. I just wanted to confirm that you were the officer who delivered the news of Dr. Stephen Hensley's death to his next of kin."

"Sure was. Sunday the twenty-fourth, 3.30 p.m., 402 East Highfield Road. Spoke to his son, Dr. Stephen Hensley, Jr."

Levi sat up straight. "His son? Not his wife?"

"Nope," said Tanaka. "She wasn't home. Her son said he hadn't seen her since the day before."

CHAPTER 14

The first thing Dominic did when he reached his parked truck was retrieve a flashlight from the glove compartment. Ignoring the odd looks he got from a couple of passing cops, he stretched out on his back on the asphalt and scooted underneath the truck, shining the light up into the undercarriage.

Back in April, there'd been a night when Dominic had used Carlos's car to pursue some leads in the Seven of Spades case. The killer themself had followed Dominic and left a calling card on the windshield at the end of the night—whether to scare him or just tease him, he still had no idea. He'd torn Carlos's car and his own truck apart the next day looking for GPS trackers and come up empty, so he'd concluded that the killer had either followed him in person or used some other means.

After what Levi had said this morning and the weirdness of last night, however, he wouldn't rest easy until he checked again.

He scanned the entire underside of the car, looking for odd wires or anything out of place. Finding nothing, he rolled out and searched all four wheel wells and the front and back bumpers before moving on to the cab. He ran his hands underneath the dashboard, emptied out the glove compartment, lifted the floor mats, and then pushed a hand beneath the front passenger's seat.

His fingers nudged up against a hard, plastic shape. He got a better grip and gave it a tug, pulling out a black rectangular device smaller than a cell phone. It was discreetly stamped with the logo of an upscale personal security brand.

"Goddammit," he said under his breath.

His faith in Levi wasn't the only reason he believed the Seven of Spades was still alive, but he'd also believed—or he'd *hoped*—that the killer had moved on. Why stay in the city after successfully framing Keith Chapman? Why continue keeping tabs on Dominic and Levi at all, still less interfere with their respective cases? If the Seven of Spades couldn't go public again, what was the point?

There was no telling how long this GPS tracker had been in his truck, and this could just be the tip of the iceberg. Dominic had extensive, if rusty, training in technical surveillance countermeasures, but he didn't have the equipment he'd need for a thorough search.

He knew where to get some, though.

McBride Investigations wasn't far from Levi's substation. Less than twenty minutes later, Dominic walked into the tech department managed by Isaiah Miller, a cute young black guy with square-framed glasses and a shy smile.

Isaiah was elbow-deep in the guts of a disassembled computer, his head bobbing along to the music he was listening to through his earbuds. He didn't look up at Dominic's greeting, so Dominic lightly touched his arm.

Yelping like a scalded cat, Isaiah leapt to his feet, violently jostling his work table. A tray full of papers fell to the floor with a crash and were followed by a travel mug that sprayed coffee in a wide arc across the linoleum as it bounced and rolled. He yanked out his earbuds and stared up at Dominic with wide, round eyes.

"I'm so sorry," Dominic said, trying not to laugh. He crouched to gather the scattered papers. "I didn't mean to scare you. I said your name a couple times."

"It's cool. Sometimes I get lost in the zone." Isaiah pulled his phone out of his pocket, turned off the music, and set it on the table before grabbing a handful of paper towels.

Once they'd put the work table back to rights, Dominic said, "So assuming you wouldn't rather just tell me to go fuck myself now—"

"What do you need?" Isaiah said with a laugh.

"A spectrum analyzer and a non-linear junction detector."

"No problem." Isaiah gestured for Dominic to follow him to his main desk, where he sat behind a sleek computer monitor. "What's the case number?"

"It's not for a case." When Isaiah blinked and opened his mouth, Dominic held up a hand. "Before you say anything, I promise that

I'll return the equipment to you within thirty-six hours, completely undamaged, with nobody aware that I had it other than you and me."

"You need professional TSCM equipment for personal use?" Isaiah said dubiously.

"Yeah. It's . . . Can I tell you something in confidence?"

"Sure."

Hovering over Isaiah like this wouldn't work to his advantage, so Dominic sat in the other chair. He leaned against the edge of the desk and lowered his voice to a more intimate tone.

"It's my psycho ex-boyfriend," he said. "We served together, and he was always jealous and controlling, but now that I'm seeing someone new he's really freaking out. I think he's been following me, maybe bugging my place—I wouldn't even be surprised if he was using hidden cameras to spy on me."

"Jesus," Isaiah said, his mouth falling open.

"He's a professional, so he wouldn't be using the cheap crap you find at a strip mall. I need similar quality counter surveillance equipment to prove I'm right."

"Dominic . . ." Isaiah's face was full of empathetic concern, but he wasn't quite sold. Dominic would have to push a little harder.

"Please," he said, letting his voice break slightly. "I know this is a lot to ask, but I don't feel safe in my own apartment. I'm afraid of what he might do next."

Isaiah bit his lip, then nodded. "Okay. If you promise to get the equipment back as soon as possible in mint condition, I can help you out."

"Thank you." Dominic reached across the desk to squeeze his arm. "And if something does go wrong for any reason, I'll take full responsibility. I'll say I snuck in here and stole the stuff without your knowledge. You have my word this won't fall back on you."

Isaiah gave him a small smile and turned to his computer. "Let me just check the inventory." He was quiet for a few seconds while he typed, and when he spoke again, it was with a too-casual air that caught Dominic's attention immediately. "I didn't know you were seeing anyone."

Dominic knew that Isaiah had a crush on him, and he'd used that to his advantage, but actually leading the guy on would be going too far. "His name's Levi," he said, letting everything he felt for Levi come through in his tone. "He's a homicide detective."

Isaiah looked at him sharply. "A cop? I'd think he'd be the first person you'd go to for help with something like this."

"I don't want to stir up too much trouble until I confirm my suspicions. I could still be wrong."

God, I hope I'm wrong.

Isaiah retrieved the requested equipment and stashed it inside a nondescript duffel bag. "You know how to use this stuff, right?" he asked as he handed the bag over.

"It's been a while, but it'll come back to me," said Dominic.

He thanked Isaiah again and headed home. Inside his apartment, he acted normally, greeting Rebel with a playful tussle and turning on a Spotify playlist like he usually did when he was home alone. Then he unzipped the duffel bag and got to work.

The spectrum analyzer would capture, map, and analyze all spectrum activity within a small area to detect transmitting surveillance devices, while the non-linear junction detector could find electronic devices hidden inside walls, floors, or any other container, even if they were turned off. Dominic hadn't used equipment like this for years, and technology had advanced since then—but even today's civilian TSCM devices didn't rival the classified military-grade ones he'd been accustomed to. It only took him a few minutes to get a handle on them.

He knew better than to rely on electronics to the exclusion of a physical inspection, so he utilized his eyes and hands just as much as the equipment as he commenced a thorough sweep of his apartment from top to bottom. He examined every door jamb, windowsill, and inch of baseboard, unscrewed every outlet plate and light switch, checked inside the smoke detectors, followed every electrical cord. Rebel followed him around, watching him with her ears pricked up and her head tilted to the side.

He didn't hit pay dirt until he reached the desk in the living room, and even with the tools at his disposal, he didn't figure it out right away.

It was the power strip.

Under other circumstances, he never would have noticed—because really, who ever looked at their power strip again after they'd set it up? He hadn't touched his in years, except for the occasional halfhearted dusting of his computer. But this wasn't the strip he'd originally bought. That had been swapped out for one with a bug built right into the internal wiring—which meant the Seven of Spades never had to come back for it, because it was plugged right into a continuous power source.

Dominic didn't make any noise to indicate that he'd found it. He turned off all the electronics connected to the strip, unplugged everything, and tossed it into a shoebox with the GPS tracker from his truck. Then he kept going, because he knew he wasn't finished yet.

This was just the beginning.

"I don't know how she did it," Levi said to Martine. "The person I spoke with at Johns Hopkins told me she was in the hospital on Monday. And I confirmed the flight manifest with Southwest—Clarissa Northridge was definitely on Flight 484 from Baltimore to Las Vegas on Tuesday morning."

"Just because she wasn't home when the local PD stopped by doesn't mean she wasn't in Baltimore," said Martine.

"I know." Levi clicked his mouse, intent on his computer screen. "But she wasn't. I can *feel* it."

Martine narrowed her eyes. "What exactly are you doing?"

"Reviewing the security footage from the Mirage. When I met Dr. Northridge, something about her struck me as familiar, and after Warner let slip that he'd seen her on Monday, I couldn't shake the idea that I'd seen her somewhere too. This seemed like the likeliest place."

He finished with one of the elevator cameras, made a frustrated noise, and moved on to the next. Martine wheeled her chair around to his desk.

"If you'd seen her in these recordings, don't you think you would have recognized her when you met?" she asked, though she sounded intrigued.

"I don't know." Levi fast-forwarded through the footage, already growing bored—then sucked in a breath and hit the pause button.

He rewound and replayed the last minute in slow motion. "Maybe not if she'd disguised herself."

He tapped the image on the screen. The tall, trim woman standing alone in the elevator was wearing gloves, sunglasses, and a head scarf like she was about to drive a convertible in the 1950s.

The height and build were right, and the way she held herself struck the same chord of familiarity Levi had felt when he greeted Northridge in person. He couldn't be one hundred percent certain it was the same woman though, still less convince a jury.

"Hmm." Martine peered closer. "Could be her. She gets off at the right floor."

Frowning at the timestamp, Levi said, "At 2:47 a.m. That's near the later edge of the coroner's window for time of death."

"But still inside it."

He fast-forwarded, looking for the point at which the woman got back on the elevator, but he reached the end of the footage without seeing her again. The cameras from the other elevators told the same story—if the woman had left the twenty-second floor before Hensley had been found dead, she'd done it by another route.

"Think she used the stairs when she left?" he asked.

"It's possible. She's in good shape—going down twenty-two flights probably wouldn't faze her. Or maybe she just went to a different room."

"I know in my gut that this is Clarissa Northridge. She saw her husband the night he died, and she's been covering it up." He rubbed the bridge of his nose. "But calling our evidence circumstantial would be too generous. We can't build a case on what we have."

Martine drummed her fingers against the desk. "You got a warrant for her cell records last night, right?"

"Yeah. They haven't come through yet, though, and we can't count on them containing anything helpful. And Carmen still hasn't been able to crack the security on Walsh's computers."

They sat in thoughtful silence for a few minutes. Levi clicked randomly though the security cameras, his mind running in circles. If Northridge had seen Hensley the night of his death and gone to such lengths to cover her tracks, she'd almost certainly been the one who killed him. And she'd get away with it if they couldn't prove that.

The woman in the elevator didn't have any luggage, only a purse. Had she just gone right up to Hensley's door and knocked? Or . . .

Levi stiffened. "The lobby," he said. "The Mirage sent us those security feeds with everything else—but we ended up not needing them once we'd identified Diana Kostas, so nobody ever looked at them. This woman must have walked through the lobby at some point. Maybe she even got a key to Hensley's room."

He hunted through the database where they logged electronic evidence until he found what he was looking for. The security cameras in the Mirage lobby covered a few different angles; he picked the one with the best view of the reception desk and skipped forward to around 2:30. Martine leaned in with him to watch.

At 2:36 a.m., the woman in the scarf and gloves approached the desk—and removed her sunglasses, leaving no doubt that she was indeed Clarissa Northridge. Levi and Martine both exhaled heavily.

"That's Alan Walsh she's talking to," said Martine.

On the screen, Northridge and Walsh talked for a minute, and then she slid a small but thick envelope across the desk. He handed her a key card in return, and she put her sunglasses back on before walking away. Walsh stashed the envelope in his inner jacket pocket.

"Oh my God, she bribed him for a room key."

"I bet you the Mirage's system records which key cards are programmed when," Levi said, reaching for his phone.

One quick call later, and he had confirmation that the card coded under Walsh's account at 2:39 a.m. on Sunday morning had been for room 2218. Levi hung up and turned to Martine in triumph.

"*This* is something we can build a case on," he said.

"That shady son of a bitch," she said, shaking her head. "I questioned him myself about whether he'd seen anything suspicious that night, and he straight-up lied to my face."

"I guess he figured he'd rather use that information to blackmail Northridge than share it with us. His supervisor was mortified—after he died, they reviewed all of his recent work activity like we asked, but they didn't double-check every key card he'd programmed. You should have heard how many times she apologized."

Martine stood and wheeled her chair back to her desk. "We have enough for an arrest warrant. Do you know where Northridge might be now?"

He checked his watch. "I do, actually. Kapoor and Warner's presentation started ten minutes ago, and she promised them she'd be there."

"Guess we're crashing the conference again."

They drove to the Mirage, checked the room assignment, and entered quietly at the back. The space was packed; the hotel had crammed as many folding chairs as possible into the room, and there were still people standing all around the edges. Levi wondered if the high turnout could be attributed more to the research itself or the notoriety of Hensley's murder.

A sheet of posterboard propped on an easel near the door bore the title of the paper being presented: *Peripheral and central mechanisms of visceral pain. S. Hensley, MD; A. Kapoor, MD; C. Warner, MD.*

Levi had read some of their research for background when the case first started. Most of the nitty-gritty science had gone over his head, but he'd gotten the gist of it. Pretty interesting stuff, though he couldn't vouch for Kapoor's statement that it was "groundbreaking."

He and Martine stayed where they were, scanning the room. Warner had the mic at the dais up front, rambling on about inflamed internal organs. He seemed sober today—in fact, he was in the best mood Levi had seen him in so far. His face was animated, his hand gestures effusive, his voice thrumming with passion for his topic. Kapoor stood next to him with a faint yet proud smile on her face.

Martine nudged Levi's shoulder and inclined her head. He looked in the direction she'd indicated and saw Clarissa Northridge sitting in the third row, hands clasped on her crossed legs, nodding along as she listened.

His phone buzzed in his pocket. He pulled it out, paying no mind to the annoyed glances he received from a few people nearby.

"What is it?" Martine asked.

"A text from Carmen," he murmured. "Northridge's phone records came in. She received two calls from a number with a Las Vegas area code on Sunday and Monday. The number is associated with a burner phone, no legitimate billing information."

"Walsh."

"We can't prove that unless we find the actual phone, but yeah, I'd put good money on it."

They both looked back at Northridge. "We should wait until the presentation is over," Martine said. "City officials won't like the LVMPD arresting a respected physician in a room full of her peers during a huge money-making conference."

Levi rolled his eyes, but he knew she was right. They hovered at the back while Warner and Kapoor took turns presenting their research. Once the doctors had finished, they wrapped things up with a touching tribute to Hensley's memory that completely glossed over what a terrible human being he'd been, and received a thunderous standing ovation.

It took a while for the room to empty out afterward; half the people present seemed to want to speak to Kapoor and Warner in person. Levi and Martine waited until there were only a few people left milling around and Northridge, Kapoor, and Warner were standing together talking.

Northridge was the first to notice their approach; she went pale, her throat bobbing harshly, but she stood her ground. Kapoor and Warner fell silent at her reaction and turned around with puzzled expressions.

"Dr. Northridge," Levi said, "we have a warrant for your arrest. Out of respect, I'm willing to forgo the cuffs until we reach the car if you're willing to cooperate."

"*Arrest?*" Kapoor exclaimed, stepping between them. "What for?"

"Stephen's murder, I expect," said Northridge. When Levi nodded, she took a shaky breath and put a hand on Kapoor's shoulder. "It's all right, Anika. Just a misunderstanding. I'll get it straightened out."

Ignoring her, Kapoor squared off against Levi and Martine. "You can't be serious. Clarissa was in *Baltimore* when Stephen died."

Warner ducked his head, his shoulders hunching as he shuffled his feet like a naughty schoolboy. Northridge closed her eyes briefly. Kapoor glanced between them, opened her mouth, and closed it without saying anything.

"If you'd come with us, please?" Martine said, gesturing for Northridge to precede her. Northridge nodded and joined them in their walk toward the door without protest.

"We'll follow you to the station, Clarissa." Kapoor turned to Warner for support, then jostled his shoulder when he didn't respond.

"What?" he said, his head shooting up. "Oh, yeah, of course."

Levi and Martine escorted Northridge to the waiting car without incident. As they helped her inside, she said, "I won't speak without a lawyer present," in a quiet, firm voice, and then didn't utter another word.

Dominic finished sweeping his apartment without finding any more surveillance devices. Besides the power strip, there were no other bugs in evidence—nor, to his immense relief, did he find hidden cameras of any kind. He threw the equipment back in the duffel bag, grabbed a notebook and pen, and took Rebel with him next door to 2G.

"Hey, Dom," Carlos said when he answered Dominic's knock. His eyes were sleepy and his hair mussed like he'd just woken up; he'd worked a closing shift at Stingray last night. "What's up?"

"I'm all out of beer. You got any?" Dominic held up the note he'd written as he spoke.

Don't react to this out loud. I need to sweep your apartment for bugs.

No longer looking quite so sleepy, Carlos blinked at the note and stared at Dominic for a few seconds before saying, "Uh . . . sure. Come on in."

Dominic entered the apartment, Rebel trotting at his heels, and set the duffel bag on the coffee table in the living room. When Carlos just stood in place as if frozen, he raised his eyebrows and jerked his head toward the kitchen.

Carlos startled, then clapped his hands. "Hey, Rebbie, you want a treat?"

Rebel spun around in an excited circle and raced after Carlos into the kitchen. Dominic unzipped the duffel bag, preparing to start the entire TSCM process from the beginning. This time, he checked the power strips first.

He was still crouched on the floor behind the TV when Rebel returned from the kitchen, settling down on the carpet with one of the crunchy organic dog treats Jasmine stocked. Carlos followed with two open bottles of Stella and handed one to Dominic.

"Thanks," Dominic said, clinking his bottle against Carlos's. He took a sip, got to his feet, and exchanged the beer for the spectrum analyzer.

Carlos hovered in the middle of the living room, his own beer hanging from one hand, and gaped at Dominic while he worked. After a couple minutes of that, Dominic sighed and set the spectrum analyzer down to grab his notebook.

ACT NORMAL!!! he scribbled.

Carlos glared at him.

"So are you all set for the proposal tomorrow?" Dominic asked. That was the only topic he could be sure would snap Carlos out of this awkward stupor.

It worked, though not the way he'd expected. Carlos cringed, his shoulders slumping. "Yeah, I guess," he said. He wandered over to the couch and flopped down.

Dominic retrieved a screwdriver from his bag and began unscrewing the plate from the light switch near the front door. "You don't sound so sure. Are you having second thoughts?"

"No! It's just . . ." Carlos waved his beer around. "I'm freaking out a little."

"I thought you guys had talked about getting married before."

"Of course we have. I wouldn't even think about proposing if we hadn't. It's just a little earlier than we'd been planning, that's all."

Dominic shone a flashlight inside the light switch, searching for any suspicious wiring. "And you're positive Jasmine's the kind of girl who will enjoy being proposed to in front of her entire family?"

"Yep," Carlos said with a grin. "You know how much she loves those YouTube proposal videos where the family and friends are in on it."

"Then why are you so nervous?"

Carlos took a long, contemplative swallow of his beer. "I don't know if I can explain it. She'll love the ring, and I know she'll say yes. But it's still one of the most nerve-wracking things I've ever done."

He trailed off into silence, though he didn't seem finished. Dominic kept listening while he closed the light switch back up.

"I want everything to be perfect," Carlos said. "I want Jasmine to have that great romantic proposal story she can tell all her friends, you know? This is . . . it's one of the most important things a man does in his entire life. I have to get it right."

Ah.

Carlos lifted a hand before Dominic could speak. "I know how heteronormative that sounds, okay? I hear it. But it doesn't change anything."

"You don't have to justify the way you feel," said Dominic. He returned to the spectrum analyzer. "Especially not to me. You're still going with the idea we came up with?"

"Yeah. Mind if I bounce what I'm planning to say off you?"

Over the next hour, Carlos rehearsed his proposal speech and jotted down notes for himself while Dominic continued sweeping the apartment, offering his thoughts along the way. They'd moved into the kitchen when Dominic started getting iffy readings on the spectrum analyzer; a few minutes of concentrated searching revealed the source of the problem. He dragged over one of the dining chairs and stood on it to access the smoke detector.

The bug was wired into the device, once again supplying it with a constant power source. It was professional equipment—not military-grade, but on par with domestic law enforcement.

With a little time and focused concentration, Dominic managed to disengage the bug without compromising the smoke detector. Carlos had been watching silently, but when Dominic hopped off the chair with the bug in the palm of his hand, he said, *"What—"*

Dominic slashed his free hand by his throat and then held up one finger. He hurried back to his own apartment, where he tossed the bug into the shoebox.

Carlos was waiting for him in the exterior hallway, Rebel by his side. "What the fuck is going on, Dom? I didn't ask any questions earlier, but you can't tell me you're sweeping my apartment for bugs and pull weird shit out of my smoke detector without some kind of explanation."

Fair enough. "Do you remember the Seven of Spades?" Dominic asked.

"The serial killer? How could I forget?"

"They're not dead."

"What do you mean, they're not dead?" Carlos said, giving him a bewildered look. "Didn't Keith Chapman kill himself right in front of you?"

"He wasn't the killer," said Dominic. "Just a fall guy. Most people in the LVMPD don't believe the real Seven of Spades is still out there, but Levi and I know the truth."

Carlos's jaw was hanging open, but he didn't say anything. Rebel moved to sit on Dominic's foot, leaning her considerable weight against his leg.

He reached down and smoothed a hand over her head. "The Seven of Spades had a weird fixation with the two of us during their spree in April, and now it seems like they never let go of it. I can't go into details, but last night they set things up to give me what I needed for my investigation with McBride while also helping Levi with one of his cases. Then this morning I found a GPS tracker in my car and a bug in my apartment, plus the one I found in yours. I have no way of knowing how long any of that's been in place. Could be a week, could be three months."

"Holy shit," Carlos breathed. "You're serious, aren't you? You really believe you're being monitored by a serial killer who everyone thinks is dead."

"I know it sounds crazy, but it's true."

Carlos raked a hand through his hair. "If it is true, are Jasmine and I in danger? Are *you* in danger?"

"No," Dominic said firmly. "The Seven of Spades was—is—a self-righteous vigilante. They only kill people who have committed a serious breach of trust that they feel is unforgivable. They're probably just keeping tabs on you and Jasmine because they know how much time I spend at your place."

"And what if they decide to make an exception for the guy trying to bust them?" Carlos asked. "Because that's what you and Levi are doing, isn't it—trying to track down the real killer?"

Dominic shrugged.

"Jesus Christ, Dominic. Have you considered *that's* the reason for the Seven of Spades's 'fixation'? Maybe they're watching you and Levi to make sure they can stop you before you get too close to the truth."

"Of course I've thought about it. But that doesn't mean that I'm going to stop, and neither will Levi." He gripped Carlos's shoulders with both hands. "If you and Jasmine were in genuine danger, I wouldn't hesitate to tell you. I'd never do anything to put you guys at risk."

Carlos studied Dominic's face for a long moment, then breathed out and nodded. Dominic released him.

"How'd this person break into our apartments without us ever realizing?" Carlos said.

"I have no idea," said Dominic. For all he knew, the Seven of Spades could have *keys*. "I'll talk to building management about installing more serious security measures. In the meantime, let's go back inside. I still need to look for bugs in your bedroom."

Carlos blanched.

Levi heard the commotion in the bullpen from the front doors of the substation. He shot a worried glance at Martine, who was escorting Northridge, and broke away from them to hurry toward the source of the noise.

Diana Kostas stood in the center of the bullpen in a towering rage as she confronted her erstwhile friend. Julie was half cowering behind the uniformed officer who must have come to transport her back to the CCDC.

"You treacherous fucking bitch!" Kostas shouted. "How could you do this to me?"

Julie's tearful apologies were lost under the continuing tirade. Everyone else in the room had stopped what they were doing to watch avidly, and nobody seemed intent on intervening. To Levi's surprise, Leila Rashid stood nearby with her arms crossed, looking bored.

"I'm so sorry, Diana," Julie said, lifting her cuffed hands in a gesture of appeasement. "Please believe me, I never meant for you to get hurt—"

"But you were happy to stand by and keep your mouth shut while I was arrested for *murder*!"

"What the hell is going on?" Levi hissed at Rashid.

"It's probably my fault," she said, though she didn't sound guilty in the slightest. "I called Kostas about dropping the charges, and when

I told her why, she cursed up a storm and then hung up on me. I knew she would come here."

"How?"

She snorted. "It's what I would do."

"How far were you planning to let this go, Julie?" said Kostas. She stood with her hands on her hips, her face flushed, her large dark eyes snapping with furious hurt. "Would you have said anything when the case went to trial? How about when I went to *prison?*"

A sob burst out of Julie. "That never would have happened! I knew you didn't kill that guy, everything would have been fine!"

"Oh, you're such a moron—"

Levi turned to see Martine and Northridge entering the bullpen. Kapoor and Warner followed a few seconds later, though they stopped in their tracks when they saw the showdown.

"I let you into my home," Kostas said, breathing hard. "I trusted you with my son. And you were ready to throw me under the bus to protect yourself and your scumbag boyfriend."

"Don't talk about him like that!"

Kostas's face twisted and her hand swung back. Levi started moving, but Rashid was faster—she darted forward and grabbed Kostas's arm even as the uniformed officer yanked Julie out of reach.

"You're in a police station," said Rashid, her tone one of mild irritation. "Don't be an idiot."

Kostas didn't move, her raised forearm still caught in Rashid's grip. She glared daggers at Julie as her chest heaved with barely contained emotion.

The spectators all seemed to be holding their breath. Levi was sure that if they'd been anywhere else, half these people would have their phones out to record every moment.

Then Kostas's shoulders relaxed, and she nodded. Rashid let go of her arm, but she didn't move away. Julie and her escort both eyed Kostas warily.

"I hope you go to prison for a long time," Kostas said. Her voice shook. "And when you get out, don't ever come near me or my son again."

She whirled around and stalked away with her head held high, leaving Julie breaking down in tears behind her. Her stride faltered as she passed Martine and the three doctors near the exit, a frown creasing her brow, and she glanced at them one more time over her shoulder as she left.

Rashid heaved a put-upon sigh. "I'll go with her, make sure she doesn't do anything stupid." When she walked by Levi, she smiled and added, "Why don't you give me a call when you find the actual murderer?"

Levi scowled after her retreating back. The uniformed officer led a sobbing Julie away—in the opposite direction—and conversation and movement resumed around the bullpen as everyone returned to their previous activities. In less than a minute, the mood in the room had gone back to normal.

"That was some serious drama," Martine said, joining him with Northridge in tow. Kapoor and Warner trailed behind.

"Can you blame her?"

"Who was that woman?" Warner asked.

"Our original suspect in Dr. Hensley's death." Turning to their newest suspect, Levi said, "I'll arrange for you to contact a defense attorney."

"I already have one on the way," said Kapoor.

They settled Northridge in an interrogation room and showed Kapoor and Warner to a room where they could wait. Thanks no doubt to the two women's combined wealth and influence, the attorney Kapoor had contacted arrived within half an hour.

Levi and Martine both groaned aloud when they saw Jay Sawyer. A member of Hatfield, Park, and McKenzie, a prestigious local law firm, he was genuinely one of the best defense attorneys in Las Vegas. He was also quite handsome in an old New England, came-over-on-the-Mayflower kind of way, but the real problem was that he *knew* how competent and good-looking he was, and it only fed his monstrous ego.

"Detective Valcourt, Detective Abrams," Sawyer said, stopping by their desks. His voice deepened as he looked at Levi. "Always a pleasure."

"For you, maybe," Levi muttered. Sawyer was bisexual, and had never made a secret of how much he'd like to get Levi on his back.

Sawyer favored him with a slow, annoyingly attractive smile. "Would you mind showing me to my client?"

Shoving himself back from his desk with poor grace, Levi stood and gestured for Sawyer to follow him. Martine wrinkled her nose sympathetically as they passed.

Levi tried not to hate defense attorneys on principle. There *were* people who were falsely accused of crimes, and he truly believed that even the guilty deserved a strong defense. It was a necessary job. But nine years as a cop had ingrained the prejudice too deeply in him to root out.

Plus, Sawyer was just a dick.

Fortunately, they made it to the interrogation room before Sawyer's innuendos could cross the line into harassment, which spared Levi the trouble of having to break his nose. He felt little relief as he left Sawyer with Northridge, though, because he knew he'd be called back in no time.

Sure enough, he was informed an hour later that they were ready to speak to him. After an unsuccessful attempt to convince Martine to do the interrogation instead—she couldn't stand Sawyer—he returned to the room and sat at the table with his notepad at the ready.

"For the record," Sawyer said, "I've advised my client not to say anything to you at all. But she insists on telling you 'her side of the story.'"

Between Sawyer's clear exasperation and Northridge's set, determined face, Levi could imagine how long that argument had gone on. There was nothing predatory or flirtatious about Sawyer's demeanor now—he was all business.

"Then let's hear it," said Levi.

Northridge took a deep breath and folded her hands on top of the table. "I'd wanted a divorce for some time; I'm sure you're familiar enough with Stephen's life by now to understand why. But Stephen refused to consent to one—not because he wanted to stay married, but simply to spite me. My family's assets are considerable, including extensive property holdings throughout the Northeast, and in a messy, contested divorce, Stephen may have been able to lay claim to portions of them because we didn't have a prenup." Her mouth tilted wryly. "You can't imagine how much I hate knowing my mother was right all those years ago."

Levi nodded for her to continue.

"I knew Stephen was in the habit of hiring call girls on his business trips. Catching him in the act of infidelity—and committing a crime, no less—would have given me leverage to pressure him into accepting a clean divorce, or swayed the court in my favor if he remained obstinate."

"You wanted to walk in on him in a compromising position with a sex worker?"

"Yes," Northridge said, and then sighed. "I made discreet arrangements to fly into Las Vegas on Saturday night. But my first plane had mechanical problems, and I ended up on a different flight. I arrived in the city much later than I'd planned. I knew there was little chance Stephen was still with the woman he'd hired, but I was determined to confront him anyway. I couldn't bear another day of our farce of a marriage."

Sawyer made a displeased noise, and it was no surprise—Northridge had just spoken to her own motive for Hensley's murder.

"What time did you arrive at the Mirage?" Levi asked.

"Around 2.30 a.m. I was worried someone from the conference might recognize me and interfere, so I covered my face as best I could. I told the clerk at the front desk I was Stephen's wife and I'd come to surprise him." She rubbed a hand over her face. "I'd expected to have to do some convincing, but he was quick to accept a small bribe. In retrospect, that should have been a warning sign."

Levi hummed agreement.

"I got a key card for Stephen's room and went upstairs. The whole elevator ride, I was planning what I would say, how I would demand that we end things. I opened the door . . ." She gazed into the distance. Then she shook herself, leaned forward, and looked Levi right in the eye. "I swear to you, Detective, Stephen was already dead when I got there. He'd been dead for at least an hour. I didn't kill him."

He was reserving judgment on that for now. "What did you do then?" he said, keeping his tone neutral.

"I must have stood there frozen for a good five minutes. I was shocked, of course, and I didn't know what to do. It took some time to process the fact that my husband was dead and I felt nothing."

"God, Dr. Northridge, you're killing me here," Sawyer said with a pained expression.

She ignored him. "Once reality had sunk in, I realized the position I'd put myself in. Flying into the city without telling anyone, disguising myself, bribing a clerk for a key to the room—I knew it would look like I'd killed Stephen. So I ran. I thought there were probably security cameras in the elevators, so I took the stairs and left through a different exit. I went to a motel that accepted cash and didn't require ID."

Quick thinking, if it were true—not unexpected for a surgeon. "You were listed on the manifest for Flight 484 on Tuesday," Levi said. "How did you manage that?"

Northridge opened her mouth, but Sawyer lifted a hand to cut her off. "Ah, ah," he said. "No. The truth about this matter would implicate somebody my client cares for in a criminal act."

Levi tapped his pen against the table, considering. "A violent one?"

"Not at all."

Sawyer's face was an impassive mask—Levi would never get the truth without some kind of deal. The guy was such an arrogant lothario that it was easy to forget he was actually good at his job.

"Give me a minute," Levi said, pushing back his chair.

A couple of phone calls later, he had paperwork in hand to guarantee immunity to the person Northridge had drawn into her cover-up. Once everything was signed, Northridge said, "The first thing I did when I got to the motel was call my sister. I told her everything and asked her to fly to Las Vegas using my identity."

"Are you twins?"

"No, but we look enough alike that with a wig and the right makeup, she could pass for the photo on my ID. I overnighted her my driver's license, and she took the flight on Tuesday."

Clever. "And how does Alan Walsh figure into this?" Levi asked. "We know he called your cell phone twice earlier this week."

They didn't actually know that, not for a fact, but who else would have been calling Northridge from a burner phone with a Las Vegas area code?

She sighed. "I spent all day Sunday worried that Mr. Walsh would tell the police he'd seen me. I didn't think he would, because it would mean admitting he'd accepted a bribe for a room key, and he'd doubtlessly lose his job for that and perhaps even be considered an accomplice to the murder. So I hoped he'd just keep his mouth shut."

"And instead?"

"Instead, he called me Sunday night and threatened to expose my presence in Las Vegas if I didn't pay him off. I agreed to his terms and had my sister wire me the cash. Mr. Walsh and I met on Monday night at a diner near my motel, and I gave him what he'd asked for."

The second call on Monday must have been to confirm the details of the meet-up, then. Levi looked at Sawyer's pinched, sour expression. "I can't believe you're letting her tell me all this."

"If you believe there's any way I could stop her, I'd love to hear your thoughts on how," he said.

"Gentlemen, please," said Northridge. "I did things that were wrong, yes, but I didn't kill my husband. I'm not afraid to take responsibility for my actions and accept the consequences, especially if it means I won't be accused of a crime I didn't commit."

"You realize that by admitting that Walsh was blackmailing you, you're telling me you had motive to kill *him*, too," Levi said.

"That's the thing." She spread her hands. "I *didn't*. I recorded both of my phone calls with Mr. Walsh, as well as our meeting on Monday. After the money had exchanged hands, I backed the recordings up to the Cloud and then played them for him. I had him on tape talking about how he blackmailed not only me, but other guests of the Mirage as well. I told him that if he ever tried to obtain more money from me, I'd bring the recordings to the police and take him down with me. Mutually assured destruction."

Levi blinked.

"Mr. Walsh and I had an understanding. I didn't mind giving him a one-time payout, and he accepted that it would end there. We parted on amicable terms. Then I read about his murder in the paper a couple of days later . . ." She swallowed hard, shaking her head. "Detective, Mr. Walsh told me that he knew I wasn't the one who killed Stephen."

Levi narrowed his eyes. "The only way he could know that is if he knew who the real killer was."

"He did. And that person killed him for it."

"Uh-huh. Any ideas who that person might be?"

She snorted. "If I knew, that would have been the first thing I told you."

Levi was quiet for a few moments while he reviewed his dense notes. Then he exhaled one long breath and looked up. "This is a great story, Dr. Northridge. You account for everything, answer every doubt." He flipped his notepad shut. "But let me tell you what this looks like from a law enforcement perspective. You have the strongest motivation to kill both Hensley and Walsh of anyone we've encountered. You went to extreme lengths to conceal your arrival and presence in Las Vegas. You bribed a hotel employee for access to the first crime scene, which by your own admission you then fled. The man who was blackmailing you turned up dead a few days later. You have the medical knowledge to measure out an overdose of Rohypnol and precisely target a man's carotid artery. And while you may have an explanation for all of that, at the end of the day, you can't *prove* any of it."

"A jury will decide that," Sawyer said.

"Yes, that is the way the legal system works, thank you," Levi said. "You think a jury is going to buy a story this full of suspicious coincidences?"

Smirking, Sawyer said, "They will when I'm through with them."

"Really." Levi smiled. "Have you met Leila Rashid yet?"

Sawyer's smirk faltered. "She's the DDA on the case?"

Levi nodded. Sawyer's lips thinned out, his eyes darkening, and Levi took some petty satisfaction at the crack in his composure.

"Well, we'll have plenty of time to strategize once my client is released on bail."

"Oh, come on," said Levi, taken aback by the depth of Sawyer's confidence. "A judge isn't going to set bail for a wealthy tourist charged with a high-profile murder. She's got flight risk written all over her."

"We'll see about that. Alternatively, you could find the *actual* killer and spare us all the trouble."

"I think we're done here." Levi got to his feet and straightened his jacket. "Dr. Northridge, you'll be transported to the Clark County Detention Center later to await your hearing."

"Don't worry, Doctor," Sawyer said, as he stood as well. "I'll expedite the process and get this all worked out in no time."

Though paler and grimmer than before, Northridge thanked them both gracefully. Sawyer followed Levi out of the interrogation room.

Expecting further blustering about the case, Levi was caught off guard when Sawyer said, "So I heard you're dating that giant bounty hunter now. Russo, right?"

Levi opened his mouth, but no words came out.

Sawyer's eyes traveled slowly down the length of Levi's body. "He must be an incredible fuck to tempt you out of a billionaire's bed."

White-hot rage coursed through Levi, tightening every muscle and setting his pulse racing. He clenched his right hand into a fist. "If you think I wouldn't risk the consequences of beating the shit out of you, you're in for a rude awakening."

"Careful," Sawyer murmured. He leaned in close to Levi as he brushed past. "I might enjoy that."

He walked away with a light, cheerful stride. Levi's nostrils flared while he watched him go, and he had to take a couple of minutes to calm himself down before returning to the bullpen.

After he'd discussed the interrogation with Martine, she said, "I don't know. Something about this still doesn't feel right. Do you really think she did it?"

"I don't know what to think." Levi rubbed his tired eyes. "All the evidence points in her direction."

"True, but let me ask you this—do you see Clarissa Northridge as the kind of person who'd lose her shit and throw up after stabbing a man?"

"No," Levi said pensively. "I don't."

"Hey, Abrams!" Gibbs shouted across the bullpen, startling people throughout the room. "Wen wants to see you in his office pronto. What'd you do now?"

Dominic arrived at his childhood home in North Las Vegas in the early afternoon. It had been a packed house when he'd grown up here with his parents, four siblings, and paternal grandmother, but now that the kids were all adults and his father had passed away, his mother and grandmother were the only residents.

As he let himself in and unsnapped Rebel's leash, he called out, "Nonna, it's me!" His mother would be at work, and his grandmother hadn't been expecting him.

Silvia ambled in from the kitchen, a frown on her face. She was by far the shortest person in their family, and he had to stoop to kiss her wrinkled cheek.

"You didn't call," she said sternly.

"Sorry about that. I was in the area and thought I'd stop by." While he spoke, he unzipped his duffel bag and withdrew his notebook, in which he'd written a similar message to the one he'd shown Carlos.

Unlike Carlos, Silvia reacted with equanimity, seeming neither surprised nor much concerned. She read the message, nodded, and eyed him critically before saying, "You're hungry." It wasn't a question.

"I could eat."

"I've been preparing arancini for dinner—I'll fry some up for you now." She nudged him, indicating he should get on with his business, and headed back to the kitchen. Rebel gazed after her longingly but stuck by Dominic's side.

While not large, his family's house was bigger than his and Carlos's apartments, and it took him much longer to sweep it thoroughly. He broke halfway through to indulge in his grandmother's arancini—stuffed, deep-fried risotto balls—and finished a few hours later.

The house was clean. He hadn't really expected the Seven of Spades to go so far as to bug his mother's house, but he wouldn't have been able to rest easy until he knew for sure.

Returning to the kitchen, where Silvia was still puttering around, he said, "Everything's fine. We can speak freely now."

"Are you in Trouble?" she asked, the capital letter coming through in her tone.

He knew what she meant. "Not that kind," he said. "I haven't been gambling, though there is something you and Ma should know. But before that, I was wondering if I could get your caponata recipe? I'm making dinner for Levi tonight and I think he'd really like it."

With a broad smile, she fetched her antique carved wooden recipe box from a cabinet and rifled through it. Withdrawing the recipe in question, she pulled a blank card from the back of the box as well and settled down at the table with a pen.

"Nonna, I can just take a picture of it with my phone—"

"Absolutely not," she said. "An authentic recipe should be handwritten. Sit down."

He obeyed immediately and without argument.

"Now," she said, uncapping her pen, "there was something you wanted to tell me?"

While she copied the recipe out in her elegant, old-school handwriting, he detailed his and Levi's history with the Seven of Spades from beginning to end. Rebel sat beside his chair with her head on his knee, her eyes half-closed in bliss as he scratched her ears and the scruff of her neck.

Once he'd told the full story, Silvia asked, "Are you sure this killer wouldn't hurt you?"

He opened his mouth to give an unqualified *yes*, hesitated, and instead said, "Not physically, at least. I know they like to play mind games, though, and I can't guarantee they wouldn't do something to mess with my mind or sabotage me in some way."

"But that isn't going to stop you, is it?"

"No."

"Nor Levi, I'm assuming."

He laughed. "Definitely not. He's even more stubborn than I am."

"That's hard to imagine." She gave him a measuring look. "And why haven't we seen Levi since that one day in April he came to the house? You could bring him to Sunday lunch, you know."

"I don't think we're ready for that," Dominic said, flustered by the sudden change of topic.

"Why not?"

He was stuck for a response. If he was being honest, the idea freaked him out a little. Bringing Levi to a friend's big family party was one thing; bringing him to his own intimate family meal was another. He'd never done that with any other guy before, and he couldn't take that step until he was sure it meant as much to Levi as it would to him.

"I'll ask him about it," he said. "Anyway, I should get going—I still have stuff to do today, and I have to stop by the grocery store too." He tucked the card she handed him into his pocket, got up from the table, and kissed her goodbye. "Thanks for everything, Nonna."

She smacked his cheek affectionately. "Make sure you use good olive oil for the caponata," she said. "None of that cheap stuff."

Levi knocked on the half-open door to Wen's office and poked his head inside. "You wanted to see me, sir?"

"Yes, Abrams, come in and have a seat. Shut the door behind you." Wen looked tired and stressed-out, the lines around his eyes and mouth more pronounced than usual.

Levi did as he was told, curious as to what this was all about. He'd mentally run through all his cases, but he couldn't think of any reason Wen would need to speak with him privately.

"I'm not going to beat around the bush," Wen said, meeting Levi's gaze across his desk. "Are you still investigating the Seven of Spades?"

On the list of subjects Levi had guessed Wen might broach, that hadn't even cracked the top twenty. His eyes widened, and he stared at Wen, at a damning loss for words.

"Goddammit, Abrams, that case is *closed*. You were specifically ordered not to pursue it!"

"Why are you even asking me about this?" Levi said, though he knew he'd already given himself away.

"Dominic Russo was seen at Dr. Angela Tran's office."

That knocked Levi even further off-balance. "He's seeing a psychiatrist, so what?"

Scowling, Wen said, "Don't insult me. You want me to believe it's a coincidence that your boyfriend just happened to choose the same shrink who treated Keith Chapman?"

"He's not my boyfriend," Levi said faintly.

"So you were kissing somebody else in the bullpen this morning, then?"

"I . . ." Levi shook his head, bewildered by how everything had fallen apart so quickly.

"You've always been honest, Abrams—sometimes *too* honest. So be straight with me now." Wen leveled him with a somber look. "Did you send Russo to see Dr. Tran as part of an independent investigation into the Seven of Spades?"

"Yes," Levi said.

"Christ." Wen leaned back in his chair, running a hand over his face. "You're suspended for a week without pay for gross insubordination. Check in your service weapon before you leave the building."

Levi clenched his jaw, breathing through his reflexive anger. He *had* disobeyed a direct and very firm order from his superior officer, and he'd done that with full awareness of what the consequences would be if he were found out. He wouldn't try to weasel his way out of them now.

"Out of curiosity," he said as he rose to his feet, "how did you know about Dominic going to see Dr. Tran?"

A hint of discomfort crossed Wen's face. "I received an anonymous tip."

"An anonymous tip?" Levi huffed out a humorless laugh. "You realize that was from the Seven of Spades themself, right? They want me to back off. I must have gotten too close for comfort."

"For God's sake—"

"Did you know Tina Chapman has received five thousand dollars in cash from an unidentified source every month since Keith died? Who do you think is giving her that money?"

"Don't start this shit again unless you want your suspension doubled," Wen snapped.

Levi shook his head and headed for the door. As he was leaving, however, he couldn't resist having the last word. "The Seven of Spades won't be content lurking in the background forever," he said. "And if we're not prepared when they return, we'll all be screwed."

CHAPTER 15

Levi knocked on the door when Dominic was almost finished with dinner. He wiped his hands on a dishtowel and moved to answer it, feeling awkward about having to let Levi into his own apartment.

Levi kissed his cheek, pet Rebel's head in greeting, and walked inside to toss his messenger bag on the dining table. "That smells amazing," he said as he stripped off his suit jacket. "What are you making?"

"Baked tilapia with a lemon-garlic sauce and my grandmother's Sicilian caponata." Dominic returned to the kitchen and peeked into the oven.

"What's that?"

"Kind of like an eggplant-based vegetable stew."

"Sounds great. Thanks for doing this."

Dominic cast him a sideways glance. Levi's body language was tense, his shoulders tight and his back ramrod-straight, his face drawn with unhappiness.

"You okay?" Dominic asked. Levi had sent him a terse text earlier about his suspension, but he hadn't answered any of Dominic's follow-up texts afterward.

Levi shrugged, unknotting his tie and draping it over his jacket on the back of a chair. "It is what it is," he said. "I could use a drink, though."

He came into the kitchen and opened the refrigerator before Dominic could do more than say, "Wait—"

Levi went still, stared into the fridge, and then closed the door and turned to Dominic. "Why is there a shoebox in my refrigerator?"

Putting a finger to his lips, Dominic fetched the box and removed the top. Levi surveyed the mess of electronic equipment inside, though he didn't try to touch anything, before looking up at Dominic with a confused expression. Dominic stowed the box back in the fridge and shut the door.

"I spent the whole day sweeping for surveillance equipment," he said. "I found GPS trackers in my truck and Carlos's car. There were bugs inside the power strip in my apartment and the smoke detector in Carlos and Jasmine's. The one here was wired into your thermostat—that was a bitch to get out, let me tell you. I was going to destroy everything, but it's evidence, so I thought you might want to bring it to the lab. Either way, we should be good now. Your place is clean, and the bugs won't be able to pick anything up from inside the fridge."

"You spent the day . . ." Levi frowned, and Dominic could see him putting everything together. "Oh my God. You manipulated me into giving you the key to my apartment. You didn't even have to ask; I just *offered*. I never suspected a thing."

"I'm sorry," Dominic said. "I didn't want to alarm you until I confirmed that I was right. You would have obsessed about it all day, and it would have interfered with your job."

Levi wrenched the fridge door open, retrieved a bottle of white wine, and slammed it shut. "You're the most talented liar I've ever met."

"Is that a compliment or an insult?"

"Both."

Dominic was standing in front of the cabinet Levi needed, so he got the wine glasses out himself and handed them over. "Technically, I didn't lie. I just postponed telling you the full truth."

Levi paused with the corkscrew halfway into the bottle. "Wow," he said.

"I know what I did was manipulative," Dominic said, "but I do believe I made the right call. I understand if you're annoyed, but if you're genuinely angry with me, then we need to talk about that."

Levi took his sweet time thinking it over while he poured two extremely generous glasses of wine, put a stopper in the bottle, and returned it to the fridge. As he picked up his glass, he said, "I'm not angry. You're right—I would have been distracted worrying about it all day, I wouldn't have been able to focus on my job, and in the end, it wouldn't have done any good anyway."

"But you're still upset."

"I'll be over it by the time I finish this glass," Levi said.

Laughing, Dominic guided him out of the kitchen. "Sit down. Dinner's almost ready."

Rebel sidled up to Levi, butting her head against his thigh. He stroked her fur with an absentminded air and sipped his wine while he watched Dominic put the finishing touches on their meal.

"So the Seven of Spades has been spying on us," he said. "For how long, do you think?"

"There's no way of knowing." Dominic gave the caponata a final stir and turned off the burner. "I'll need to check your car for a GPS tracker tomorrow morning. And I should probably sweep Martine's house too, if you think she'd agree to that."

"Yeah, I can imagine that conversation going well." Levi knocked back half his glass in one go. "You know, even when I bring all that stuff into the substation, Wen will find another explanation for it. He doesn't want to believe. None of them do."

Dominic set up two plates with tilapia, large helpings of caponata, and chunks of fresh crusty bread. He carried them over to the dining table, where he'd already laid out napkins and silverware. "At least being suspended means you know nothing will interrupt our plans tomorrow."

"Don't be a dick," Levi said, but he was smiling, just like Dominic had known he would.

Levi placed his fork and knife on his empty plate and sighed in satisfaction. He'd been irritated with Dominic earlier, but a bottle of wine and an excellent meal had gone a long way toward appeasing him.

He couldn't shake his bad mood entirely, though. The news of his suspension had ripped through the substation like wildfire before he'd been able to leave. Between Gibbs's smart-ass comments, the others' pitying looks, and a whispered argument with Martine in which he could see her physically restraining herself from saying *I told you so*, it was a wonder he'd gotten out of the building without throwing a chair through a window.

There was no relief to be found at home, either, because now he knew that the Seven of Spades had been *in his apartment*, his privacy violated in one of the worst ways imaginable. Tomorrow he'd be spending the day at a party full of strangers, and on Monday he'd have to tell a courtroom full of people about how creepy little Drew Barton had gotten the drop on him and assaulted him at gunpoint.

There was only one reliable way to purge this much stress. Levi finished his wine, stood up, and moved to stand beside Dominic's chair. Getting the hint, Dominic scooted back far enough for Levi to straddle his lap. Rebel was gnawing on a rawhide bone under the table, content to ignore them for the time being.

"Hey," Dominic said, his arms encircling Levi's waist.

"Hey." Levi brushed the backs of his fingers over Dominic's cheek. "Thanks for dinner."

He leaned in for a kiss, unbothered by the taste of garlic. As their embrace intensified, however, pain lanced through his busted lip, and he jerked back with a grunt. Shrugging it off, he dove back into the kiss—only to pull away again a few seconds later when the throbbing refused to be ignored.

"Fuck, I can't," he said. "My lip hurts too much."

Dominic smoothed a hand up his back. "Do you want to stop?"

"No, I just don't want you to kiss me," Levi said, and then winced at how that sounded.

Dominic only looked intrigued. "No-kiss sex, huh?" he said. "That's a little kinky."

Levi's hands tightened on Dominic's shoulders as he was momentarily overwhelmed by sheer *want*. Dominic made everything feel easy; he never seemed bothered by Levi's sharp corners or rough edges. It still astonished Levi every time.

"You could kiss me other places," he suggested.

Lust flared in Dominic's eyes. "Is that right?" he said, his voice husky. He grabbed Levi's ass with both hands and yanked him even closer, then nuzzled the underside of his jaw and pressed an open-mouthed kiss to his skin. "Like here?"

"Mmm."

Dominic's mouth traveled down the side of Levi's neck, strong hands kneading Levi's ass. "How about here? Or maybe here?" He sucked lightly at the hollow of Levi's throat.

Levi rolled his hips, rubbing his swelling cock against Dominic's stomach and enjoying the sensation of Dominic stirring beneath him. "A little lower."

"Oh, you mean here?" Dominic asked, as he unbuttoned Levi's shirt. He bent his head and mouthed at one of Levi's nipples.

Moaning, Levi arched his spine. One of Dominic's arms came around to support his back, and he trusted his weight to Dominic's strength while Dominic sucked both of his nipples in turn, flicking them with his clever tongue until Levi was writhing in his lap. Then Dominic surged back up, burying his face in the side of Levi's neck and biting hard.

"Ah!" Between the two of them, Levi was usually more of a biter, but it looked like Dominic was planning to make up for the fact that Levi couldn't use his mouth for much tonight.

"You drive me crazy," Dominic growled into his ear. "The sounds you make, the way you move against me—"

He reached around Levi and swiped his plate to the side, then lifted Levi up and sat him on the edge of the table without ever getting out of his own chair. He stripped out of his T-shirt and Levi followed suit, throwing his own shirt off to the side.

Sliding his chair closer to the table, Dominic braced himself on Levi's spread thighs and leaned forward to place a trail of hungry kisses down Levi's chest and abdomen. When he reached Levi's waistband, he let go to wrench Levi's belt open and lower the zip on his trousers, and Levi groaned as that hot mouth descended on his cock through the thin layer of his boxer briefs.

Dominic inched Levi's underwear further down, but just as Levi was sure he was going to get his cock sucked, Dominic abruptly veered off course and suckled on his sensitive hip bone instead.

"Fuck!" Levi's hips bucked off the table, but Dominic shoved him back down and held him there, his teeth scraping the hollow of his hip.

Panting, Levi fell back on one hand. He had to push the other one into his underwear to free his erection and give it a few strokes.

"God, Dominic, please—"

Dominic turned his head to rub his cheek against Levi's shaft. "So if you can't kiss, I'm guessing there's no chance of getting my cock in your mouth?"

"Not tonight. Sorry."

"That's too bad." Pushing Levi's busy hand away, Dominic kissed the head of his cock. "I've never been with anyone so eager to learn how to deep-throat me."

"I'll get there eventually," Levi said. It was a point of pride for him, because Dominic could deep-throat *him* like a porn star. Granted, there was a significant size difference to consider, but he was still determined to return the favor someday.

"That's okay," said Dominic. "I like watching you struggle with it."

Levi was still processing his shocked arousal when Dominic pulled him off the table, spun him around, and shoved him back onto it face-first. He gasped as Dominic yanked his trousers and underwear down to mid thigh and sank his teeth into one ass cheek.

"Should I take it easier on you?" Dominic said teasingly, after he released the bite.

Levi twisted around to scowl at him over his shoulder. "Don't you dare."

Dominic grinned, obviously accepting the challenge, and got back to work. He squeezed Levi's ass with forceful, grasping hands while he lavished his flesh with sloppy kisses and playful bites. Levi watched, mesmerized, spreading his legs as wide as he could within his pulled-down trousers. He was ready to scream in frustration by the time Dominic finally pried his cheeks apart and kissed his hole.

Rather than eat him out, though, Dominic pulled Levi back onto his lap. Levi went with it, relaxing against Dominic's chest and savoring the slide of bare skin. He groaned his appreciation when Dominic grasped his cock and began jerking him off briskly.

"I seem to remember making you a promise about tonight," he said in-between rapid breaths.

"Rings a bell." Dominic nibbled on his neck. "Something about not trying to escape if I managed to pin you?"

"Well, I'm a man of my word." Levi craned his head around to kiss Dominic hard on the mouth, just once. "Let's go in the bedroom, though. I feel weird doing this with Rebel watching."

A few minutes later, they were tussling naked across the bed, all the covers and pillows shoved off onto the floor. Levi was too turned on to put up much pretense of resistance, more interested in clutching greedily at Dominic's thick muscles and frotting his aching cock against Dominic's warm skin. Once the lube came into play, he gave up altogether.

"You're not even trying to stop me," Dominic said at one point. He was holding Levi facedown on the bed, both arms restrained behind his back, and had two fingers working in his ass.

"Why the hell would I want to *stop* you?" said Levi, canting his hips.

Dominic laughed and dropped a kiss on Levi's shoulder blade. He got a third finger inside and Levi keened, rising onto his knees though his chest was still trapped flat against the mattress.

"God, look at you." Dominic's tone was rich with admiration. "Are you ready for me?"

"I've been ready."

Dominic released Levi's arms, eased him onto his back, and resumed finger-fucking him. "There's something I want to try," he said conversationally, like he wasn't tormenting Levi's prostate. "An old wrestling fantasy."

Levi's eyelids fluttered at a particularly pleasant twist of Dominic's fingers, and he had to force himself to concentrate. "What is it?"

Dominic told him, and he frowned.

"That'll never work," he said.

"Yes, it will. Trust me. You've just never been with a guy my size before."

Levi's eyes darted down to where Dominic's cock jutted thick and swollen between his thighs.

"That's not what I meant, but thanks," Dominic said with a chuckle. "You've said yourself you've only slept with guys who were built like you. You have no idea the opportunities a size difference like ours can open up."

"I'll try it." Levi was game to try almost anything once, especially when it came to sex with Dominic. "But I still think you've watched too much porn."

They disengaged long enough for Dominic to roll on a condom and lay on his back. Levi sat astride his hips, facing away, and carefully lowered himself backward to stretch out along the length of Dominic's body. Dominic helped him adjust the position until his entire torso was resting on top of Dominic's, his head near Dominic's collarbone and just his feet planted on either side of Dominic's hips.

"You're sure you can breathe like this?" Levi asked.

"Yeah, I'm fine," Dominic said, sounding amused. "Lift your legs."

Levi grasped the backs of his thighs and pulled them toward his chest. Dominic didn't even grunt; Levi could feel him breathing slow and easy.

God. Levi was struck then with the reality of how strong Dominic truly was. While Levi was thin, he was almost six feet tall and strung with sinewy muscle from head to foot—his weight wasn't insignificant. Yet Dominic was supporting all that weight on his chest and abdomen without any apparent effort whatsoever.

"Fuck," Levi said, realizing that this *was* going to work after all. He shivered at the thought.

Dominic gently urged Levi to spread his lifted legs further apart. Levi flushed with heat but allowed it, his breath coming shorter.

"Ready?" Dominic asked. At Levi's nod, he placed one hand on Levi's stomach and reached down with the other to feed his cock into Levi's hole.

It took a few minutes, as it always did, but soon Dominic was fucking up into Levi at a leisurely pace. In this position, the shallow upward angle meant that Dominic's cock dragged over Levi's prostate with every thrust, lighting him up from the inside out.

"Told you," Dominic said smugly. Now his breathing was labored, though Levi suspected that was more from arousal than physical strain.

Levi groaned in response, rocking his hips mindlessly while his hands slipped in the sweat on the backs of his thighs. The stimulation was so intense it was almost too much. "What—what makes this a wrestling fantasy?" he said in-between bright sparks of pleasure.

Dominic pushed all the way inside and stilled his hips. He disengaged Levi's grip on his legs, then hooked his own arms underneath Levi's armpits and joined his hands behind Levi's head. Levi tamped down on the muscle memory compelling him to prevent the hold and cried out as Dominic started fucking him again in a horizontal version of a full Nelson.

"Oh my God." Levi put his hands on Dominic's wrists, though he didn't try to free himself. He brought his knees up against his chest and gazed down his own body to where he was spread open and stuffed full.

He knew that Dominic would release him in a second if asked, and that certainty was why he was able to enjoy this, why he could take pleasure in indulging Dominic's display of raw physical power. Every one of Dominic's rapid bouncing thrusts hit him in the exact right place to blur his vision and draw broken moans from deep in his chest.

"I'm going to fall out if you don't stop squirming," Dominic said, a hint of breathless laughter in his voice.

Levi could fix that. He wrapped his ankles behind Dominic's knees, locking their thighs together, and tensed his legs, adding his own strength to the mix as he met Dominic thrust for thrust. Dominic made a choked noise beneath him.

With his arms trapped by Dominic's hold, Levi couldn't touch his cock, which was slapping angrily against his belly and demanding his attention more ferociously with each passing second. "*Dominic*," he said, twisting in delirious need.

Dominic let go of his arms but got to Levi's cock first, pumping it hard while he rabbited away at Levi's ass. Levi reached up blindly to touch Dominic's face, knowing how much noise he was making but unable to control himself.

"That feel good?" Dominic kissed Levi's palm. "You gonna come for me?"

"Call me baby again," Levi said unthinkingly.

He felt a frisson of surprise run through Dominic's body; then Dominic groaned, and his hips sped up even more. "Come on, baby," he rumbled, and it was perfect, it was exactly the way Levi had pretended not to imagine it. "I know you're getting close, I can feel you tightening up on me. Let me hear how good you feel taking my dick, come on, show me how much you get off on it—"

Levi's muscles coiled up tight and released all at once in a shattering orgasm. His loud cries echoed off the bedroom walls as his hole pulsed around Dominic's thick shaft and come splattered hot and messy across his stomach.

Dominic stroked him through it, then gripped his hips with both hands and kept thrusting. Levi lay panting and wrecked on top of him.

"I can't—I need to go deeper than this," said Dominic, a little frantic now.

Blissed-out and generous in the aftermath of his climax, Levi said, "You can do whatever you want."

Dominic pulled out and brought Levi along as he shifted them both into an upright kneeling position. Sitting on his heels with Levi still straddling his thighs, he guided Levi back onto his cock until Levi's ass was flush with his hips.

This time, his huge cock sank *much* deeper than he'd been able to go when they'd been lying down. Levi gasped, falling forward onto one hand. Dominic froze.

"Don't stop." Levi pushed back on him, relishing the stretch and the sensation of fullness. "Don't hold back, Dominic, I don't want you to."

Groaning, Dominic wrapped both arms around Levi from behind, buried his face in Levi's shoulder, and snapped his hips. Levi stayed braced on one hand and clutched Dominic's thigh with the other.

"That's it," he said. They hadn't been doing this long enough for him to admit to Dominic how much he loved being fucked after he came—feeling a cock sliding in and out of him while he was still raw and sensitive. "Come on, harder, fuck me up—"

He squeezed his ass around Dominic's pistoning cock, pleased when Dominic let out a hoarse shout.

"God, do that again," Dominic said. "Levi—*baby*, please."

Levi obliged him, rhythmically clenching and releasing his muscles, basking in Dominic's moans and curses and animalistic grunts. It was no time at all before Dominic bit down on Levi's shoulder and slammed home, muffling his cry of completion in

Levi's flesh. His hips never stopped moving, grinding in slow circles as he came.

When Dominic relaxed and lifted his head, Levi slumped back against his chest, leaning his head on Dominic's shoulder. Dominic pressed several fervent kisses to his temple and the side of his face.

"You good?" Dominic asked.

"Nngh."

"I'll take that as a yes."

Dominic lifted Levi off his cock to lay him on the bed, discarded the condom, and hung over the side of the mattress to retrieve the pillows and blankets. Levi rolled onto his side, peaceful and boneless, letting Dominic create a cozy nest around them and then spoon up behind.

"Don't fall asleep," Levi said, though he was halfway there himself. "It's still early, and I'm not done with you yet."

Dominic's soft laugh reverberated against Levi's back. "I hope not."

CHAPTER 16

Levi's ringing cell phone woke him in the morning. He slapped at it blindly, his muddled brain thinking it was his alarm before he remembered he hadn't set one—not only was it Saturday, he'd also been suspended.

Rubbing the sleep out of his eyes, he peered at the screen to see it was Natasha calling. It was a little after eight thirty, which was practically sleeping in for him, but he was surprised she'd call him so early on a weekend.

He answered the call and rolled out of bed. "Hey, hold on a second," he whispered as he padded toward the door. Dominic was out cold and didn't even stir, and Rebel only pricked her ears halfheartedly as she watched him go.

"Is everything okay?" Natasha asked. "I'm sorry, I know it's early."

Out in the kitchen, Levi could speak at a normal volume. "It's fine. It's just that Dominic is still sleeping."

"Ooh."

"Shut up," he said amiably. He started warming up his Breville espresso maker, which had been a birthday gift from Stanton and was the most expensive thing he owned besides his car.

She laughed, but when she spoke again, her tone was more somber. "I heard about the suspension. How are you doing?"

"It's not the end of the world."

"I had no idea you were still investigating the Seven of Spades."

"Well, it's not something I was spreading around." He dumped dark roast coffee beans into his grinder, set it to French press, and stepped away so the noise wouldn't drown out their conversation. "I know everybody thinks I'm crazy."

"You're not crazy, Levi; you're passionate," she said.

He glanced at the dark armoire against the wall, shut up tight to hide the evidence of his obsession within. "I guess that's a matter of opinion," he said. "Did you call to check up on me?"

"Actually, no. I was calling about Adriana."

"Is something wrong?"

"I'm having more trouble finding her a place here than I anticipated," Natasha said with a sigh. "The group home she's staying in temporarily is already stretched past capacity, and she's not even supposed to be in our system—she's in Reno's."

"I thought you were trying to find her a foster family." Returning to the kitchen, he poured the coarsely ground beans into his French press.

She was silent for a moment. "Here's the thing. A lot of foster families are hesitant to take in a teenager with a history of running away, not to mention a history of abuse allegations."

"Abuse *allegations*?" Levi said, pausing in the act of filling a carafe with hot water from the espresso machine. "What the fuck does that mean?"

"In Reno, Adriana reported that her foster father had been physically rough and sexually inappropriate with her. Her caseworker investigated and judged the claim to be false."

He set the carafe down hard on the counter. "It wasn't, Natasha. If anything, 'physically rough and sexually inappropriate' *undersold* what happened to her. I know an abused kid when I see one—"

"So do I," she said grimly. "I don't know the specifics of what happened, but now Adriana's file has a note that she made an unsubstantiated abuse claim."

"Did they leave her there?" he said, his stomach churning with the beginnings of an acidic rage he knew all too well. "After they decided the allegations were false, did they leave her in that same house with that same man?"

"Yes."

He had to put the phone down to keep from throwing it. Gripping the countertop, he hung his head between his arms and breathed in through his nose and out through his mouth. It didn't help.

Adriana's foster father was probably the man Dominic had reminded her of. He'd be a big guy, and strong, but that wouldn't matter. The only reason Dominic was an even match for Levi was because he was a highly trained veteran Army Ranger. Chances were this other man was just a bully used to getting his way because of his size, but a bulky frame and simple strength alone wouldn't be enough to protect him from Levi.

He could imagine it in vivid detail; he knew exactly what it would feel and sound like. The thudding impact of flesh on flesh, the crunch of bone, the spurt of blood from a busted nose . . . He'd break the man's face, kick him in the ribs, choke him out, and let him see how *he* liked being the one who was helpless and afraid—

Through the haze of his violent fantasy, Levi became aware of a tinny shouting coming from his phone—Natasha urgently repeating his name. He picked it back up and said, "I'm here. I'm fine."

"You're not fine," she said. "I know you, Levi. Right now, the only thing you can think about is tracking that guy down in Reno and tearing him apart."

"You're half right. I'd like to do the same thing to the caseworker."

"Levi—"

"I won't actually do anything. You know that. Doesn't mean I can't imagine it."

The water had cooled off too much, so he emptied out the carafe and refilled it. He let the necessity of pouring the water into the French press at a slow, steady rate keep him calm and focused.

"True, but the problem with you is that whenever you have that kind of retribution fantasy—which every human being has to some extent, by the way—you always feel ashamed afterward."

He shrugged irritably even though she couldn't see him. "I'll deal with it. It's just . . . what kind of fucked-up system do we have where a vulnerable child is put in a situation so horrible she thinks it's a better option to run away and live on the streets of Las Vegas, combing through Dumpsters for food? God knows what else happened to her here. Even if they thought she was making everything up, why take the chance and leave her with him? Why didn't they move her anyway?"

"You're asking me questions I don't have answers to," Natasha said quietly. "The system is broken in more than one way. We just have to do the best we can with what we're given."

He put the top on the French press and left it alone to steep, then reset the grinder with a smaller batch of beans on the espresso setting. "And what is the best we can do?" he asked.

"I'm not sure. I pulled every string and called in every favor I could to keep Adriana in Vegas this long. If I don't find a more permanent solution soon, they'll send her back to Reno. There'll be nothing I can do."

He closed his eyes and exhaled. "All right. I'll see if I can figure out any way to help. I do suddenly have a lot of free time on my hands, after all."

Chuckling weakly, she said, "Thanks. I'll keep trying and call you with any updates."

"Okay. Talk to you later."

"Levi," she said, just as he was about to hang up.

"Mm?"

"It's okay for you to want to hurt Adriana's foster father for what he did to her. It's a completely natural emotional reaction, especially to child abuse. Most people would feel something similar. You don't have to be ashamed of it."

"I know," Levi said. "Thanks, Natasha."

They ended the call, and he put down the phone. Natasha was right, in a way, but Levi wasn't *most people*. For most people, revenge fantasies were idle ones, events that couldn't realistically come to pass.

If Levi decided to hurt that man, he easily could. He could hurt him badly, quite possibly kill him, and there were very few people who would be able to stop him if he tried.

He cracked his neck from side to side, pushed those morbid thoughts to the back of his mind, and returned to one of his favorite rituals—making coffee.

He finished up the French press, then warmed two mugs with hot water while the espresso machine pumped out a perfectly infused double shot. After he filled both mugs with strong, fragrant coffee, he poured the espresso into one and steamed milk for the other. The final step was to grab some supplies from the pantry that he'd bought with Dominic in mind—raw sugar and vanilla-flavored coffee syrup. He mixed the syrup, steamed milk, and sugar into the second mug, then tasted it and almost gagged.

It was disgusting—Dominic would love it.

Carrying both mugs, Levi went back to the bedroom and nudged the door open with his foot. Dominic was still asleep, but he grunted and shifted around beneath the covers when the smell of coffee hit the air. Even Rebel perked up.

"Hey," Levi said, settling on the bed. He put his mug on his nightstand and waved the other above Dominic's face.

"It's too early," Dominic said without opening his eyes.

"You have no idea what time it is."

"I know what *too early* feels like." Dominic cracked one eye open. "What's that?"

"An abomination I refuse to dignify with the title of coffee."

Dominic pushed himself upright, accepted the mug, and inhaled deeply. "This smells great," he said. He took a sip, and a smile of pure delight broke across his face like a child on Christmas morning. "You made this for me?"

"Yeah," Levi said, suddenly embarrassed. Was it too much? He picked up his own coffee to hide his discomfiture.

Brushing his fingers against Levi's jaw, Dominic said, "You're sweet."

Levi snorted. "I can say with confidence that you're the only person who's ever thought that."

Dominic smiled, but as his eyes traveled over Levi's body, his gaze sharpened and became assessing. "Something's wrong. What happened?"

Damn his observational skills. "I don't want to talk about it," Levi said. Then, because he also didn't want to hold Dominic at an arm's length the way he had too frequently with Stanton, he added, "I'll tell you later, though."

"Okay," Dominic said. He arranged his pillow behind his back and whistled for Rebel, who shimmied up the bed for a belly scratch. "You know, we don't have to leave for the Andersons' until two. That's hours from now."

Levi shifted closer with a small smile. "How *ever* will we pass the time?"

The Andersons lived in the eastern outskirts of Henderson, on three desert acres in the foothills of the River Mountains. As Dominic turned onto the street where their property line began, Levi gazed out the window at a group of horses gathered beneath a wooden shelter to enjoy the effects of a cool water mister.

"Horses?" he said.

Sitting on the bench seat between them, Rebel snapped to attention, leaning over Levi and putting her front paws on his door so she could look out the window too. She went nuts for horses; the word alone was enough to rile her up.

"Yeah, Jasmine's parents run a small horse farm—boarding and breeding, plus an equine therapy program." Dominic slowed down on the approach to the main gate. Rebel huffed and dropped back into her seat when the horses faded from sight. "Her mom's a big animal vet, and her dad teaches animal physiology and behavior at UNLV."

The gate stood open, and the winding, dusty drive was lined with cars. Dominic parked in the first available space, hopped out, and patted his thigh to signal Rebel to follow. Only when he went to close the door did he realize Levi was still sitting in the passenger seat, his seatbelt buckled and his eyes unfocused.

"What's wrong?" Dominic asked. Levi hadn't yet shared what had happened this morning to upset him, and Dominic hadn't pushed—neither of them were the type of person to easily talk about what was bothering them. They'd managed to have a fun morning regardless; Levi had seemed fine until right this minute.

"People don't like me," said Levi.

Dominic blinked, wondering if Levi was fucking with him.

"I don't mean that to sound self-pitying. It doesn't matter to me if people like me or not. I don't care what most people think at all. But you do."

"Thanks," Dominic said, a little stung.

Levi unbuckled his seatbelt and turned to face him. "In a good way. Being liked is important to you; you want to make the people around you happy and for everyone to get along. You're a naturally nice person, and people gravitate toward that. But me . . . even when I try to be nice, it comes out wrong. I can't even explain this to you right now without offending you."

Shaking his head, Dominic said, "I'm not offended, Levi, I just don't understand what you're getting at. Especially at this particular place and time."

"I . . ." Levi dropped his eyes to his hands. "I don't want to embarrass you."

Oh. Dominic rocked back on his heels, astonished. He knew that Levi was uncomfortable around strangers, but he'd never expected Levi's anxieties to take this form. "You couldn't embarrass me."

"No?" Levi said, looking up again. "These people know you well, and I'm sure they love you as much as everyone else does. They're going to think it's weird that someone like you is with someone like me."

"No, they—"

"Carlos and Jasmine do. Please don't deny it. I'm not the kind of guy they imagined you being with."

"Carlos and Jasmine couldn't give two flying fucks who I'm with as long as I'm happy," Dominic said, exasperated. He leaned forward into the truck. "You make me happy, Levi. I won't pretend it's not important to me for my friends and family to like you, because it is. But I'm not worried about it. They'll see the same things in you that I do."

"You didn't like me until we started sleeping together," Levi said.

"Whoa, hey," Dominic snapped. "That's not true and you know it. I liked you as soon as I started getting to know the real you instead of the assumptions I'd made about you. That was before sex ever entered into it. Don't cheapen that."

Levi yielded immediately. "You're right, I'm sorry. Don't you see this is exactly what I mean, though?"

Dominic climbed back into the truck, leaving Rebel watching him quizzically from the ground. He took both Levi's hands in his.

"You're prickly and uptight and a little caustic sometimes," he said. "But I *like* those things about you because they make you who you are. You also care deeply about the people close to you. You're fiercely committed to your job. You're heartbreakingly compassionate. And even when you're kind of a dick, you ultimately treat people with respect unless they start shit with you first. I'm not looking for a nice guy, Levi. I want a *good* guy. That's way more important."

Levi stared at him, his eyes wide with more astonishment than Dominic thought was warranted by what he'd said.

"What?" Dominic asked.

With a sound that was half laugh, half surprised exhalation, Levi said, "Believe it or not, you're not the first person to tell me something like that."

"Because it's true." Dominic kissed him briefly, careful of his bruised lip. "Now have a little faith in me and help me get this crap out of the back of my truck."

Levi smiled and nodded. They got out of the cab, and Dominic opened up the truck bed, where he'd strapped down two three-gallon beverage dispensers full of homemade sangria as well as Levi's contribution, a cooler packed with bottles of Blue Moon. Drinks in hand, they walked the rest of the way up to the house, a pale stucco Southwestern ranch that sprawled out in an upside-down U shape.

Rock music could be heard blasting from the backyard, along with a hubbub of laughter, shrieking kids, and the sound of dozens of voices raised in conversation. The front door stood ajar, only the screened storm door in place. Dominic opened it with his elbow and stepped into the house with Levi and Rebel right behind him.

"Dom, Levi!" Jasmine broke away from a group in the kitchen and hurried over to greet them. She looked radiant in a sundress that displayed her tattoos beautifully, her rainbow braids flowing loose down her back. "Oh yum, you made sangria."

Carlos came up behind her, relaxed and smiling, a pair of sunglasses perched on top of his head. Dominic handed him one of the beverage dispensers.

"We've got a classic red and my own mango-peach recipe," he said. "Levi taste-tested them both. Actually, if I hadn't stopped him, there might not have been any left."

Levi rolled his eyes and hefted the cooler he was carrying. "I'm more of a shopper than a cook myself."

"Any alcoholic beverage will be a hit with this crowd, believe me," said Jasmine. "Come on, let's go out back. I'll introduce you around."

As Jasmine and Levi headed for the backyard, Dominic hung back to speak to Carlos privately. "You seem calmer today. Everything set for the proposal?"

"Yeah. We're gonna do it during dessert."

Dominic slapped Carlos's back with his free hand and walked out into the large backyard. A variety of folding tables had been set up for a casual buffet; scattered seating arrangements were shaded by canvas awnings and cooled down by huge industrial fans. Dominic and Carlos set the sangria up where Jasmine directed, and Levi set his cooler down beside a few others.

After Jasmine excused herself to fetch her parents, a group of elementary school-aged children ran past with a couple of happily barking dogs. Rebel whined, stamping her feet in place as she watched. "Go ahead," Dominic said, and she was off like a shot.

Levi was surveying the backyard with an expression of slight surprise, and Dominic knew he was struck by the incredible diversity of the people milling around, the same way he'd been himself the first time he came here.

"These are all Jasmine's relatives?" Levi said.

"Well, you know Jasmine is multiracial herself, but the Andersons have also been foster parents for decades. A lot of those kids come back to these reunions as adults with their own spouses and children."

Levi turned to Dominic, his eyes sharp with sudden interest. "The Andersons are foster parents? Do they still take kids?"

"Yeah," Carlos said, "they've got two right now."

That obviously held meaning for Levi that Dominic didn't understand, but just then, Jasmine approached with her parents Marcus and Wendy in tow. There was a strong resemblance between parents and daughter, though Marcus's skin was much darker than Jasmine's and Wendy's a few shades lighter. Both were athletic, outdoorsy people, as well as the most welcoming individuals Dominic had ever had the pleasure of meeting.

"Dominic, it's great to see you," Wendy exclaimed, as he kissed her cheek and shook Marcus's hand. "And this must be your new boyfriend?"

Levi went still. Dominic met his eyes, thought *sure, what the hell*, and said, "Yeah, this is my boyfriend Levi Abrams. Levi, this is Marcus and Wendy Anderson."

Levi shook their hands and pleasantries were exchanged all around. Wendy's gaze lingered on his injured mouth, but she was too polite to mention it. Levi must have noticed, though, because he brushed his fingers against the bruise and said, "I was in a physical altercation with a suspect the other night. It looks worse than it is."

"Levi is a homicide detective with the LVMPD," Jasmine put in.

"That must be an intense job," said Marcus. "Are you from Las Vegas originally, Levi?"

"New Jersey, actually."

Dominic slipped an arm around Levi's waist as he and Marcus continued talking. Levi looked up at him with a smile and returned the gesture, pulling him even closer.

They passed a couple of pleasant hours under the hot sun and clear sky, gorging themselves on barbeque and chatting with Jasmine's various relatives. Dominic stuck by Levi's side, knowing he wouldn't want to be left alone among strangers, but multiple glasses of sangria eventually had their expected effect. He murmured an apology as he excused himself to the bathroom; Levi just waved him off impatiently.

When Dominic returned, he found Levi deep in conversation with the Andersons' two current foster kids, Josh and Rima. Both teenagers were smiling and gesturing effusively with their hands while Levi listened in contemplative silence.

Curious, Dominic stayed back, but it was impossible to watch Levi for long without him noticing. He twisted around in his chair a few seconds later, waved at Dominic, and said something to the kids. Then he pushed away from the table and came to stand by Dominic's side.

"Do you know where either of the Andersons are?" he asked. "I need to speak with them about something important."

"I think Wendy's in the kitchen," Dominic said, even more intrigued now.

Levi headed back into the house, Dominic trailing behind. Wendy was indeed in the kitchen, emptying fresh bags of chips into big serving bowls.

"Dr. Anderson," Levi said.

"You can call me Wendy, hon." She stuffed the chip bags into the garbage can. "What's up?"

"I've been talking to your foster kids all afternoon. They were all happy here, even when things got off to a rough start. You and your husband made a real difference to them, changed their lives for the better."

"Well, sadly it doesn't always work out that way, but we do try our best with every kid who comes through our door."

"I believe that," Levi said. "And I know a young woman who could really use your help. Would you possibly have room for one more?"

"So what do you think?" Levi asked, after he finished his story about how he'd met Adriana and the dilemma she was facing. He, Marcus, and Wendy had retreated to Marcus's home office for privacy.

"Sounds like she's been through hell," Marcus said.

"She has. I don't even know the full extent of it."

The Andersons exchanged a glance, and then Wendy nodded. "Why don't you give us this Natasha's phone number, and we'll see if we can set up a meeting with Adriana tomorrow? If everything goes well, we'd be happy to take her."

"Thank you," Levi said, light-headed with relief. He fished his phone out of his pocket. "You have no idea how much this means to me."

"It's very sweet of you to take such a personal interest in her welfare."

That was the second time Levi had been called *sweet* today, when he couldn't remember having ever heard himself described that way before in his life. He didn't know how to accept that kind of compliment, so he just smiled awkwardly and read Natasha's number out so Marcus could jot it down.

Shortly afterward, they returned to the party, where various members of the extended Anderson clan were clearing up the remains of lunch and putting out a bountiful dessert spread that was sure to have Dominic's sweet tooth itching. Unlike the lazy summer mood of earlier, the crowd in the backyard was buzzing with a strange nervous energy that put Levi's senses on high alert.

It took him a minute to find Dominic, standing off to the side and whispering to Carlos, who was a little pale. Dominic stopped and smiled when Levi joined them. "How'd everything go?"

"Good, I think. What's—"

Carlos signaled to someone behind Levi, and seconds later, Marcus called out, "Jasmine, can you please help me in the kitchen?"

Seeming puzzled, Jasmine put down her drink and disappeared into the house. The moment the back door shut behind her, the rest of the party burst into frantic activity like a kicked anthill.

Tarps were thrown off a cluster of crates that had been stacked in one corner, and Wendy dug through them, handing out objects to the family members who rushed up to her—picture frames, Levi saw upon closer inspection. Carlos gave Dominic a fist bump and moved to stand about thirty feet from the back door, fiddling with something in his pocket. The people with frames raced to line up on either side of him in a wide V formation while the rest of the family amassed around them.

"Oh my God," Levi said. "Is he proposing?"

"Yep." Dominic grinned, kissed Levi's cheek, and strode away to collect his own frame and take position in the line to Carlos's immediate right.

Levi drew closer with everyone else. The framed pictures were all of Carlos and Jasmine, and he could tell from the changes in their appearances that they extended throughout many years, with the oldest at the front of the two lines and the most recent in the back. Standing to Carlos's left, Wendy held an empty frame with today's date engraved on it.

The music from the speakers cut off abruptly. When the back door opened, a new song started up, a quiet arrangement of strings and piano that sounded oddly familiar. It wasn't until a few bars in that Levi realized it was a version of "All I Ask of You" from *Phantom of the Opera*.

As Jasmine emerged into the backyard with Marcus, she stared in open-mouthed confusion at the spectacle before her. Her father gently encouraged her to keep moving, and she glanced from side to side while she walked, taking in the photographs. Levi saw the exact moment she understood what was happening.

Already misty-eyed, she proceeded down the aisle of pictures to where Carlos was waiting for her. He'd looked nervous earlier, but now he was beaming, watching her like she was the only person in the entire backyard.

A hush fell over those assembled, so the only sound was the song playing softly in the background. Even the dogs were quiet.

"Jasmine," Carlos said, "when we first met, I was afraid to be the person I knew I was supposed to be. You were the one who taught me how to embrace the parts of myself I'd tried to ignore, who showed me that I didn't have to hide or be ashamed of who I was. You've always been my strength, my solace, my safe place."

He choked up then and had to pause to clear his throat. Jasmine was crying silently, tears sliding down her cheeks. Levi looked at Dominic, who had a soft smile on his face.

"I learned about unconditional love from you," Carlos went on. "And when my family rejected me, yours didn't hesitate for a moment to welcome me with open arms and open hearts. That's why I wanted to do this here, in one of the few places I've ever felt truly safe and loved, surrounded by the people who have become my family too."

Wendy reached out to squeeze his shoulder from behind. He flashed her a quick smile, then lowered himself to one knee. Jasmine cupped her face with both hands.

"I love you, Jasmine." He pulled a ring box out of his pocket. "I want us to be family forever. Will you marry me?"

He opened the box. Levi couldn't see the ring well from where he stood, but Jasmine gasped aloud, her hands dropping in shock. She nodded, murmuring, "Of course," through her tears, and Carlos slipped the ring on her finger before rising to pull her into a kiss.

The crowd exploded with whoops and cheers, closing in around the happy couple in a deluge of hugs, kisses, and congratulations. Levi slipped through the exuberant mass of people until he reached Dominic.

"That was beautiful," he said, looking up at Dominic's suspiciously bright eyes. He'd found the proposal incredibly moving himself, and he didn't even know Carlos and Jasmine that well; he could only imagine how Dominic was feeling. "Did you know about it in advance?"

"I helped Carlos plan it," said Dominic.

Levi pulled him down into a kiss. They couldn't go for long because his lip still hurt, but he pressed their foreheads together for an extended moment once they'd separated and just breathed Dominic in.

Everyone at the party wanted a few minutes to speak with Carlos and Jasmine and snap some pictures, but eventually Levi and Dominic made it to the front of the line. "Mazel tov," Levi said, smiling, while Dominic hugged them both.

Jasmine threw her arms around Levi, wrapping him up in a tight embrace. He was startled but recovered quickly, returning the hug. Once she let go, he shook Carlos's hand.

"Look, isn't it gorgeous?" Jasmine said, showing them her ring, which consisted of a large solitaire diamond framed by platinum filigreed in an elaborate geometric pattern. "It was my great-grandmother's in the 1920s—perfect vintage Art Deco."

Levi glanced at Dominic and could tell he had no idea what that meant either. "It's really pretty," Dominic said.

With everyone in giddy spirits, the party revved into a higher gear after that. Marcus cued up a more energetic playlist over the speakers, and some people started dancing while others put together an impromptu flag football game. One of Jasmine's aunts broke out sparklers for the kids, who ran screaming and giggling around the backyard.

After an hour or so of that, Levi needed a break from the socialization. He excused himself and retired to a relatively quiet corner, sipping a cup of coffee and watching Dominic wrestle around in the patchy grass with Rebel and the other dogs.

"Hey," Carlos said, approaching from the side with a bottle of beer in one hand. "Mind if I sit?"

"Sure."

Carlos settled in the chair next to Levi, and they drank in companionable silence for a while.

"That was a really thoughtful surprise you put together for Jasmine," Levi said eventually.

"Thanks. She deserved it." Carlos glanced toward the main hub of the party, where Jasmine was surrounded by relatives *ooh*ing and *aah*ing over the ring, before turning back to Levi. "So, um, I need to talk to you about something, and it's a little awkward."

Levi arched an eyebrow, waiting for him to continue.

"Dominic was acting weird earlier this week. Tense and anxious, not like himself at all. At first, I thought it might have something to do with this whole serial killer thing—and yes, I know about that. Dom kind of had to clue me in when he found a bug in my smoke detector."

"You and Jasmine aren't in danger," Levi said, feeling guilty that they'd been dragged into this mess. "The Seven of Spades wouldn't harm you."

Carlos waved a hand. "It's okay. Dom broke it down for me, and I trust him to keep us safe if anything changes." He looked down to where his thumbnail was worrying the label on his bottle. "After he told me about the Seven of Spades, I wondered if that was why he'd been nervous before. But the thing is, Dom doesn't *get* nervous, at least not about normal things like serial killers and life-threatening danger. There's really only one thing in the world that puts him on edge."

He stopped there, leaving his true question unspoken. Levi drank more coffee while he stalled for time.

How much was acceptable for him to share? Carlos was clearly concerned, and he was looking for either reassurance or confirmation of his fears. It wouldn't do anyone good for Levi to brush him off.

"He hasn't been gambling," Levi said. "He just had a close call this week, and it threw him a little bit. He'll be okay."

Carlos nodded. Out in the yard, Dominic was flat on his back, laughing as he warded off the dogs' enthusiastic tongues. Levi couldn't help smiling at the sight.

"Look, Levi, you didn't really know Dominic back when he was gambling," said Carlos. "But Jasmine and I were there for the entire thing, the whole terrible downward spiral. Gambling turns Dominic into a different person. It makes him irresponsible and even more reckless than he is naturally. And he gets . . . mean."

"*Mean*?" Levi said, shaking his head in bemusement. He could barely imagine it. "I'm almost curious about what that would look like."

"Don't be," Carlos said flatly. "It's scary as fuck. I'm ashamed to admit this, but Jasmine and I weren't as close to him then as we are now, and it got so bad we almost gave up on him. If Rebel hadn't gotten sick, I don't know where Dom would be today. Maybe in jail—you know what happens to gamblers who can't stop."

Frowning, Levi asked, "Why are you telling me all this?"

"Because I think he's falling in love with you, and I want you to promise that if he does start gambling again, you *won't* give up on him. That you'll remember that the person he becomes when he gambles isn't the real him, and you'll help him find his way back no matter how difficult it gets."

Levi stared at him, speechless. Carlos gave a self-conscious shrug.

"I understand that's a lot to ask someone who's only been dating him three months. And I know you guys aren't at the point in your relationship where you're ready to make promises like that. Dominic is my best friend, though, and you—you seem like the kind of person who never gives up on anything. I just need to hear you say it."

Levi looked across the yard again. Dominic was sitting up now, scruffing Rebel's ears and kissing the tip of her nose. A sharp, tender pain lanced through Levi's core as he watched.

"I wouldn't let anyone hurt Dominic," he said to Carlos. "That includes Dominic himself. You have my word."

"Thank you." Carlos clinked his bottle against Levi's mug.

Dominic stood up, brushed the dirt off his jeans, and headed in their direction with Rebel at his heels. "Hey, guys," he said, circling around behind Levi's chair. He draped his arms over Levi's shoulders and bent to kiss the side of Levi's neck.

Back when the Seven of Spades had just been getting started, Martine and Levi had wondered how the killer had been able to get behind Phillip Dreyer to slit his throat when he'd been seated in a wide-open office. *How many people do you trust to stand behind you while you're sitting down?* Martine had asked.

Levi's response had been *Enough to count on one hand and have fingers left over*, because that list had been limited to his parents and Martine herself. He wouldn't even have felt comfortable with Stanton in that position.

Right now, he didn't feel an ounce of anxiety. He put a hand on Dominic's arm and rested his head against Dominic's stomach, warm with contentment.

"What were you guys talking about?" Dominic asked.

"Nothing important, just taking a break from all the excitement," Carlos said.

"Mmm." Dominic nuzzled Levi's neck. "It is a lot. Do you want to go home?"

"I'm fine. We don't have to leave early on my account."

"My reasons are totally selfish, trust me." Dominic nipped at Levi's ear, and his voice dropped to a lower register. "I want to take my *boyfriend* home and do nasty, unspeakable things to him."

"Dominic, for fuck's sake," Levi said, both embarrassed and a little turned on.

Carlos grinned. "Right, I'll take that as my cue to be elsewhere." He winked at Levi before returning to the party.

Dominic's attentions to Levi's neck became more aggressive, and he slid his hands over Levi's chest in a way that hinted at delicious things that lay in store. "Come on, baby. Let's go."

A full-body shudder ran through Levi at the husked endearment.

"God, I'm never going to get over how hot that is," said Dominic. He moved to the front of Levi's chair to pull him to his feet. "It's gonna take us a while to say goodbye to everyone. Let's get started before I have to drag you into the bathroom and suck your cock up against the wall."

"You say that like it's supposed to be some kind of disincentive," Levi said, and laughed as Dominic playfully shoved him back toward the crowd.

CHAPTER 17

I t was still light out when they left the Andersons', the sky just beginning to glow orange with the first strains of a summer sunset. Rebel lay between Dominic and Levi, panting and happily exhausted. Levi idly stroked her ears as he sat with his eyes closed and his head tilted back on the seat.

Dominic kept glancing sideways at him while he drove west through Henderson. He'd loved having Levi with him today, introducing him around and, frankly, showing him off. Levi was right—his brusque, reserved manner didn't appeal to everyone—but even when people didn't like Levi, they respected him. Dominic had overheard more than one admiring comment about Levi's intelligence, his dedication to his job, and of course his killer cheekbones.

Maybe it was time to invite Levi to his family lunch.

Levi's cell phone rang, startling them both. Dominic turned off the radio so Levi could answer it.

"Hello?" His brow furrowing, Levi said, "Ms. Kostas? Wait, slow down, I can't understand anything you're saying."

Dominic gave him a questioning look, and Levi put the phone on speaker.

"Sorry," said a woman's voice, sounding out of breath. "I'm freaking out. Detective, I think you arrested the wrong person for Dr. Hensley's murder."

"Why?"

"When I was at the station yesterday, I thought I saw . . . but then I wasn't *sure*, and I didn't want to say anything until I was. There have been enough false accusations thrown around already."

"Ms. Kostas—"

"I'm sure now," she said. "I remember clearly. Dr. Hensley's wife didn't kill him. She's not the person I saw that night."

Levi bolted upright. "*What?*"

"I—"

There was a loud crash on the other end of the line, the unmistakable sound of shattering glass, and Kostas yelped in surprise and fear. Dominic's hands tightened on the steering wheel.

"What is it?" Levi said urgently. "What's going on?"

"Oh my God," she said, terrified now. "How did you—no, get out! Get away from me! No! Help, *help*, somebody help me!"

Her voice grew fainter, as if she'd dropped the phone, but they could clearly hear the sounds of a violent struggle—thunderous bangs and thuds along with her piercing, panicked screams. Then the call abruptly disconnected.

Dominic and Levi stared at each other. Levi's face was bloodless.

"Where does she live?" Dominic asked.

Checking the nearest street sign, Levi said, "Just a few blocks from here."

Dominic hit the gas and followed the directions Levi gave him, breaking every traffic law on the books while he barreled through the streets of Henderson.

"Dominic, I don't have my gun," Levi said as he waited for his 911 call to go through.

"Mine's in the glove compartment."

A minute later, they peeled into the driveway of a small, charming house. Levi jumped out before the truck was even in park, holding Dominic's Glock in a two-handed grip. Dominic and Rebel followed right behind.

A quick circuit of the house revealed what had happened: a rock had been thrown through a window by the back door, allowing the intruder to reach inside and unlock it. The door was half-open, and Dominic heard nothing from inside, but he threw out an arm to bar Levi's entrance anyway.

"Wait," he said. "Rebel, *danger.*"

She'd already picked up on that, her body language stiff and wary, but at his command, she crouched down lower and slunk inside the house. Her ears flicked back and forth, and then she looked up at Dominic before trotting further inside.

If she'd sensed an immediate threat, she would have barked. Dominic jerked his head, indicating for Levi to precede him.

They followed Rebel through the kitchen and into the living room, where a tall, dark-haired woman lay unconscious amidst the wreckage of tossed furniture, smashed lamps, and scattered dirt and ceramic shards from a potted plant. Her throat was swollen and red.

While Levi cleared the room, Dominic dropped to his knees beside her, heedless of the sharp debris slicing into his jeans. He lay two fingers along her wrist and bent his ear near her face.

"She's got a pulse, but she's not breathing," he said. He tilted her head back, then lifted her chin forward to open her airway. "Someone strangled her and didn't see it all the way through."

Rebel gave one short, sharp bark and darted down a hallway that led to the side of the house. Levi ran after her.

"What—" Dominic started.

"She has a son!" Levi called over his shoulder as he disappeared around the corner.

Shit. Dominic stayed focused on Kostas, pinching her nostrils shut and giving her two slow rescue breaths, making sure her chest rose like it should. He checked her pulse again.

It had stopped.

"Goddammit!" He rose up on his knees, placed his hands in the center of her chest, and pushed straight down with his upper body weight, counting out the chest compressions in his head. It had been a long time since he'd last performed CPR, but he remembered the basics.

Halfway through his count, he heard an ominous crack as one of her ribs broke under the force. He cringed and snatched his hands away.

Kostas lay still, her face white and her lips turning purple. A few feet away was a picture frame that looked like it had been stomped on; underneath the spiderwebbing glass, Kostas was holding a cute toddler and beaming at the camera.

"Okay, come on," Dominic said grimly, getting back to it. "Come on, girl, I know you're not ready to go yet."

He was administering rescue breaths again when Levi hurried back through the living room with a small, curly-haired boy on one hip. The boy was bawling at the top of his lungs, and Levi had one hand cupped over his eyes to shield him from the sight of his mother on the floor. Levi carried him out the front door, Rebel following close behind.

Dominic performed another round of chest compressions, and another creak sounded from Kostas's rib cage. He gritted his teeth and kept going. He didn't believe in God, not the way Levi did, but he found himself praying anyway. She was too young to die this way. It wasn't fair—

She coughed, then drew a weak, gasping breath. Dominic grabbed her wrist; her pulse was thready but continued on as her shallow breathing evened out.

"Oh fuck," he said, almost toppling over as he was flooded with bone-deep relief.

Paramedics burst into the house then. He scrambled to his feet, gave them a brief rundown, and stayed out of their way while they worked. Levi and Rebel rejoined him a minute later.

"Mason's with one of the local cops," Levi said. He watched with a worried expression as Kostas was loaded onto a stretcher. "She's alive?"

"Yeah," Dominic said. "But there's no telling how long she went without oxygen. There could be permanent damage. And . . . and . . ." Hysteria bubbled up in his chest. "Levi, I broke her ribs, I heard them crack—"

"Hey." Levi pressed his hands to either side of Dominic's face. "Ribs can be fixed. Death can't. I can tell you right now that she'd rather be alive with every bone in her body broken than dead."

Dominic nodded and took a shuddery breath. The paramedics wheeled Kostas out the front door, leaving him, Levi, and Rebel alone in the destroyed living room.

"Before she was attacked, she said she knew who killed your guy," he said.

His gray eyes clear and cold, Levi said, "So do I."

Levi didn't have to wait long in the parking lot outside the emergency department of St. Rose Dominican. Even at dawn on a Sunday, the lot was far from empty, but fortunately there were no people walking around.

Except one. Levi watched his quarry hurry down the line of parked cars, shrugging into a white doctor's coat. Slipping out from behind the concealment of an SUV, Levi said, "Come to finish the job?"

Craig Warner whirled around.

"D-detective," he stammered, his eyes huge behind his glasses. "What are you—I mean, hi. I'm just, uh, here on a hospice consult for a colleague I met at the conference."

"Actually, I'm pretty sure you came here to take a second whack at killing Diana Kostas," said Levi.

Warner shook his head frantically, his mouth working open and shut.

"After all, I went to a lot of trouble to have the news of her attack, survival, and hospitalization here splashed all over every news media outlet in the Las Vegas Valley over the past ten hours. Couldn't have you skipping town, and we had no other reliable way to track you down since you checked out of your hotel." Levi smiled. "Of course, Ms. Kostas isn't actually at this hospital."

Warner's jaw dropped. He jumped about a foot in the air when Martine emerged from a nearby car, gun at the ready. Other doors slammed around the parking lot as uniformed officers hopped out of unmarked cars and moved to establish a perimeter and keep any civilians at bay.

Warner's eyes darted around in a panic, and then he plunged his hand into the jacket beneath the doctor's coat, withdrawing a small gun of his own that he aimed shakily at Levi.

"Seriously, Warner?" Levi said, taking a few steps closer. "Poison, stabbing, strangulation, and now a gun—what, are you going for murder bingo?"

"I haven't killed anyone," Warner said.

Martine snorted. "Yeah, waving a gun at a cop gives that a lot of credibility."

Tilting his head to the side, Levi studied Warner's nervous, twitchy body language. He didn't think Warner would shoot him head-on like this—the man seemed to favor taking his victims by surprise—but he couldn't be sure of that. He continued advancing slowly while he spoke.

"I didn't put it together until Ms. Kostas called me last night. See, the only reason we suspected Dr. Northridge to begin with was because you told me you'd seen her on Monday. Then it turned out that she had been in the city all along, so that checked out. But when she told me her story . . . she was smart, and she'd been very careful. If she'd killed Hensley, there's no way she would have let you catch so much as a glimpse of her. So how'd you know she'd been here? My guess is Alan Walsh told you, and you 'accidentally' let it slip to me to cast suspicion on her."

Warner's face had been steadily draining of color and was now a sickly gray. He licked his lips but said nothing.

"Should I keep going?" Levi asked. He took Warner's stony silence as a *yes*. "On the posterboard at your presentation on Friday, you were named in the research—but I saw the original program for the conference, and you weren't named on the paper then, nor were you scheduled to speak at all. In fact, your name is missing from a lot of the background reading I did for this case. Because that was Hensley's game, wasn't it? He cut you out of research you'd been a part of, took credit for your work, verbally abused you, and generally made your life miserable at every turn. So you decided enough was enough."

"No," Warner whispered.

"You knew Hensley would hire an escort his first night in Vegas, and you must have read about trick rollers somewhere. It seemed like the perfect plan. Your room wasn't far down the hall from his, so all you had to do was keep an eye on the people coming and going and wait for his escort to leave. Once she had, you hurried to his room, convinced him to drink with you, and made sure he got a lethal dose of Rohypnol in his champagne. Then you stole his valuables as the finishing touch."

Warner closed his eyes briefly.

Levi had almost closed the distance between them. "Problem is, Alan Walsh saw you sneaking those valuables out the service exit at the Mirage the next morning. He photographed you, realized later what he had proof of, and blackmailed you. So you had to kill him too."

"You can't prove any of this," Warner said, his nostrils flaring.

"I can prove all of it." Levi counted the points off on his fingers. "First of all, the people you were with all vouched for the fact that you were falling-down drunk that night. Even your girlfriend agreed. And there's no way a guy that wasted could pull this plan off. Which is why you paid the bartender to give you non-alcoholic drinks all night and *pretended* to get drunk. She's a temp, so she was a little hard to track down, but she was happy to tell us all about it once she found out you strangled an innocent woman."

"That's crazy. She's—she's lying—"

"Then there's the steak dinner you ordered from room service Tuesday night—the night Walsh was killed with a steak knife in a design made exclusively for the Mirage."

Warner opened his mouth, but Levi held up a hand.

"I'll admit—circumstantial at best," he said. "What's less circumstantial are the multiple calls on your cell phone records from burner numbers Dr. Northridge has confirmed belonged to Walsh. Plus, you're a doctor. I'm sure you're aware that DNA can be obtained from vomit, especially when the dumbass who left it at a crime scene didn't clean it up thoroughly."

Warner blanched.

Moving in for the kill, Levi said, "The photographs I mentioned earlier, the ones of you leaving the Mirage with Hensley's belongings? That wasn't guesswork on my part. I've seen them with my own eyes, because a couple of hours ago, our tech analyst was able to break through the encryption on a backup hard drive Walsh had hidden in his bedroom."

"No, you—you've got it all wrong. I can explain—"

"Most damning of all," Levi said, talking right over him, "is that when Diana Kostas recovers—which she will—she'll name you not only as her attacker last night but as the person she saw going into Dr. Hensley's room the night he was murdered. That's why she called me; it's why you tried to kill her. You were in such a rush to kill Hensley that you didn't give her enough time to leave the hotel. The two of you were in the hallway at the same time and she *saw* you. She just didn't realize what she'd seen or how you were connected to him until she saw you again at the substation on Friday."

Quiet fell over the parking lot as it was bathed in pink light from the sun cresting the mountains to the east. The three of them stood in a motionless tableau—Martine with her gun trained unwaveringly on

Warner, and Warner pointing his gun more shakily at Levi, who was barely more than a foot away from him now. The uniforms hung back at the perimeter, guns drawn but making no other move to interfere.

"She was in the elevator," Warner said, his voice cracking, and Levi had to swallow hard to suppress a triumphant shout. "The doors hadn't closed yet, and she saw me knocking. She was too far away to know which room I was at, though, and she had no idea who I was. It shouldn't have been a problem."

"Getting away with murder isn't as easy as you expected, huh?" Levi said.

"I didn't want to hurt her or Walsh! Nobody was supposed to die except Hensley." He looked pleadingly at Levi. "He deserved it, you know he did. He ruined *lives*. I did everyone a favor."

"Yeah, you should get an award for your humanitarianism," Martine said in disgust. "Put your gun on the ground and get on your knees with your hands behind your head."

Warner clenched his jaw, panicked determination sparking in his eyes. Holding his gun inches from Levi's chest, he said, "I don't think so. Put down *your* gun or your partner gets hurt."

Martine chuckled. "Oh, you poor bastard. He's not the one who's gonna get hurt."

Levi leaned to the side as his arms shot up, his left hand grabbing the muzzle of the gun and his right wrapping around the butt. He kicked Warner viciously in the balls while whipping the gun out of his grip, then backed up a few steps to disengage. He aimed the gun at Warner himself, though he needn't have bothered—Warner was doubled over and groaning in agony.

"How's that, Ms. Rashid?" he called out.

Leila Rashid sauntered out from behind another parked car, put her hands on her hips, and surveyed Warner, who blinked up at her with eyes dazed from pain and shock. "Not bad. I do love a good solid confession. Makes my job a lot easier."

"Dr. Warner, meet Leila Rashid, the deputy district attorney who'll be prosecuting your case. Or cutting you a plea deal, which you might prefer now."

"What?" Warner tried to straighten up, winced, and said, "No! You saw what he did, he—he coerced me, entrapped me—"

"He coerced you into a confession while you were holding a gun on *him*?" Her voice was cool with disdain. "Good luck selling that one."

Keeping said gun trained on Warner, Levi nodded to Martine, who holstered her own weapon and moved forward to place him under arrest. Levi didn't relax until she carted him away to one of the unmarked squad cars.

"I need to bag this," he said to Rashid, as he ejected the gun's magazine and emptied the bullet out of the chamber.

She accompanied him to his car, which hadn't been his intention, but he didn't see how he could stop her. He retrieved an evidence tag and bag from the supply in his trunk and started filling them out.

"Yours must be the shortest suspension in the history of the LVMPD," she said, leaning one hip against the trunk.

"Wen wasn't happy about it, but he didn't have much of a choice after Diana Kostas chose to call me. Plus, Martine argued on my behalf. We needed all hands on deck to make this case airtight and set up the trap." He dropped the tagged gun into the bag and sealed it shut. "Don't worry, though—everyone still knows why I was suspended in the first place. I'm still the obsessed freak nobody believes."

Rashid shrugged. "I believe you."

He fumbled the bag, just managing to catch it before it hit the ground. "You what?"

"There's no way Keith Chapman was the Seven of Spades," she said calmly, as if she were discussing what she'd had for dinner the night before. "The real killer set him up and is still at large. I've always believed that."

It took him a few seconds to process his shock, and then anger set in. "If that's true, then why give me such a hard time about it? Why haven't you ever spoken up yourself?"

"There are more people who believe you than you might think. We're just not all bent on committing career suicide."

"Defending your beliefs is more important than a job," he snapped.

"Is that why you tried so hard to hide your little side investigation?" she said with a smile. Before he could respond, she added, "Besides, ultimately it won't matter that I kept quiet, because you'll be vindicated sooner rather than later. A killer as theatrical and desperate for attention as the Seven of Spades can't hold out much longer. That craving for recognition must be unbearable by now, even if they've been killing people in other ways this whole time. They'll reappear at some point, and everyone will know you were right."

"You realize that will mean that someone else has been killed," he said, staring at her.

She wrinkled her nose. "Rapists and wife-beaters and corrupt public officials? What a shame."

"I guess that's one way of looking at it," he muttered.

Pushing herself off his car, she said, "Just give it time. Meanwhile, when it comes to Warner, make sure you have every *I* dotted and every *T* crossed. No shortcuts and no mistakes. Between the evidence you've collected and a confession made in front of two detectives and a DDA, any competent defense lawyer will advise him to take the plea I'll offer. We can all spare the taxpayers the expense of a trial."

He nodded. "I'll leave it in your hands, Ms. Rashid."

"Call me Leila," she said, flipping her long black hair over one shoulder. She turned and walked away with the easy, graceful athleticism he'd noticed the first time they met.

Once she was gone, he stored Warner's gun in the trunk, then gave himself a moment to appreciate the fact that the case had been wrapped up with little chance of the killer escaping justice.

Time was, a successful solve had been cause for celebration, not to mention a great sense of accomplishment. Since the Seven of Spades had burst onto the scene, however, Levi's other cases had dimmed in importance. He still gave them everything he had, but it didn't feel the same anymore.

Until he caught the Seven of Spades, every other victory would ring hollow.

CHAPTER 18

Monday morning, Levi found himself strolling along the Andersons' property line despite the blazing summer sun overhead. Adriana had wanted to go for a walk, and he hadn't had the heart to say no.

"I know it's been less than a full day, but how has everything been so far?" he asked.

"Pretty good." Adriana walked beside him with her hands stuffed into the pockets of a new pair of jeans. "The Andersons are nice."

"What about Josh and Rima?"

"They're okay."

Despite what sounded like faint praise, Levi could see the changes in her already. She still had a hunted air about her—she probably would for a long time—but she looked more relaxed, less likely to bolt at the drop of a hat. When he'd arrived at the house, she'd been talking and laughing with her new foster siblings in the kitchen, and she hadn't flinched when Rima had touched her arm.

He nodded toward a group of horses that were quite sensibly hanging out in the shade. "Have you been around horses before?"

"No. The Andersons said I could earn extra money helping out with the farm, though, and Wendy's going to teach me how to ride." She shrugged nonchalantly and kicked a clod of dirt. "That'll be kind of cool, I guess."

Levi hid a smile.

They arrived at the corner of the property, and Adriana hopped up to sit on the wooden fence. Levi leaned against it, his suit jacket draped over one arm.

It was so hot that the air was hazy, the dust an inch thick on the parched earth. Good thing he'd thought to stash an extra shirt in his car; this one would soon be soaked through with sweat.

"I'm glad you caught the guy who killed that doctor," Adriana said. "He's not gonna get away with it, is he?"

"Definitely not. The DA's office is offering to avoid seeking the death penalty if he agrees to life in prison without parole."

Levi thought that was a ballsy move on Rashid's part. Though Nevada technically had dozens of men sitting on death row, the state hadn't executed anyone since 2006. He knew for a fact that the government's stockpiles of one of the drugs used for the lethal injection was about to expire, too, and pharmaceutical companies weren't exactly jumping at the chance to participate in executions these days.

But Rashid knew as well as Levi did that Warner was a coward at heart. He'd take the deal.

"Confirming that the bag you found was the same one in those photographs was a big help," Levi added. "Thank you."

She smiled and swung her legs back and forth as she sat atop the fence. He could tell there was more she wanted to say, so he gazed out across the horse pasture while he waited.

"Did your boyfriend hit you?" she asked abruptly.

Startled, he raised a hand to his lip. The healing cut and lingering bruise still looked bad, but it barely hurt anymore so he tended to forget about it.

"No," he said. "I was searching a suspect's apartment and her boyfriend came home and attacked me."

She didn't apologize for suspecting Dominic, and he didn't scold her for it. "Did you win the fight?"

"Yes."

She looked him up and down, then nodded. "I asked Natasha about you. She said you study some kind of Israeli martial arts and that a few months ago you took down three guys in like twenty seconds."

"It's called Krav Maga," he said, hoping Natasha hadn't hyped him up *too* much. "It was created for the Israel Defense Forces in the 1940s. I train under the IKMF—the International Krav Maga Federation."

"Are you a black belt or something?"

A smile tugged at his lips. "Uh, no. Krav doesn't use belts. There's fifteen levels—five Practitioner, five Graduate, and five Expert. I'm an E1."

She was silent for a minute while she absorbed this. Then she said, "You told me you'd teach me how to defend myself. Did you mean it?"

"I did. If you're still interested."

"I am," she said, but she hesitated, chewing on her lower lip. "It's just . . . do you think people will think it's weird, you spending time with me? Like maybe it's inappropriate?"

He shrugged one shoulder. "Would people think that, knowing I'm gay?"

"*Are* you?"

"You know I have a boyfriend."

"That doesn't mean you're gay," she said archly.

That surprised a laugh out of him, and he said, "You're absolutely right; I stand corrected. But I am gay, no doubt about it. I've only ever kissed one girl in my entire life—Jessica Stein, at my bar mitzvah. I think she only did it out of pity though, because later that night I caught her making out with Danny Chen."

"Ouch."

"Honestly, it was a relief. They ended up dating for a few years too." He straightened up. "We'll just be straightforward with the Andersons and your caseworker about what we're doing and why. I doubt anyone will have a problem with it."

"Okay," she said, grinning. "Thanks."

"You're welcome. Now let's head back. I have to be in court in a couple of hours."

Adriana jumped off the fence, and they started toward the house. Halfway there, she said, "You didn't have to help me. You don't have to help me now. What are you getting out of this?"

It was a fair question, so Levi gave it thought before he answered. "It makes me angry to see people get hurt, especially by someone they should have been able to trust. The best way to deal with that anger is to address the problem head-on."

She scuffed her sneaker along the ground, sending up a cloud of dust and dirt. "Huh."

"What?"

"Nothing. It's a good reason, maybe the best reason. It's a little weird though, because if you think about it, isn't that kind of the same reason that serial killer slit all those people's throats?"

Levi didn't have a response for that.

Dominic knocked on the half-open door to Room 227 and peered around it before entering. The woman in the first hospital bed was asleep; he walked quietly past her to where a drawn curtain separated off the room's second occupant.

Diana Kostas was flipping through a magazine, the head of her bed raised at a gentle incline. Her throat was mottled with vicious dark bruises, but she was breathing unassisted. The only equipment hooked up to her was an IV line.

He cleared his throat and said, "Excuse me, Ms. Kostas?"

She glanced up and sucked in a breath, her fingers tightening around the edges of her magazine—not an unexpected reaction to a man his size in a woman who'd just been brutally assaulted. But her anxiety quickly turned to confusion as her eyes fell on the enormous bouquet of dahlias and yellow roses he held in one arm.

"I'm Dominic Russo. Detective Abrams's boyfriend?"

Her eyes went wide. "Oh my God," she said, her voice so hoarse and ragged it was painful to hear. "You're the one who saved me." She struggled to sit up, then gasped and grabbed the side of her rib cage.

"Um, yeah, I—wait, let me help you." He set the flowers on the side table and moved to the bed, using the controls to lift the top half so she could keep her body still.

"Thanks," she said, still holding her ribs. "Sometimes I forget they're broken."

"I'm the one who broke them," he said quietly. "I'm so sorry."

She gave him an incredulous look. "Please. You saved my life. If you hadn't given me CPR, I'd be dead. My son would have lost his mother. A couple of cracked ribs is a small price to pay."

By the time she finished talking, she was panting for air and her voice was barely audible. It must have been agonizing for her to speak.

Hovering over her with his bulk while she was injured and immobile felt rude, so Dominic backed away. He spied a cup of water with a straw sitting next to the flowers he'd brought, and handed it over to her before settling into the visitor's chair. She thanked him with a nod and sipped slowly.

"I just wanted to make sure you were okay," he said.

She gave him a thumbs-up as she drank. He smiled.

There was another knock on the door, and Levi rounded the curtain a couple of seconds later. He and Dominic had arranged to meet here, so he showed no surprise when he saw them sitting together.

"How are you feeling, Ms. Kostas?" he asked.

"I'm okay," she whispered.

"Glad to hear it. You should know that Dr. Warner is in police custody now, and it looks like he'll be taking a plea deal. If he does, you won't have to testify against him in a public trial."

Profound relief flashed across her face. Dominic couldn't blame her—he and Levi were about to do exactly that, and neither one of them was looking forward to it.

"Where's your son?" Levi asked.

"Staying with a cousin of mine. Someone I can be pretty sure wouldn't stand by while I was framed for murder." Her snort turned into a cough, and she took another sip of water. "I should be out of here in a day or so."

That brought them to the other reason for Dominic's visit. Leaning forward in his chair, he said, "The police taped over the broken window Warner used to get inside your house, but it's still a vulnerable point. If you're okay with it, I'd like to replace it with reinforced glass, so this kind of thing is less likely to happen again in the future."

She blinked at him, obviously taken aback. Levi stood silently at the foot of the bed.

"You don't have to do that," she said.

"I know, and I won't if it would make you uncomfortable. You're going to be laid up for a couple of weeks with those ribs, though, and you won't be able to do it yourself. A professional company will charge you an arm and a leg. It wouldn't be any trouble for me."

Her hand fluttered over her rib cage, and then she smiled and nodded. "Okay. If you're sure, I'd really appreciate that. My cousin brought me my house keys; they're in that cabinet there."

Dominic retrieved the keys and put them in his pocket. "I'll get these back to you tomorrow once it's finished."

"Thank you," she said. "Both of you."

Levi inclined his head solemnly, Dominic wished her a speedy recovery, and they left her alone to rest. Out in the bustling hallway, Levi said, "Will fixing her window make you feel better about cracking her ribs?"

"It'll do for a start." Dominic could see that Levi thought he was being ridiculous—but Levi also wasn't going to argue with him about it, which he appreciated. "Besides, you can't expect me to believe that *you'd* be okay with her and her son going back to a house with a busted window right next to their back door."

"It's a stupid fucking place for a window," said Levi. "If you want my opinion, she should just brick the whole thing over. Now let's go get this bullshit trial over with so I can go home and get drunk."

"What a sweet-talker," Dominic said, grinning, and followed him to the stairs.

CHAPTER 19

Drew Barton may have been a sniveling, wife-killing little weasel, but unlike Craig Warner, he was willing to take risks. He'd rejected the plea deal offered by the DA's office and had entered pleas of "not guilty" for both his wife's murder and his armed assault on Levi.

It was a tough sell, but Barton had a good lawyer—George Durham, a partner at the same firm to which Jay Sawyer belonged. Levi soon learned that Durham's defense strategy was to propose that the LVMPD had unfairly accused Barton after the Seven of Spades killed his wife, then followed, harassed, and intimidated him until he'd tried to talk things out with Levi at his hotel, at which point Levi had attacked *him*.

Melinda Wu, the DDA prosecuting the case, called Martine to the stand first. Martine detailed the investigation of Patty Barton's murder in layman's terms the jury could easily digest, ending with her account of how she'd called Levi to warn him after she'd learned that Drew Barton had slipped away from the uniformed officers keeping an eye on him. Durham's cross-examination was short and polite, and Martine stepped down looking a little confused—Durham was usually a bulldog on the cross.

Levi was next up. He'd testified in countless trials in the past, of course, and he and Wu had already rehearsed what he would say. He kept his voice cool and dispassionate as she led him through his explanation of his own role in the investigation, including his interrogation of Barton and how they'd obtained the evidence that had granted them an arrest warrant.

It was more difficult to remain detached when they reached the part of the story where Levi had emerged from the bathroom of his hotel room to be confronted and threatened at gunpoint. Barton had tried to make his wife's murder look like the Seven of Spades's work, and when Levi had seen right through that, his last-gasp desperate plan had been to do the same thing to Levi. He might even have succeeded if the electricity in the hotel hadn't gone out at an opportune moment, allowing Levi to evade him for a few critical seconds. They'd tussled for the gun until Dominic had arrived on the scene and taken Barton down.

When she was finished, Wu stepped back and gave Levi a smile and a small nod. He knew better than to let his guard down, though, because Durham was already rising from his seat.

This wasn't the first time Levi had been cross-examined by Durham, an older white man with a thick head of salt-and-pepper hair and sharp, assessing blue eyes. Still, he didn't know what to expect.

"Detective Abrams," Durham said pleasantly, "could I ask how you sustained that injury to your mouth?"

"I was involved in a physical altercation with a suspect last week," Levi said warily. He wasn't sure where this was going, but he was sure he didn't like it.

"Would this suspect be Kyle Gilmore?"

"Yes . . ."

"The same Kyle Gilmore who was treated the following day for a broken nose, two lost teeth, multiple lacerations to the arms and hands, and testicular contusion?"

Sitting the row behind Wu, Dominic winced. The men in the jury shifted uncomfortably in their seats.

Levi clasped his hands together in his lap where nobody could see the evidence of his tension. "Mr. Gilmore assaulted me with a knife while I was performing a legal, warranted search of his apartment. I disarmed him and used non-lethal force to subdue him. Given that he was extremely intoxicated at the time, it required more force that might have been otherwise necessary."

"Mmm." Durham walked back and forth in front of the witness stand with slow, confident steps. "What about the 'physical altercation' you were involved in on April twelfth of this year?"

Levi couldn't place the date right away, but when Dominic stiffened, he knew.

"I'm referring, of course, to the three men you beat so badly they were all admitted to the hospital with head injuries," said Durham.

Wu stood up. "Objection, Your Honor. Relevance?"

Judge Sanchez raised an inquiring eyebrow at Durham.

"Speaks to Detective Abrams's temperament and behavioral patterns," he said, unfazed. "It's vital to my defense."

Sanchez weighed this for a moment, then nodded. "Proceed, counselor. *Circumspectly*."

Wu sank back into her seat, shooting Levi an apologetic look.

"You're presenting the situation out of context," Levi said, struggling to retain his composure. "I had caught those men in the middle of an active burglary. I was outnumbered, they were all armed, and I couldn't reach my own weapon. My partner had been critically injured. The only way for me to survive was to render those men unconscious, and yes, that unfortunately meant they sustained *minor* head injuries. They were all fine within a couple of days. No lasting damage whatsoever."

Durham stopped right in front of him. "Indeed. Can the same be said for Dale Slater?"

Levi's body went cold. Out in the courtroom, Dominic rose halfway out of his seat before Martine pulled him back down.

"For those who aren't aware," Durham said, turning to the jury, "Dale Slater is the man that Detective Abrams shot dead on March seventeenth."

"That was a hostage situation!" Levi said, over the low murmur running through the audience. He was dangerously close to losing his temper, but he couldn't just keep his mouth shut. "He was using a little boy as a human shield, I had no choice but to shoot him—"

Wu spread her hands wide. "Your Honor—"

"Mr. Durham, either make your point quickly or abandon this line of questioning," said Sanchez.

"Of course, Your Honor." Durham smoothed out his jacket. "Detective, Dale Slater's death was ruled justifiable homicide due to the circumstances. However, you were mandated to receive six sessions of counseling after that incident, correct?"

"That's required of any officer who uses lethal force in the line of duty," Levi said stiffly.

"As it should be. But you're no stranger to the use of force, are you, Detective? On or off duty."

Levi narrowed his eyes.

"You're a highly trained, accomplished practitioner of Krav Maga, the fighting system used by the Israeli armed forces," Durham said.

"Yes, I am." Levi risked a glance at the jury, where he saw several intrigued expressions.

"And during this alleged assault where you claim my client attacked you, you kicked him with so much concentrated force that you shattered his right kneecap. His leg hasn't been the same since. You, on the other hand, walked away from this confrontation completely unscathed."

More whispers rippled through the courtroom. Dominic and Martine were both watching Levi with concern, waiting for the inevitable moment when he would snap. They knew he didn't handle provocation well.

But he *had* to. Durham was painting a picture of him as aggressive and unstable, trying to destroy his credibility and the case along with it. The only way for Levi to counteract that was to present a calm, composed front.

"Mr. Barton broke into my hotel room while I was in the shower," he said, each word measured and deliberate. "He lay in wait and then ambushed me, threatening me at gunpoint. He told me he was going to tie me to a chair and kill me."

Despite his best intentions, Levi's breath quickened as he remembered that night—the horror of what should have been a safe space being invaded, the fear of facing a gun at a distance too far to disarm, the knowledge that Barton was desperate and couldn't be reasoned with. He had never given up, but he had known there was a good chance he would die. Just like Patty Barton, who'd been stabbed half a dozen times in her living room by her own husband.

"Barton killed his wife and then came after me. He made his intentions very clear." Levi glowered at Barton, who smirked back at him from the defendant's seat. "Considering everything he'd done, he's lucky that his knee is the only thing I broke."

Durham smiled. Wu leaned back in her seat, rubbing her temples, and Martine looked at Levi with pure exasperation. Dominic just seemed like he was trying not to laugh.

Levi pressed his lips together and strove to shove the anger back down.

"I suppose he is," Durham said. "Let's talk about luck, since you brought it up. We haven't heard Dominic Russo's testimony yet, but earlier you alluded to the part he played in all this. You said that he was alerted to your alleged predicament by text messages from someone claiming to be the serial killer known as the Seven of Spades."

"That's correct."

"And by the Seven of Spades, of course, you mean Keith Chapman."

Levi's breath stilled in his lungs. His eyes darted toward Dominic, who no longer looked the slightest bit amused.

Even if Levi was willing to lie about this, he couldn't. Durham's self-satisfied expression made it clear that he knew exactly what he was doing. It would be easy to catch Levi in a lie—all he had to do was bring up the reason behind Levi's recent suspension. If Levi perjured himself, his testimony could be thrown out altogether.

"No," he said. "I don't."

"No?" Durham raised his eyebrows in exaggerated confusion. "You'll have to forgive me, Detective Abrams. It's my understanding that the LVMPD closed the Seven of Spades case with all five murders attributed to the deceased Officer Chapman."

Levi's stomach rolled. He felt like he was poised on the edge of a cliff, and any step he took, any decision he made, would result in a total free-fall. There was no good choice here.

He looked at Dominic one more time—steady, rock-solid Dominic, who had never doubted him for a second and didn't doubt him now. Dominic gave him an encouraging nod.

"Keith Chapman wasn't the Seven of Spades," Levi said.

The courtroom exploded with noise. Sanchez banged her gavel several times, calling for order, while Durham happily waited out the chaos he'd created.

"Can you explain what you mean by that, Detective?" he asked once the furor had died down.

Levi was in it now, so he might as well commit. "Keith Chapman was framed by the real Seven of Spades. He'd been poisoned and manipulated into believing he might be the killer, but he wasn't. The true killer is still at large."

This time, the crowd's shocked reaction took even longer to get under control. Levi sat still, his fingernails digging into his palms, glaring directly into Durham's eyes the entire time.

Durham wasn't so easily intimidated. "That seems like an enormous secret for the LVMPD to keep from the public. But then, that's not the LVMPD's official stance, is it? It's just your own. In fact, you were suspended this past Friday when your sergeant discovered you'd been conducting your own independent side investigation into the Seven of Spades against his direct orders."

"That suspension was lifted less than forty-eight hours later—"

"You've been claiming the Seven of Spades is still alive for months, with no evidence to show for it," Durham said. He moved closer and closer to Levi as he spoke. "Last week, you insisted that the Seven of Spades *helped you with a case*. But nobody believes you—not your own sergeant, not your fellow homicide detectives—"

"Objection!" Wu snapped. "This is all hearsay."

"Sustained," said Sanchez.

Durham nodded and placed his hands on the edge of the witness stand. "My apologies, Detective. I can see that you're angry. So angry, indeed, that you're shaking."

Levi clenched his jaw.

"But I don't think that's unusual for you." Durham's eyes bored into Levi's. "You're angry and violent and unpredictable, and you're obsessed with a dead serial killer to the point of self-delusion. Who knows what a man like that is capable of?" Pushing off the stand, he said, "No further questions, Your Honor."

"You may step down, Detective," Sanchez said. There was a note of sympathy in her voice.

Still reeling with shock, Levi stood, buttoned his jacket, and left the stand to join Dominic and Martine while everyone in the room openly stared at him. Dominic rubbed a hand over his back.

Wu rifled through her papers, scribbling notes and conferring with her co-counsel for a few minutes. Then she said, "The prosecution calls Dominic Russo."

Levi had to get up again to let Dominic out of their row, because there was no way Dominic could squeeze past him. When he sat back down, Martine linked her arm through his and patted his hand.

In direct contrast to Levi, Dominic was an attorney's dream witness—charming but never smarmy, playfully self-deprecating without crossing the line into false humility. His roguish good looks didn't hurt either.

Wu started by establishing his credibility as a witness, discussing his two terms of decorated service with the Army Rangers, his honorable discharge, and his years spent as a bounty hunter getting fugitives off the street. Within five minutes, Dominic had the entire jury regarding him with hero-worship, dazed lust, or both.

Once she had the jury where she wanted them, Wu led Dominic through his account of the night in question. He'd been driving home when he'd received text messages from an unknown number. The sender had claimed to be the Seven of Spades, warned him that Levi was in immediate danger, and asked for his help. Dominic had driven straight to Levi's hotel, where he'd convinced a hotel employee to bring him to Levi's room and unlock the door. After hearing a gunshot and the sounds of a struggle inside, he had broken through the door and tackled Barton, subduing him with a chokehold until he'd surrendered.

By the time she finished her questioning, Wu looked pleased again. It *was* a great story—and most importantly, it reinforced Dominic's trustworthiness and dependability, clinching the jury's clearly high opinion of him.

Durham began his cross-examination by saying, "Mr. Russo, you stated that you had a hotel employee with you to unlock the hotel door, so why did you need to break through it?"

"The security chain was fastened."

"And you . . . broke it?" Durham said with an expression of polite disbelief.

"Well, I had to throw my weight against the door a few times, but yeah, it snapped eventually." Dominic casually crossed his massive arms over his chest as he spoke. In his suit, the effect wasn't the same as it would have been with bare arms, but it got his point across. One of the women in the jury was practically drooling.

"I see," Durham said, momentarily flustered for the first time all afternoon. "Ah . . . so when you entered the room, you saw Detective Abrams and Mr. Barton fighting, believed Detective Abrams was in danger, and came to his aid by attacking Mr. Barton yourself."

Dominic gave him an easy smile. "Nah. If I'd wanted to attack him, I would have just knocked him out, you know? Truth is, I had no idea *what* was happening, so I was trying to separate them. A chokehold seemed like the easiest way to do that."

Durham stared at him for a few seconds. "Mr. Barton has stated that once you had him in the chokehold, you threatened his life."

"No, definitely not. Although he was panicking at the time, so I can see how he might have misunderstood me." Shifting so he was addressing the jury as well, Dominic said, "A strong choke can easily cause injury, even if you don't mean it to. Barton was thrashing and flailing around so much, I was worried I might hurt him by accident. I warned him to stop moving so that wouldn't happen."

Several members of the starry-eyed jury nodded along with his explanation. Durham frowned, then glanced briefly at Levi and back at Dominic, his brow furrowing deeper.

Levi suddenly realized Durham's predicament. He must have intended to present an image of Levi and Dominic as partners-in-crime, an aggressive, intimidating duo who had attacked Barton and cooked up this story to cover their asses. No doubt he had assumed Dominic's size and military history would make that easy, but he hadn't expected Dominic's mellow personality.

Now it was too late. The jury was firmly on Dominic's side, and a few jabs wouldn't change that. If he pushed too hard, they'd turn on *him* instead.

"Mr. Russo, let's return to the beginning of the story, if you don't mind," he said. "When you received the texts warning you that Detective Abrams was in danger, you didn't doubt they were genuine?"

"Actually, I was split fifty-fifty. I wasn't convinced that the danger was real or that the texts had come from the actual Seven of Spades."

"Yet you went straight to the hotel anyway? You didn't even call 911?"

"The texter said they'd already called," Dominic said with a shrug. "I figured that if the texts turned out to be fake, the worst that would happen is I'd be the butt of someone's practical joke. No big deal. But if the danger was real and I ignored it? Detective Abrams could die. I couldn't take that risk."

Durham returned to the defendant's table to sip from a bottle of water. Levi felt spiteful glee at the frustration on his face—everything he did was just making Dominic look *better*.

Durham put the bottle down, turned back, and said, "You and Detective Abrams are involved in a sexual relationship, isn't that right?"

There were a few scattered murmurs of surprise. Dominic smiled at Levi.

"We're in a committed romantic relationship," he said. "Sex is part of that, sure." He winked at the jury, and Levi could swear that one of the older women straight-up swooned like a Victorian maiden.

"Oh my God," Martine said under her breath. She pressed her face against Levi's shoulder to stifle a laugh.

"Ah, well." Durham cleared his throat. "Were the two of you involved, romantically or sexually, the night of the events in question?"

"Not yet."

"But you had feelings for Detective Abrams then."

"I liked him," Dominic said, meeting Levi's gaze across the courtroom. "I respected him. I'd spent the previous week getting to know him better, and I'd learned what a good heart he has, and how dedicated he is to protecting the people of this city. So yeah, you could say I had feelings for him then."

Durham looked like he was fantasizing Dominic's ugly and painful demise, but he kept it together. "Do you believe the Seven of Spades interfered that night to help protect Detective Abrams?"

"Yes. As I stated earlier in my testimony, I believe the Seven of Spades was angry with Mr. Barton for trying to pin his wife's murder on them. They told Detective Abrams themself that they would kill Barton if it looked like he might get away with it. I think they saw Barton give his tail the slip and break into the detective's hotel room, felt guilty for their role in the whole thing, and contacted me for help. Then they shut off the electricity in the hotel as a final protective measure. They knew Detective Abrams's training would give him an edge in the dark that Barton wouldn't have."

"That's quite an interesting interpretation," Durham said, clasping his hands at his waist. "And do you, like Detective Abrams, believe that Keith Chapman was framed, and that the real Seven of Spades is still alive?"

"Yes, I do," Dominic said without a moment's hesitation.

Durham waited for the crowd's reaction to die down. "You must have a lot of faith in your partner."

"He's the kind of man it's easy to have faith in," said Dominic.

Levi swallowed past the ache in his throat. He dropped his gaze to his hands, but he could see Martine smiling in his peripheral vision.

"I also have my own reasons for believing that, though. Detective Abrams and I were two of only a handful of people who were with Keith Chapman in his final hours. I heard his story firsthand, saw his behavior up close, realized how incredibly sick he was. I don't know how much sense this can make to someone who wasn't there themselves, but there's no way Chapman was capable of the Seven of Spades murders. It's just not possible."

Durham stood in front of the witness stand, absolutely flummoxed, having to revise his approach yet again.

"Mr. Russo, I'd never question your integrity," he said, as if he hadn't spent the past ten minutes doing exactly that. "Like everyone here, I appreciate your service to this country, and the personal sacrifices you've made to protect our freedom."

"Thanks," Dominic said dryly.

"You're obviously a man of great honor and loyalty. But sadly, there are people out there who will take advantage of good men such as yourself."

Dominic gave him a blank look.

"You heard the gunshot from Detective Abrams's hotel room, but you didn't see what actually happened. The truth about that encounter is purely the detective's word against Mr. Barton's. The gun found at the scene was unregistered and couldn't be traced, and it had both men's fingerprints all over it."

"That's true, but Barton's hands tested positive for gunshot residue after he was arrested that night."

"Isn't it possible that Mr. Barton fired at Detective Abrams in self-defense?"

"No," Dominic said.

Durham raised an eyebrow. "That's it? Just *no*?"

"That's right." Dominic's body language wasn't so casual anymore.

"Oh no," Levi muttered. It was extremely difficult to provoke Dominic, but he *did* have sore spots. His biggest weakness was his gambling, which Durham must not know anything about or he'd already have brought it up.

His other weakness was Levi himself, and Durham was zeroing right in on that.

"We've heard from Detective Abrams's own testimony that he's a skilled fighter capable of and willing to commit serious violence. His preoccupation with the Seven of Spades is such that it endangered his job. Meanwhile, your feelings for him are so strong that you rushed to his aid on nothing more than an anonymous text message and have supported him unwaveringly ever since."

"Make your point, counselor," Sanchez said, while Dominic stared at Durham with a face like stone.

"Isn't it possible that Detective Abrams brought Mr. Barton to his hotel room with the malevolent intentions my client has described, then sent you those texts himself, knowing that you would never question his version of events?"

"That's insane," said Dominic. "You can't seriously be suggesting that Levi would impersonate the Seven of Spades."

Durham shrugged. "Maybe Detective Abrams *is* the Seven of Spades."

The resulting uproar was instantaneous and deafening. Levi rocked in his seat like he'd been punched in the gut, his back slamming against the wood. Martine's hand tightened on his arm as if she thought he might leap up, but his legs wouldn't have supported him even if he'd wanted to. Up on the stand, Dominic's expression was dark with anger.

Sanchez called repeatedly and uselessly for order. Over the din, Wu was shouting, "Objection, Your Honor, for God's sake! This is wild, baseless speculation."

"Withdrawn," Durham said before Sanchez could respond, but the damage was already done. Once something had been said, the jury couldn't unhear it, regardless of the judge's instructions to disregard the statement.

Sanchez got the room under control eventually. Levi didn't dare look at anyone but Dominic, but Dominic wasn't looking back; he was scowling at Durham instead.

"You have no idea what the fuck you're talking about," he said.

"Mr. Russo, please watch your language," Sanchez said, sounding pained.

"Sorry, your Honor. But I can't just sit here and listen to this." Dominic leaned forward, speaking directly to Durham. "Drew Barton killed his wife. Detective Abrams proved that, so Barton tried to kill him. It's that simple. Now you're trying to assassinate the character of one of the best men I've ever known to protect this piece of shit—"

"*Mr. Russo.*"

"—but it's not going to work, because you've gone way too far. The Seven of Spades has put Detective Abrams through hell, and what you just implied is one of the most sickening things I've ever heard. You should be ashamed of yourself." He sat back, folded his arms, and said, "I'm sorry, Your Honor. It had to be said."

She nodded wearily. Durham, who had taken a couple of steps backward during Dominic's speech, scanned the jury.

He'd miscalculated. The angry outburst he'd provoked from Levi had been self-defense, which some people would find off-putting or even frightening. Dominic's outburst, on the other hand, had been in defense of someone he cared for, which came across much differently. Now Dominic looked like an upset but protective boyfriend while Durham looked like a bullying asshole.

"No further questions," said Durham.

"Good." Sanchez rapped her gavel. "I think that's enough for today. We'll reconvene tomorrow morning, at which point I expect to hear the presentation of more solid facts and fewer wild theories."

Chastened, Durham withdrew to the defendant's table. As soon as the judge had taken her leave, Levi whispered, "I have to get out of here," to Martine and slipped out of the courtroom as quickly and quietly as he could, considering that everyone in the vicinity was staring at him.

He left the Regional Justice Center through the public entrance, trotted down the first flight of steps, and took refuge under one of the two dozen palm trees planted in front of the building. Leaning his shoulder against the trunk, he raked a hand through his curls and took a few deep breaths.

A knot of uniformed officers were standing down by the curb, Jonah Gibbs amongst them, chatting and laughing with each other. Levi hoped they didn't notice him; Gibbs's attitude was the last thing he was prepared to deal with right now.

"Hey," Dominic said behind him. "You okay?"

Levi turned around to face him and Martine. "Well, I was just accused of being a serial killer in a public courtroom, so no, I'm not having the best day."

"He didn't mean it," said Martine. "He was just trying to get a rise out of Dominic and make you both look bad. Everyone could see that."

That was true, but it did nothing to improve Levi's mood. He'd always anticipated wanting a few drinks after this trial; now that need was imperative. "I just want you to take me home and get me so drunk I can't see straight," he told Dominic.

"It's barely four—"

"I don't care."

Durham and Barton emerged from the building then, their heads angled close together in conversation. Levi's body tensed from head to foot.

Durham saw their group, smiled, and walked right up to them with Barton in tow. "What a surprise running into you out here, Detective."

Levi was searching for some response other than loud angry cursing or punching him in the face when he was distracted by the slam of a car door down the street. A van from KTNV-TV had just pulled up, and a reporter and cameraman jumped out as he watched. They were joined within seconds by vehicles from three other news outlets.

"Did you call the press?" he said in disbelief.

"My client would like to make a public statement, as is his right."

"You're not going to get away with what you did to me," Barton said to Levi, though the facade of innocent victim was ruined by his nasty little smirk.

Levi lunged forward without thinking about it. Dominic stepped in front of him, gripped him tightly by both elbows, and said, "Do. Not. Move."

"You're turning this trial into a circus," Martine said, giving Durham her best scornful glare. "Don't you have any respect for your profession?"

"You mean like a cop who breaks bones and beats people unconscious?"

Levi strained against Dominic's hold until Dominic shook him hard and hissed in his ear. "I swear to God I will throw you over my shoulder and carry you out of here if you don't calm the fuck down."

"You wouldn't," said Levi, outraged by the very idea.

"To keep you from making a career-ending mistake? You bet your sweet ass I would."

Before either of them could say anything more, the steps were inundated with a flood of clamoring reporters and flashing cameras. The commotion caught the attention of the cops by the street, though they stayed out of the way to observe from a distance. Levi tried to retreat himself, but as he was hemmed in by reporters on all sides, he ended up stuck close to Barton with Dominic beside him.

"Ladies and gentlemen, thank you so much for coming," Durham called out. "All over the country, we've seen evidence of corruption inside our police departments. We've seen how unscrupulous officers abuse their power to intimidate, harass, and even physically assault the innocent citizens they're charged with protecting."

"Oh no, he did *not*," said Martine. Levi could only imagine her fury at hearing one wealthy white man say that about another.

"But I for one will not stand for this injustice. My client, who has been unfairly targeted—"

Crack.

Barton's head exploded, spraying Levi with blood and bone shards. He'd barely recoiled when Dominic dove atop him and bore him to the ground, bellowing, "*Sniper!*" at the top of his lungs.

The steps of the justice center erupted in utter pandemonium. Frantic screams rang through the air as people fled in every direction, mowing each other over in their panicked rush to escape. One reporter stomped on a dropped camera, shattering it to pieces; another slipped in the pool of Barton's blood and went down hard.

Staying low, Dominic dragged Levi's motionless body behind the shoddy cover of a palm tree. Martine crouched behind the next trunk over, her gun in one hand while she spoke urgently into her radio. Down by the road, the cops had taken cover where they could and were returning fire toward the source of the shot, a parking garage diagonally across the street.

"If you don't have eyes on the sniper, stop *shooting*!" Dominic shouted at them. "You're firing into a populated building! *Idiots*."

Levi stared at Barton's corpse where it lay crumpled on the steps. The sounds around him faded into the background like the roar of a distant ocean.

"Levi. Levi!" Dominic tapped his cheek. "They wouldn't let me bring my gun into the courtroom. I don't have it on me."

Levi didn't really hear him. There was only one thing he was listening for, and he hadn't heard it yet—a second rifle round.

Dominic said his name a few more times, but when Levi didn't respond, he said, "Sorry about this," reached into Levi's jacket, and pulled his gun out of his holster. "Jesus Christ, Martine, don't your people know how to deal with an urban sniper?" he asked as he checked the magazine.

"Only in theory," she said grimly. "They've never been in this situation before." She began yelling orders, urging the officers to follow protocol, which was to break into teams and flank the sniper's suspected position from multiple angles.

Levi stood up.

"Whoa!" Dominic's free hand shot out and closed around his wrist. "Levi, what the hell? Get down!"

After disengaging with a simple wrist grab defense that was as natural as breathing, Levi walked over to Barton's body. Blood dripped down his face and into his mouth; he spat it on the ground without pausing.

He was wide open, completely exposed, but he didn't care. Whether the Seven of Spades had taken the shot themself or hired someone else, they'd gotten what they wanted.

Barton's head was like a burst melon smeared across the concrete, even messier than when Keith Chapman had blown his own brains out. Durham was nowhere to be seen.

Amidst a storm of cursing, Dominic ran out beside him, putting his body between Levi and the parking garage. Since Levi knew any danger had passed, he allowed it.

"What the fuck are you doing?"

"It doesn't matter," Levi said. His voice sounded mechanical even to his own ears. "Barton was the only target. The shooter is long gone by now."

"You don't know—"

A frightened cry behind them made them both whip around, but the officer in question wasn't hurt. She was pointing across the street.

A few months ago, the city had installed three-sided ad kiosks on certain streets, the kind that played simple video advertisements on a loop. As they watched, every single ad on each kiosk on Lewis Avenue blinked out one by one, replaced with the same image: a three-dimensional seven of spades card rotating on a black background.

Awash in unreality, Levi slowly walked down the remaining steps to the curb, drawn closer against his will. Barton's blood was hot and sticky on his face, his chest, but it was a distant discomfort, as if his consciousness was hovering outside his body. With Dominic and Martine standing on either side, he stopped and waited for what would come next.

The entire street had fallen silent.

A message in shimmering gold script appeared beneath the card on every screen simultaneously:

ALL BETS ARE OFF

Explore more of the *Seven of Spades* series:
www.riptidepublishing.com/titles/series/seven-spades

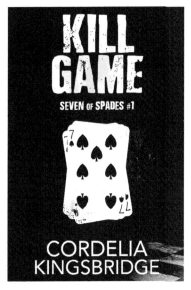

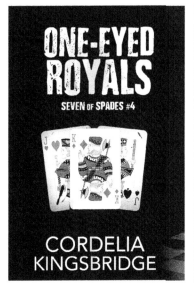

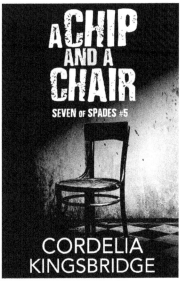

Dear Reader,

Thank you for reading Cordelia Kingsbridge's *Trick Roller*!

We know your time is precious and you have many, many entertainment options, so it means a lot that you've chosen to spend your time reading. We really hope you enjoyed it.

We'd be honored if you'd consider posting a review—good or bad—on sites like **Amazon, Barnes & Noble, Kobo, Goodreads, Twitter, Facebook**, **Tumblr,** and your blog or website. We'd also be honored if you told your friends and family about this book. Word of mouth is a book's lifeblood!

For more information on upcoming releases, author interviews, blog tours, contests, giveaways, and more, please sign up for our weekly, spam-free newsletter and visit us around the web:

Newsletter: tinyurl.com/RiptideSignup
Twitter: twitter.com/RiptideBooks
Facebook: facebook.com/RiptidePublishing
Goodreads: tinyurl.com/RiptideOnGoodreads
Tumblr: riptidepublishing.tumblr.com

Thank you so much for Reading the Rainbow!

RiptidePublishing.com

ALSO BY CORDELIA KINGSBRIDGE

ABOUT THE AUTHOR

Cordelia Kingsbridge has a master's degree in social work from the University of Pittsburgh, but quickly discovered that direct practice in the field was not for her. Having written novels as a hobby throughout graduate school, she decided to turn her focus to writing as a full-time career. Now she explores her fascination with human behavior, motivation, and psychopathology through fiction. Her weaknesses include opposites-attract pairings and snarky banter.

Away from her desk, Cordelia is a fitness fanatic, and can be found strength training, cycling, and practicing Krav Maga. She lives in South Florida but spends most of her time indoors with the air conditioning on full blast!

Connect with Cordelia:

Tumblr: ckingsbridge.tumblr.com

Twitter: @c_kingsbridge

Facebook: facebook.com/Cordelia.Kingsbridge

Enjoy more stories like
Trick Roller
at RiptidePublishing.com!

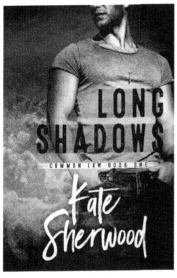

Long Shadows
ISBN: 978-1-62649-526-5

Friendly Fire
ISBN: 978-1-62649-482-4

Earn Bonus Bucks!

Earn 1 Bonus Buck for each dollar you spend. Find out how at RiptidePublishing.com/news/bonus-bucks.

Win Free Ebooks for a Year!

Pre-order coming soon titles directly through our site and you'll receive one entry into a drawing for a chance to win free books for a year! Get the details at RiptidePublishing.com/contests.

Printed in Great Britain
by Amazon